PLATINUM
Dreams

A novel
by

Jacki Kash

Platinum Dreams Publishing

Platinum Dreams Publishing—Michigan

Published by:
Platinum Dreams Publishing
P.O. Box 320693
Flint, MI 48532

Visit our Web site at www.platinumdreamspublishing.com
for information or submission guidelines.

Library of Congress Control Number: 2006902371
ISBN-10: 0-9779317-0-6
ISBN-13: 978-0-9779317-0-5
Book Design: Florence Dyer
Cover Design/Graphics: Mike Evans, Promotions Ink
Hair stylist: Kassandra Buyck

First edition.

For information regarding special discounts or bulk purchases, please contact:
jkash@platinumdreamspublishing.com

Printed in the United States of America

To my children—Cimone, Tre'Von, and Xzavion

From here on, it only gets better!

—J.K.

PLATINUM

Dreams

He sat there becoming aroused at the sight of her. She was a portrait of beauty, standing there nervously, preparing to perform. Her tight silk dress clung to her perfect hourglass shaped figure like a second skin. Her shoulders, dusted lightly with glitter, sparkled against the bright lights. Her lip gloss made her lips look as if she'd just run her wet tongue over them, letting him know that she'd anticipated this moment just as much as, if not more than, he had. He rejoiced silently at this miracle that was all for him. He knew she would give him everything she had because she was all his tonight.

He dimmed the lights and all that existed was her. She owned the stage. She was a single star radiating throughout the whole galaxy. He couldn't help but smile wickedly. It began down in the innermost parts of his stomach and traveled through his entire body until he could no longer contain the joy that radiated from within him. He bit his lip hard in his struggle to control his excitement. The anticipation of her performance was overwhelming.

As the music began to drift softly from the speakers, his palms began to sweat. She slowly slid her delicate fingers around the large microphone, silently praying for the strength to perform perfectly. Her life depended on this. She had to make a perfect impression. He had to feel that she really loved him or it was over.

CHAPTER ONE

"Help me!" I screamed, my throat ragged from the high pitched pleas for help. "Help! Help!" I screamed again, hoping for someone to hear the desperation in my voice and come to my rescue, but my throat was raw from crying and the screams fell into oblivion. My feet were heavy and the wind whipped right through my bones, but I tried to keep my focus. Other than the bright full moon, there was no light and I could see no way to escape. The darkness embraced my fear hungrily, chiseling away at my sanity. If I could just hold on to my sanity, I knew everything would be alright. But thinking it and doing it were two different things. I ran as fast as I could and swung blindly at tree branches to clear my path but I could barely see in front of me. I had to catch myself from catapulting over the steep ravine. My breath came in short, sporadic breaths as I made a sharp left to avoid a fall.

Running downhill, I checked over my shoulder to make sure I hadn't been spotted. I paused but only long enough to rest my hands on my knees and take a deep breath. Horrible trembles shook my body, but now was not the time to nurse my hysteria. Getting to safety was at the top of my to do list, so trembling hands, stomach cramps, and shortness of breath would have to wait 'til I was out of harms way.

The slippery road glistened as the rain poured down like cats and dogs. Forced to abandon my shoes back in the woods, I now almost-regretted the decision as my feet hit every nook and cranny in the muddy, rock laden ground but the stilettos would've made my getaway even more difficult. The bloody gash below my eye stung incessantly and my obscured vision signaled that it had begun to swell. The mud streaked, once pail yellow dress was now

1

blood-stained and ripped and the rain caused me to slip, losing my footing like those silly chicks always did in horror flicks.

I needed help and fast but the road was deserted. No signs of life existed.

Gulping for air, my chest heaved up and down. Horrifying thoughts played themselves in my mind, thoughts of death and despair that I couldn't shake off. Was this how my story would end? The headline flashed across my minds eye, "Single black female, found dead at the age of twenty-three."

Even through my powerlessness, I couldn't let that happen, no matter what. Dying simply was *not* an option. I was too fly and had too much to live for to end up on the late night news, especially since my destiny was yet unfulfilled. I was helpless against the thoughts of death that forced themselves on me, but even so, I couldn't accept it, I wouldn't. My life wasn't supposed to end like this. There was so much to accomplish, so many unfulfilled dreams. Bowing down to a death sentence just wasn't my style, not when there was so much left to do. Being the survivor that I am, I knew I'd make it through this, no matter what.

Forcing myself to block out the bad seeds, I forced myself to recall the only song that gave me hope in hard times: "Survivor" by Destiny's Child. I pictured myself in the Destiny's Child video along with the other girls, surviving the woes of the jungle, taking on anything that came our way. The song gave me the strength I needed to take a deep breath, gather up all my might, and scream for help again. Someone had to hear!

The big full moon gave a soft yellow glow to my wooded surroundings. Taking inventory of my whereabouts didn't help at all. I was still all alone. One thing was for sure, I couldn't give up, not when I was *just* starting my new life. I straightened up and decided to pray up.

"No matter what, God is for me," I reminded myself, carefully navigating my way through the forest.

My only hope was in waiting on the supernatural answers from Him, if nothing else, I'd definitely learned that. Clasping my hands tightly together momentarily, I prayed for His help, not knowing how He would answer or when but just knowing that He would. "Survivor" by Destiny's Child replayed in my head as I walked expectantly along the dark path but, still, nothing. I forced myself to not lose hope, not when I'd come this far. God would answer. He had to.

"God, help me!" I demanded, looking towards the heavens, knowing that if He could hear the simple prayer of a child that surely He would answer me, but I was left there feeling stupid with no direction.

"If you're there," I softened my tone this time, bowing my head in prayer, "I need you." But the words made no sound. They were like trees falling in a forest full of nobodies.

My body shuddered from sobbing uncontrollably and my cold hands felt wet and clammy as I buried my face in them.

"Why is this happening to me?!" I cried for my own benefit, wondering what in the world I could've done to deserve this. Walking slowly, I tried to redeem myself, each step repenting for every bad thing I'd ever done or even thought about doing. Lately, my life had turned into a series of repenting.

"Dang, how bad could I have been for you to do me like this?" I asked God, feeling that no matter how much I repented it would never be good enough. I was always being punished.

God knows I'd tried to become a better person, especially after reading all the curses that came upon evil people in the Bible; I definitely didn't want any part in that. It was crazy. I was trying to do right, not like some of the hypocrites I observed, demonstrating on Sundays and back to business on Monday, in exchange for the rights to claim "I'm so saved," even as they went about their wicked ways. But even so, I couldn't judge them. I had more than enough issues of my own to deal with.

3

"Issues, issues, issues," I breathed, disgusted at this mess I was in. Drudging along slowly, I gathered the flimsy material above my knees to continue my lonesome journey, shaking my head in disgust at my newest set of problems.

Was being faithful to God worth all this? I wondered, 'cause I'd been faithful to the best of my ability and the more I tried, the more bad stuff came against me. I mean dang, was I the subject of some wilderness experiment that God was conducting to see how much I could take? If that was the case, He could call it off because I was about to lose it wandering around out here in the middle of nowhere. I thought about pulling my hair out. If I thought it would solicit a reaction from Him I would've.

"Just curse God and die!" A voice growled angrily at me.

The grim suggestion echoing in my head had to come from Satan, an attempt to aggravate me as I lost my balance and plunged forward, falling into a pool of muddy water. I tried to crawl out, but the cold muck pulled me in like quicksand.

"Somebody help me!" I screamed angrily, punching the air with tightly balled fists as my voice echoed through the blackness. My sanity spiraled downward, forcing me to cry out. The high pitched scream permeated the air so intensely that I barely realized the shrill sound had escaped from my own throat, penetrating the thick, horrific silence that was denser than the fog on this dark stretch of deserted highway.

My neck snapped back and I shot straight up as a flash of lightning ripped through the sky and tore into a nearby tree. The branch screeched as it let go of its foundation and hit the ground. My breathing became more labored even as I attempted to disguise my whereabouts, feeling the presence of evil stalking me. An ear piercing crash of thunder followed, cracking violently down from heaven in wondrous fury. But when it exploded a second time, I knew that it was not thunder, but the blast of a gunshot ripping through the air.

4

Though sitting straight up, fear paralyzed my body. I could do nothing but recite the 23rd Psalms over and over.

"Yea, though I walk through the valley of the shadow of death, I will fear no evil," I began praying. I longed desperately for an escape from this ghastly darkness that engulfed me.

I sensed danger as a shadow approached from far off, beating through the branches that threatened to slow him down. The swishing of his shoes, splashing against the puddles of rain made the hair on my arms and the back of my neck stand at attention. Even in the darkness, I realized that *he'd* unleashed the thunder.

I turned to run but the mud was like quicksand holding me down.

His stride quickened and his intense gaze locked onto me as if he was taking an x-ray of my fear. His steps turned into a sprint as he cut through the distance separating us like the swipe of a butcher's knife slashing through tender flesh.

"Run! Run!" my inner voice yelled but that gaze, visible even in the darkness, remained locked onto me and kept me frozen to the spot. I heard the voice but stood there helpless, dazed like a deer blinded by the glare of oncoming headlights. I was unable to move, unable to breathe but eerily conscious of every beat of my heart thumping uncontrollably inside my chest. An eerie feeling passed through my veins as things began to travel in slow motion. Even the tears sliding down my cheeks obeyed the command as one dropped slowly behind the other, disappearing into the puddles of rain.

The beating of my heart and the stomping of his boots, splashing the puddles of rain, were the only signs of life and they grew louder and louder, magnified by my fear. *Swoosh...swoosh...Swoosh.* He was close. I began counting down the last few seconds of my life.

"Yea, though I walk through the valley of the shadow of

death," I recited, as the figure neared closer. "I will fear...no...evil...for...thou...art...with me," I stammered, barely able to catch my breath, trying to lift my feet from the quicksand with no luck. "Oh, Lord."

The stranger raised the gun slowly, smiling from behind his fur lined hoodie. He pointed the gun directly at my chest and his gaze penetrated me, glaring into my soul. My breathing stopped and my eyes fixed on the shiny tool that would soon snatch my life away. Little gasps of air escaped my throat as I tried to scream Jesus' name but my lips felt like they'd been sewn together. My stalker laughed as if he could read my thoughts and knew my lips were bound. I'd never been so scared in my life. What was he waiting for? I succumbed to the fear, letting my feet sink deeper into the quicksand, knowing he would over power me, possibly making the end worse.

His stride adjusted back to the agonizingly slow, deliberate steps as he came within five feet, and then four feet, and then three feet of me.

This was really it.

There was no way out and even if there was, I was frozen to that spot. He was close enough to reach out and touch me yet he prolonged my suffering, torturing me with silence that forced me to wonder what he was going to do to me.

Even disguised by the black hoodie, I recognized him from the wicked smile planted on his face. He seemed to take pleasure in my fear. I looked into his eyes to see if I could find any mercy but there was none. His black eyes were ice cold. His appearance was frightening. His features had been altered and there was a blur where his face should've been, disguising his identity, one of the many tricks he'd used to push me over the edge. He cocked the gun and laughed, letting me know that he had won and that I was his and he was free to do whatever he wanted, even kill me. I closed my eyes and stood there helpless, anticipating my impending doom.

A blast of air swept past me, spinning my body around and lifting me off my feet and into the air. The stalker stood there perplexed, waving the gun wildly as he let off a shot. He stomped the ground angrily and squeezed the trigger, letting off another shot. The bullet whizzed past my head, barely missing me as I ducked. Without a doubt, I knew it was the Lord protecting me. He *hadn't* forsaken me. He'd come right on time, swooping me away to safety. His angels took charge over me just like He'd promised in His scriptures, rescuing me from the deranged stalker who threatened to erase my existence. He was disappearing out of sight, still madly waving the gun which had become a tiny speck from far above where I was soaring.

The angel had a firm grip on my shoulders as we ascended into the sky. Visibility was limited through the thick fog but, even so, I dared not to look back as the angel carried me away. I heard small, muffled gasps and realized they were coming from me as I gulped hungrily for air. My heart pounded hysterically, almost bursting through the confines of my chest cavity. Even as the angel had carried me away to what I knew had to be a safe place, my palpitating heart continued to jump around frantically with the force of a caged animal fighting desperately to break free.

In a desperate struggle, I threw blows with all my might as a pair of strong hands shook me desperately, refusing to loosen their grip on my shoulders. But the hands were familiar and even in the midst of being confounded, I was sure they didn't belong to the stranger. These hands were strong and comforting.

"Baby, wake up!" A voice demanded, as the darkness began to subside and the cobwebs inside my head became less fuzzy. "Wake up!"

The sound of my husband's raspy voice penetrated the silence with urgency and his muscular arms wrapped tightly around me like a security blanket, coaxing me out of the dream realm and back into reality. He smoothed my hair and wiped away the beads of sweat that had formed on my forehead.

The blanket of terror that had wrapped itself around me like a snug winter coat slowly began to lift and the fear loosened its deathlike grip. Warm, salty teardrops formed in the corners of my eyes and rolled down my cheeks onto my lips as I cried softly into my husband's chest. He kissed away my tears and I took solace in his arms when he drew me closer. His gentle touch always eased the pain into submission.

I *hated* reliving the gruesome nightmare. Even as I regained consciousness, realizing I was safe, I couldn't help but remember the chain of events that would forever change my life.

CHAPTER TWO

My agent called a few days ago alerting me to the big news. She'd arranged for me to meet a writer from BET *Reel Stories* today. I would be spending a lot of time with Sonji Hawkins over the next few weeks, possibly months, pouring over the details of my life story or, in my real opinion, scrutinizing every detail of my life and how to make it into my big screen debut as she translated my story into a blockbuster screenplay.

"Kayla," she squeezed my hand warmly as we met up on the brick lined pavement leading up to the deck, "it's a pleasure to finally meet you," she said as I smiled in return.

Sonji, seemingly in her late-twenties with flawless chocolate skin, slim figure and cover-girl looks, was sharply dressed in a 2-piece crème linen suit and possessed a professional demeanor without giving off an air of superiority. Her warmth and friendliness instantly put me at ease with her, making me feel as if I'd just reconnected with an old friend from my childhood. The good vibe between us added the assurance I needed if I was going to share my story with her. Of course, she'd heard the rumors like everyone else but she was about to get the *real* deal and then BET was going to tell it to the world.

I was still trippin', thinking back to when I was a little girl prancing around the house in my dress-up clothes, gaudy jewelry and sunglasses with dreams of being a famous writer and singer whose name would be known in every household on my mind. My singing would bless the ears of all who listened and thousands of people would stand in line to see me perform and my stories would keep my readers hooked 'til the last word.

Way back then, I dreamed of writing about other characters whose lives I'd imagined and bringing them to life through my books. I never thought I'd be telling my own story to the world. It was a trip to think that my name had blown up and was a household word. On top of that, knowing that my life was newsworthy felt like a surreal experience. Hearing and reading about events on the news, you never actually think they could happen to you. But here I was, the network actually wanted *my* story and it was gonna be on T.V.! I smiled at the thought. I'd come a long way from being that little girl with big dreams. The reality of it made me rejoice on the inside. This is what true success felt like. I'd always wanted to be a star but I never thought it would happen like this, never in a million years.

*　*　*　*　*

Mama and Granny or, G as we affectionately called her, had instilled in me the danger of strangers at a young age. They warned about the child molesters, the kidnappers and the worst of 'em all, those who pretended to be something they weren't only to get what they wanted. They called them wolves in sheep's clothing. They were strangers too although they were a different type. They were the ones you knew but who were deceiving about their true identities. Yeah, those were *definitely* the worst, the ones you had to really watch out for.

The warnings started when we were no older than three or four and continued throughout our teenage years. "Don't talk to strangers" and "never get into a car with a stranger," were at the top of the list among other things. My sister and I used to joke about it after they'd left the room.

"Dang, do they have to say it so much, it's already embedded in my brain," we'd giggle. But the older I got and the more often the television news stories portrayed teenage girls as the victims of abuse, molestation and disappearances, the more I understood their need to protect us by preaching those words over and over again. After a girl from school went missing and everyone blamed her Mama's boyfriend, the message really hit home. Andrea Johnson. I'll never forget that name, especially after they found her body discarded like trash in a field a few months later.

Of course as I grew older, my judgment became keener and I found that listening to my heart, my most reliable instinct, always yielded the best results. I trusted my heart to lead and guide me with the wisdom to make the right decisions. Though I admit, a few times I didn't follow my first mind and it was in those instances that the worst situations arose. What lay ahead was definitely one of those times.

Now ordinarily, I wouldn't even dream of puttin' my business all in the streets but the twists, turns and loops I'd been through had drastically altered my viewpoint. If what I'd experienced could help even one young sister or brother make a wise decision or take time to analyze situations before acting, then giving people a sneak peak into my private life would be worth it. And if everything happened for a reason, the only reason I could see for me having to go through my trauma was to help someone else. That's why I'd decided to sell BET the rights to my story. It wasn't about the money but I wasn't about to turn it down. I was on a whole new level now. I'd finally realized that everything wasn't about me.

Sonji listened intently, asking few questions, as I gave her the background on my life with the tape recorder spinning, pen and pad in hand and with the intensity that filled people's eyes when they were soaking in the details of others' misfortune.

My big dreams had come when I was a little girl. I never knew what it was, just that there was something different about me. I wanted to be famous when I grew up. At the top of my list were my goals to become rich and famous as a singer/songwriter and author. I didn't know the terms platinum and best-selling author then but once I gave my desire those names it was on and poppin'. I could *already* see myself blowin' up in the music industry and as a writer. When I was supposed to be coppin' z's so I could get educated the next morning, I was staying up until the wee hours of the morning writing songs and stories that people could relate to, songs that I envisioned them dancing, laughing and crying to. And with hip-hop exploding the way it was, I knew that was the avenue I'd use to exploit that special something in me.

My vision was clear. I was going to be rich *and* famous, like the hip-hop version of Anita Baker or Aretha Franklin. I could see myself walking across the stage to receive my songwriter of the year and best female vocalist awards. Then when I turned thirty, I would put some icing on my cake by settling down with a fly husband and giving him a couple of kids, coppin' a mansion and some bling and living *happily ever after*. I had faith in my plan and I was going to go all the way to the top with it. I definitely had star potential and letting it go to waste was simply not an option.

Even though I hadn't been in any productions yet, acting would probably come naturally to me, too, since I had the blood *Type-E* for entertainer flowing through my veins. I could definitely see myself opposite Will Smith on the big screen. He'd been the object of a huge crush I'd had since back in the day. He was hot! My success story would make a blockbuster movie, with me playing myself and Will Smith playing my man. No doubt, I would also write the screenplay and sing on the soundtrack. Like I said, I had big plans.

Back when I used to read the Bible I stumbled across a scripture that said God had blessed me with the power to get wealth. I typed it up and framed it and I was going to use the gifts and talents I'd been blessed with to get rich 'cause to me that sounded much better than just sittin' on my talents and letting them go to waste. Bump that, I was going for mine.

Don't get it twisted, I wasn't trying to toot my own horn, but knowing I was blessed was a blessing in itself; and it was that feeling of being different from everyone else that motivated me. Some people took my confidence as conceit but I didn't let it faze me. Haters would always hate, those who didn't have would always talk about those who did and the world would keep on spinning. The haters didn't faze me but the killer part was that my own sister came at me trying to knock me off my square.

"Girl, maybe you should listen to Mama and leave them platinum dreams alone," she chirped, programmed by Mama to be a dream killer. I couldn't even believe she said that. My mama had her doing her dirty work and now I had to reprogram her thinking. Mama had that poverty mentality but I wasn't going to let her poison my sister.

"Kenya, if you don't believe in yourself, no one else will. You have to have a dream or what's the point of living?" I asked her.

"Yeah, Kayla, that's cool to have a dream. But have a dream you can actually achieve," she said, actually trying to convince me that my dream was too far fetched to become a reality.

No she didn't.

"My dream may seem impossible to you but I know I'm going to get where I wanna be. I can only show you and I'm tellin' you now, if you can't be down with me while I'm tryin' to get there, I'm goin' to remember that when I make it," I replied. "I'm your sister, if nobody else in the world believes in me, you should."

"Dang, you're making me feel bad now," she commented.

"You should!" I laughed, but I could see she was coming around.

"Kay, I do admit, I admire you for not having an ordinary dream. That really does make you stand out. It's just that Mama makes it seem like you gotta go to school and get that degree to amount to anything," she admitted.

"I ain't knockin' anyone that goes to school, more power to 'em,'" I explained. "But that route isn't for everybody and everyone's success doesn't come that way. Sometimes you just gotta be a trailblazer. I'ma get mine, you'll see and I ain't gonna let Mama and nobody else kill my dream," I finished.

"You're right, I'm sorry for even comin' at you like that. I mean, you probably could make it if you put your mind to it, you sing better than half the chicks with record deals," she added.

"Well, I sure am gonna try, that's all I can do," I said, glad that I'd made some kind of positive impact. I thought about her comment. Platinum wasn't bad, I could think of lots of worse kinds of dreams to have, but platinum dreams weren't bad at all.

"Ladies and gentlemen, coming soon to a theater near you, *The Kayla Coleman Story*. Starring, produced and directed by Kayla," Kenya laughed, teasing me now without that dream killing banter while illustrating my name on a billboard. Then she pretended that a reporter was interviewing her.

"So," she said into her fake microphone, "what inspired you to write this movie?" Then turning to her left side as if switching to my character, she slowly put her hand to her throat, "Me, me, me, me, me," she sang and then burst into giggles like she'd just told the joke to end all jokes. My sister was definitely crazy.

I refused to let her teasing deter me from what I had to do, though; she'd see when I became a big star and my dreams came true. I'd wait until she was right there, oozing with the desire to hang out with me and my wealthy friends. That's when I'd take the opportunity to remind her of all her stale jokes and then I'd laugh. It was all good though, if nobody else believed in me, even with all the stale jokes, Kenya certainly did...now. I smiled to myself thinking of how I had to convince her to see it my way.

14

Sonji listened and we laughed over Kenya's silliness. "Shoot, we had never been around people that were multi-talented, so when I found out I was as talented as the people we watched on TV. I was just proud to be one of them," I told her, illustrating how my confidence had been mistaken for conceit. "I always imagined myself as the type of chick who would push Benzes, Jags, have a nice home and be a major star!" Sonji gave me a "me too" look. And trust me, when I imagine all the endless possibilities that my new life will afford me, I know I won't settle for less.

My major goals won't allow me to sit around and wait for something good to fall out the sky like lots of folk or, worse, watch life as it passes me by. I was 'bout my biz, at least I could say that. How many people got to sit down and tell their life stories? I'm sure it wasn't many.

I always kept my eyes and ears on the pulse of the music industry, taking in any and everything I could. I was hungry for success and I could taste it. Every time a new artist came out, I worked even harder to claim my spot, writing and doing whatever just to get noticed and get around other singers, local rap acts and producers since they were doing what I wanted to do.

I entertained my friends with my urban tales, feeling a rush every time someone acknowledged my writing skills. When I heard the over night success stories, it fueled my drive and determination, a winning combination that was a necessity for me to make my mark. Besides that, I stayed in the studio when I could, soaking up everything I saw and heard like a sponge.

"Opportunity plus preparation," is what I told myself each morning. "That's the key."

I wasn't going to get caught off guard when my opportunities arose and I had a feeling it would come soon. My heart told me I had what it took to take over the industry and that's exactly what I planned to do.

My cousin Tika had an ill flow and she let me sing hooks

on her single, giving me my first taste of the recording studio. After that, I was addicted but Tika was more of a behind the scenes type chick, wanting to run the company instead of it running her, so she was trying to get her feet wet as a writer and A&R assistant for an independent record label instead of pushing that single. But I was still going for mine and I knew that when Tika got that plug, I was in, too.

Tika introduced me to people. She told me what books to read, she helped me to write when I first got started and she had business knowledge of the game. I'd heard of too many people getting ganked with shady contracts, only to be on lockdown with a label or having their projects shelved. I wasn't gonna let that happen to me though, I had a plan.

The industry was crankin' out studio manufactured wanna-be's and one hit wonders but I was gonna be the one that made it, 'cause music was in me. I could see the headlines, 'Kayla *The Real Deal* Coleman takes over R&B and hip-hop.' As long as I stayed focused on the prize, I would be a star.

Along with the discovery of the gifts God had placed in me came the discovery of my purpose, to bless people through songs and books. Since my childhood singing had been my thing and since I'd been destined for greatness, I was going to capitalize on my talents.

Mama used to be a gospel music junkie, ordering all kinds of gospel tapes off of T.V. and as soon as they'd arrive, I'd break out my microphone and sing until my heart's desire. My microphone was really the remote control, an ink pen or whatever I could wrap my hands around and sing into, but it didn't matter. As long as I was singing, I was happy. I'd gather the family around, step onto the stage and captivate my audience. I knew at an early age that I had IT! A gift from God, talent, the blessing, you know, IT! And *IT* was going to take me places.

See, 'round here, it was easy for a girl to get stuck. If you didn't get straight out of Troy after high school, chances are, you would be stuck here life. I definitely didn't plan on being stuck here for life. And if a sister got caught up with some guy or even worse, a scrub and fell into the baby Mama trap, well let's just say that would turn a simple ride thru into the scenic route. Guys always tried to knock the cute girls up, like they were tryin' to make sure nobody else came near their girl. But they weren't the ones who had to be on lockdown with a baby, so they didn't care.

I'd seen females get sidetracked big time but I didn't plan to go that route. This wasn't the worst place on earth, but for a woman like me, it could make all the difference between living the life of my dreams or settling for whatever crumbs life threw me. I knew the world was filled with all the good stuff I wanted out of life and I planned to discover it and make my mark. I vowed to myself a *long* time ago that no matter what it took or how long, I was *going* to make it and *nothing* was going to stop me.

My skills were known around town since I'd played the talent show circuit, taking advantage of every opportunity to perfect the gift and showcase my talents. But Mama was so strict; it was hard pursuing my dreams when she would hardly let me go anywhere. When I did get out of the house, she wanted me back before I could get off into anything. It was a tight situation, that's for sure.

Accomplishment might as well have been deleted from my dictionary, 'cause anything that had to do with accomplishing my dreams was cut out by my Mama. She was a *real* hater. Shoot, sometimes I felt like I was stranded on Alcatraz. Mama was trying to choke the life right outta my dreams, and I felt almost powerless to save them. I thought parents were supposed to support their children in pursuing their dreams, but not my Mama. Her idea of the good life was me getting some job, staying there for twenty-five or thirty years and retiring. To me, that sounded like working on a plantation somewhere.

"Yessa, massa, no suh, massa."

Nah, that was not how I envisioned my life. I was going to make my own choices, do my own thing and what made me happy. Why work for someone else and then at the end of it, they tell you, *"Oh, your 401k is gone, our accountants have not adhered to the standards set forth...blah, blah, blah"* or *"Sorry, we know you've given us your life, but we're downsizing and we just won't be able to keep you on."* Yeah right! I could see that every day of the week on the five o'clock news. They could save that for the birds, 'cause I definitely wasn't going' for it.

Mama was probably trying to protect me and Kenya from making the same mistakes she did but I wasn't her and she couldn't live through me.

At seventeen, Mama found herself pregnant, marrying my daddy at eighteen and having Kenya two years later. If you asked me, Mama acted like she resented my daddy for dashing her dreams of becoming a nurse, a dream she'd postponed shortly after my birth, opting to settle down and take care of us instead. Not that she couldn't do both. She tried at first, with Daddy working at Ford while she went to school part-time, but Daddy even messed *that* up and then she had to go to work full time and put school on hold.

Mama had never gotten over the betrayal she'd witnessed when she came home early from school that day, seven months pregnant and sick as a dog, to find Daddy laid up with another woman in *our* house.

From the stories I heard, Mama straight snapped, nearly blowing his and the stupid chick's head off that had the nerve to lay up with him in his wife's bed. From then on, I think Mama hated *all* men. She divorced Daddy after Kenya was born and although he paid child support for us, he wasn't there for us the way I thought a daddy should be.

After the divorce, Daddy moved to Detroit for his job, so he said, but Mama figured he went to shack up with his home wrecking girlfriend after she'd kicked him to the curb. The only time we really saw him was during the holiday season, birthdays and family reunions.

Mama was dead set against marriage. Her boyfriends didn't stand a chance and they didn't even know it. This latest one, Rodney, was cool though. He'd outlasted all of them, hanging in there for a full two years but Mama was never satisfied with having to deal with his hectic schedule with him being a doctor and all. I was secretly hoping he'd pop the question so she'd have a life of her own to obsess over. Sometimes, I felt like my Mama resented me because if she wouldn't have had me, she wouldn't have married Daddy. Instead, she would've finished school and become a nurse. She may have even ended up with someone like Rodney sooner.

She got on my nerves, taking out her resentment for Daddy by keeping me on lockdown. Shoot, it wasn't my fault he'd treated her bad and not all men were like him. But she didn't see it that way. She was just set on running my life, but all she did was make me rebel.

"Teenagers need to get out and mingle," I tried explaining to her the night she forbade me to go to my 10 p.m. studio session.

"Kayla, you're really not old enough to frequent recording studios, anything could happen in those types of places," she said, turning her nose up like I was going to a gutter studio, which wasn't even the case. But my Mama didn't trust me to make the right decisions, so she figured if she didn't let me hang out, then I couldn't get into any trouble. Her bad, 'cause I'd sneaked out a few times. She wasn't about to ruin my life.

Yeah, my Mama drank double doses of hater-aide and she was definitely a trip.

"I can't live like this," I sighed, slamming my bedroom door. Her over-protectiveness was driving me mad. I couldn't even talk to Kenya, with her always-living-up-to-Mama's-perfect-

19

expectations-self. She even graduated a semester early and was leaving for Cali the day after her going away party. That was all good but, as for me, I was going to do my own thing and what made me happy. I wanted to be a singer and that was that!

CHAPTER THREE

As planned, Kenya was leaving in a couple of days to pursue Mama's dreams and people were already pouring in to wish her farewell. The music was blasting as friends and family poured in from Saginaw, Michigan to Columbus, Ohio for Kenya's big bash. We invited everyone we knew, Daddy even showed up. Mama had been acting funny, ignoring him since he stepped through the door.

"The house looks nice, Pam," Daddy complemented her on her pride and joy which was the two-story, red brick, three-thousand square foot home that she'd purchased after receiving her share of Granddaddy's estate when he passed five years ago. "The lawn looks like you could just lay on it and take a peaceful nap," he smiled, referring to the beautifully manicured yard with the lush grass that perfectly accentuated the lavish landscaping.

"Thank you," she stated dryly as she walked right past him to greet my aunt Teri with a hug. You'd think Mama would've gotten over what he did but after all these years, she still gave him the cold shoulder.

"Daddy, did you do that yet?" Kenya inquired, obviously trying to keep something on the down low.

"Almost ready, baby girl," he smiled, grabbing a soda and heading through the French doors in the family room leading to the deck.

"Girl, I'm gonna miss you," I confessed to Kenya, applying *MAC's Lipglass* to my perfectly shaped lips as I dolled up for the celebration.

"I'm gonna miss you, too." She said, her eyes tearing up just at the mention, causing me to look up in surprise. I didn't know leaving was affecting her like that.

21

"Come here," I said, hugging her, "You'll probably get to L.A. and meet some fine doctor or athlete and forget all about your big sister," I teased.

"Uh, uh," she frowned, "That's the only thing that's making me not wanna go, I don't know anybody out there. I'm scared that I'm gonna feel like a fish outta water."

"Ken, don't cry, you'll be okay," I comforted her. "Just think about how going to school is going to help you to reach your goals in life."

"I know that but I just don't wanna leave you behind," she sniffed.

"Girl, don't even trip. I'ma be alright," I said, "And anyway, you're not leaving me behind! I'm gonna be all over once I get on."

"I know," she managed a laugh while wiping her tears. "And I want everybody else to know too, so I need you to do me a favor, alright?"

"Depends, what is it?" She'd piqued my curiosity. "I hope you don't want me to give a speech or something."

"Yeah, right, we're not even gonna go there. I want you to sing."

"Are you serious?" I smiled, "Girl please, I thought you were about to ask me to do something major."

"Nah, I just want everybody to hear you," she beamed, motioning for me to look out the bedroom window. I peeped between the blinds. Daddy was in the backyard working hard to make our deck into a stage. My cousin Scotty brought in speakers and a microphone as I stood in the window flabbergasted. Kenya knew how much I loved to perform.

"Fa sho," I agreed. I have the perfect song, too, I thought smiling, floating on cloud nine. And not just because my sister wanted me to sing for her and her guests but also because even though I was going to miss her, I was happy that she was getting out before she got caught in the trap.

"Girl, we'd better hurry up, I see your peeps arriving." I smiled. Cars circled our cul de sac as more guests arrived. Our block hadn't been this hot since my graduation party.

"Um, who is that fine brother with Tika?" Kenya asked squinting and licking her lips as an Escalade pulled up in the circular drive and our cousin Tika stepped out as the GQ brother extended his hand to help her.

"I don't know but he looks like a gold-diggers dream."

"Right," Kenya hi-fived me. "And the killer part is I bet she ain't even trippin' off him, I bet she's got him caterin' to her,"

"Um, hmmm. That's 'cause guys know when chicks have dollar signs flashin' in their eyes. They respect independent women with their own." We cut our conversation short as the couple approached. I had to admit, she had good taste in men. He was dressed in Polo gear, lookin' so fresh and so clean, and smellin' good. I wondered where she met him, 'cause he was fine with a capital F.

Cars lined our suburban block as guests poured in to send Kenya off in style. Scotty, DJ'ing as we mingled, announced that I was about to bless my sister with a song, causing my palms to sweat up instantly when I heard my name. I hoped I looked more confident than I felt as I walked to the deck, taking the mic that Scotty held out to me.

"This is for my baby sister. It's a song that I wrote and I hope y'all enjoy it."

A smile lit up Kenya's face as I gave Scotty the instrumental track. Kenya threw her hands up and started bouncing to the beat after he popped it into the audio system.

"That's my sister," she laughed, clapping along with the beat. I tucked her smile away in my chest of memories as I hit the final notes.

Kenya ran up to me, throwing her arms around me in a big

23

hug.

"Girl, that was *the bomb!*" she gushed, "When did you write that?"

"Oh, I don't know, that was just a lil' somethin' I had tucked away in my treasure chest." I bragged.

"You are so silly," she laughed.

"Awww, I made you cry again," I teased, wiping a tear from her cheek.

"Girl, please," she said, wiping at her eye, "I think I had a lash in my eye," she tried to play it off, all of a sudden distracted by someone across the yard.

"Yeah, right," I laughed, looking over my shoulder to see who had captured her attention.

"Oooh, Kayla, I got somebody I want you to meet," her high pitched voice squealed in excitement as she waved to someone across the yard and motioned for them to come over. "Come here, come here!" she hollered across the yard. "Um, wait right here Kay," she said, meeting the stranger half way across the yard, smiling from ear to ear as they approached.

I stretched my neck to see who she was inviting to join our private moment and was caught off guard by a smile that revealed a perfect set of pearly whites.

"Kayla, this is Rashad's roommate, Andre'," she said, nudging me with her arm. It was the, 'he's fine, right?' nudge.

"Hi, Andre'," I blushed. He *was* fine!

"Hey," he replied with a hint of a southern accent, "it's nice to meet you, Kayla," he was smiling, reaching for my hand and bringing it to his sexy lips. He brushed his lips lightly across my hand, almost making me melt on the spot. I felt my temperature rise as he repeated my name. "Kayla," sounded perfect rolling off his tongue. He was tight! I gave him a quick once over, admiring his sexiness. He was dressed in crisp dark blue Sean John jeans, a matching tee, Air Force 1's, with a diamond encrusted cross

24

draped from an iced out platinum chain and a Cartier watch on his outstretched wrist. Kenya thought she was slick, trying to play match maker but I wasn't mad. Dre' was all that *and* a bag of chips standing there looking like he'd just stepped out of the pages of GQ! Kenya excused herself as Dre' began telling me how much he'd enjoyed my song.

"Thank you," I smiled shyly, drowning in the chocolate centers of his eyes.

"You're welcome."

"So where are you from?" I asked, his hint of a southern accent enticing to my ears and his gorgeous smile captivating me.

"Alpharetta, Georgia, 'bout forty-five minutes outside of Atlanta," he responded, looking into my eyes as if they held everything he'd ever dreamt of in them. I was instantly drawn to him like a bee to honey. His finely chiseled features set against his smooth chocolate complexion were just the tip of the iceberg. God had blessed him with lips that looked as if they were made to meet mine in sweet, lingering kisses. His eyes twinkled as if they were on the verge of a smile and his bald head, oooh, I could just picture myself rubbing my hands over it and bringing it to my lips for a sweet kiss. No doubt, he was hot! He reminded me of the model, Tyson Beckford, who'd been the object of my crush since I'd first laid eyes on him posing for Polo ads. I observed my female cousins nudging each other as they witnessed my exchange with Dre'. I hoped no one could tell I was blushing.

Dre' took my hand, "Come on, let's dance," he invited me to join him as Alicia Keyes wooed us with her song, "Fallin'."

We looked into each others' eyes as we moved to the song. The chemistry flowing between us was crazy, making my heart palpitate as his hand massaged my back. I wondered if Dre' felt it too. I caught a glimpse of Kenya smiling across the backyard like she was the one sharing this moment with this fine stranger. I hated for the song to end and Dre' must have too because instead of walking away when it was over, he kept my hand in his as he guided me to the bench in the secluded corner of the yard where I often retreated to write.

"So what are you going to school for?" I asked as Dre' and I chatted, conversation flowing smoothly between us like two old friends.

"To get knowledge in my field," he grinned.

"I mean…"

"I know that's not what you meant," he laughed, "I'm majoring in marketing," he smiled, those lips inviting me to kiss them. "I moved here to complete my Bachelor's Degree and that's how I met my homeboy, Rashad," he explained.

"Yeah, Rashad is all about them books though," I giggled, remembering how the very same girls who'd thought he was a nerd in school were trying to get with him now that he had a good job and a degree and had grown into a sexy, caramel skinned, six-foot-five man who was always perfectly groomed, looking and smelling good. It also didn't hurt that he knew how to treat the ladies.

"Yeah, that's my dawg, though. He's cooler than a fan." Dre' grinned, licking his sexy lips as he slid a little closer to me on the swing.

"So are y'all going to keep your apartment since he's graduated?" I inquired.

"I don't know, Boo, it all depends," he smiled, a glint of humor in his eyes.

"On what?" I asked.

"On whether I decide to make you my wife and move ya cousin on up outta there," was Dre's response.

"I thought you were crazy but now I know for sure," I laughed, excusing myself to get some punch.

"Girl, what you think?" Kenya harped on me before I could even make it to the punch table.

"You're party was off the chain!"

"Quit playing, Kay, I'm talkin' 'bout Dre'. What you think about him?"

"He seems cool," I said, glancing in his direction. Sure enough his eyes were locked on me. I smiled at him.

"Cool, huh, I guess that's why y'all been hugged up over there on that swing for over an hour," she said, hand on her hip.

"Girl, whatever," I said, playfully giving her the "talk to the hand" sign. "I might clue you in later but, right now, let me get back to my date," I teased as I turned to walk away but not before she let out an audible gasp and stood there with her mouth open.

Dre' captivated me with his conversation. He wasn't lame nor was he stupid and immature like most of the guys I'd gone to school with. Probably 'cause he was two years my senior. After he transferred schools, he'd landed a coveted internship position with one of the top urban marketing firms in metro Detroit. His whole demeanor showed that he wasn't some broke, lame, no game brother. I liked that.

I don't know what it was but there was definitely something different about him. Maybe it was his sexy looks that had me thinking about him long after the party was over. Or maybe it was just his boyish charm that melted my heart. Whatever it was, I liked it. I knew there was something good on the horizon for us, too, just from that first meeting. He was a breath of fresh air in the midst of the smog filled city of lames with no game. He was definitely sucker-free and when I got a chill just thinking about him, I knew I was gone already.

"So, tell me, tell me!!!" Kenya prodded for answers later that night, as we kicked it about the party.

"Girl, tell you what?" I laughed at her childlike curiosity.

"The low on you and Andre', that's what," she laughed. "Don't play," she said, brush in hand, head cocked to the side as if she would hurl it at me if I didn't give her some answers.

27

"Nothin', I gave him my number," I responded nonchalantly as I went about writing in my journal.

"You gave him your number?" disbelief laced her voice as she covered her mouth. I didn't give most guys my number, which is why she was making such a big deal about it. "I knew it," she smiled, folding her hands behind her head.

"Knew what?" I asked.

"Knew you and Dre' would be perfect for each other," she stated matter-of-factly, repositioning herself in my lounge chair to face me and revealing a big grin.

"Girl, you're a mess," I laughed at her well orchestrated attempt to make sure I met Dre'.

"Well, at least my mission's accomplished," she yawned, "now I can go off to college knowing my big sister is in good hands."

I finished writing in my journal about how sexy I thought Dre' was and how I was happy that Kenya had played match-maker this time. I closed my journal, ready to talk to Kenya about Dre' some more but she was already out like a light. I kissed my little sister's cheek goodnight. The next time I see her she will have become a woman.

CHAPTER FOUR

Dre' was definitely diggin' me, I could tell by the way he said my name when we talked. The way he looked at me across the table sent chills down my spine. I felt all giddy inside as we enjoyed our dinner at Fishbone's, which one of my favorite restaurants located in downtown Detroit's Greektown district. You could've knocked me over with a feather when, after Dre' didn't use my number for a whole week, he surprised me with an invite to dinner and a movie for a double date with Rashad the weekend after Kenya's party.

Dre' held my hand under the table as we chatted with Rashad and his date. I kept wondering what Dre's lips tasted like all through dinner. I'll bet they tasted like watermelon Jolly Ranchers. I knew I was trippin', having thoughts like that but Dre' was so different. I had to be careful though. The fly types already thought they could get any woman and I wasn't about to let him turn me into a statistic. I was happily satisfied with things just the way they were.

The thought of being with someone like Dre' scared me, especially since I was feelin' him the way that I was. Guys were usually cool until they found out they had your heart. Then it was over. The dog would come out. I had seen it happen too many times. Dre' was cool but I wasn't about to let my guard down, not yet anyway. I sipped my lemon flavored water to cool myself down. Dre' would trip if he knew what was going through my head, which was exactly why I made up my mind to keep it on the low and take it slow.

Time flew by and as the end of summer approached. Even though my plan was to kick it with Dre' from a distance, meaning without getting' my emotions involved, that's not how it turned

29

out. Even though I didn't mean to, I was hangin' out with him almost everyday, just kickin' it. He was so cool and he definitely possessed the qualities that attracted me: fine, intelligent, nice build, financially fit and fine. Plus, he wasn't actin' pressed to get intimate with me. That was definitely different. He earned a couple of cool points for that alone. Most guys were all about one thing, but if Dre' was pressed, he didn't show it. His Daddy had definitely raised him right. A lot of preacher's kids were buck wild but Dre' was the exception. He always treated me like a lady. That's why I finally gave in to my feelings and let him be my man.

Kenya laughed as I told her the latest news on me and Dre'.

"Girl, that ain't news, I knew that was gonna happen the first time you saw him. You should have seen the sparkle in your eyes. You were gone at first sight."

"I know, I hate to admit it but I'm glad you invited him to that party, I'm feelin' him."

"Good but, girl, I have to go. I don't mean to cut you off but I'm studying for a major biology exam."

"Okay, love you," I said, a little saddened at not having more time to talk to my baby sister.

"Love you, too, bye." She hung up.

That was about the size of our conversations since she'd moved to Cali. No more late night chat sessions, no more giggle sessions, it was all about studying. Not that I didn't understand, that was the college life, at least for Kenya. I was all the more thankful for Dre', he'd become my new best friend.

Needless to say, my Mama, the hater, was presented with another dream to squash. My happily ever after dream with Dre'. She tried to blow the top off our relationship, always blockin'. She was enough to drive a person batty. Dre's schedule with school and work was hectic enough without Mama trying to come up with busy work to take up my time. And Dre' didn't make it any better. He was always on her team; talkin' about maybe she was just lonely, trying to help me to see her point of view. I'll bet she would like him if she knew how hard he defended her. I wasn't even gonna trip, she wasn't about to ruin my relationship.

We walked hand in hand into our little corner of the backyard after satisfying her curiosity about when I was coming home. Dre' and I fired up the grill as we cooked dinner together and we kicked it in the backyard since it had become one of our favorite weekend destinations.

The hours we spent in the swing made me look forward to weekends. Laying my head on Dre's muscular chest and inhaling his hypnotic cologne as the swing glided back and forth was like heaven on earth. He held me close like no one had ever done 'cause I'd never let anyone get that close. It scared me to fall in love but I couldn't help it. Dre' was a dream come true and I wanted him more than anything. Almost as much as I wanted be the best thing to hit hip-hop since Mary J. Blige. I luxuriated in the bliss I felt as we laughed and talked under the star lit sky until I finally let him leave as the moon began to disappear and the sun made its presence known.

Mama was at it again as I woke up in a good mood from having spent the past couple hours dreaming about Dre's arms wrapped around me as we watched the sunrise.

"Kayla," she yelled in that loud and irritating voice, "Get outta that bed. Half the day is gone and you're still in bed!"

I looked at my bedside clock. It was only 9:15 in the morning. This chick was trippin'.

I pulled my pillow over my head in an attempt to muffle her voice as my door swung open and Mama strutted into the room, opening the blinds, inviting the sunshine to infiltrate my room.

"Kayla, get up, I need you to take my car to be serviced and they close in an hour. Get up!" her voice boomed.

"I'm up," I responded to her rude invasion on my savory

31

dream.

"Staying up with that boy all night, you need to be in at a reasonable hour," her voice sounded like fingernails dragging across a chalk board.

All she could see was this man that, according to her, was trying to steal her daughter away, when in actuality, she was pushing me towards him. I felt sorry for her. She needed to get a life. Maybe if she could get Rodney to settle down with her she could spend more time concentratin' on her own relationship and less time in my business. She gave me plenty of material to write in my journal, that's for sure.

"Dang Mama, we were just in the backyard."

"Doin' God knows what!" She shook her head as if the thought was too much for her to even entertain.

She was on some other stuff, was all I could think as I crawled out of bed and dragged myself into the shower, allowing the hot jets of water to beat against my back to wake me up.

What was her deal? It wasn't just Dre', she was a hater. She was a perfect example of "misery loves company" but it wasn't my fault that her man didn't spend quality time with her. It must be awful to wake up miserable everyday and only be able to ease the pain by trying to cause the people around you to feel the same way.

As I massaged my skin with the Victoria's Secret scented loofah, picturing myself hugged up against Dre' last night, I anticipated the moment I'd see him again.

"Kaaaaayla!..." Mama's yell cut off my reverie.

"Yes, Mommy dearest," I answered under my breath. "I'm almost done, Mama," I yelled through the door, frowning at the interruption.

Happy to get out of the house for awhile, I zoomed into the Lexus dealer's parking lot. After this morning's episode of Mama trying to run my life, I decided that what I really needed to focus on was my future. The sooner I made some moves, the sooner I could get paid and then I wouldn't have to deal with the Mama drama. I knew just what I was going to do to. There was a music conference coming up and I was going to be there! I was ready to kick down some doors in the music industry.

Even though Mama had been buggin' this morning, I wasn't going to let it stop me from having a good day. Tika and I hooked up and we enjoyed a day of beauty at the spa, her treat. I'd gotten my hair fixed in spiral curls, had my nails filled, received a freshly air-brushed French manicure and to top off my beauty treatment I got a facial, massage and pedicure.

My new Baby Phat outfit was hot, too, accentuating my curves in all the right places! I had to look fly for tonight. As soon as nightfall hit, me and my home girls were hittin' open mic night at Paradise's, the local hot spot where for five bucks up-and-coming artists could showcase their talent.

I was surprised to see Dre's tall physique as I rounded the corner near our house. He was posted up by the garage looking sexy in his Roc-a-Wear jeans and tee. I checked my appearance in the mirror, licking my lips, and smoothing my fiery auburn hair back just to make sure my curls fell perfectly as I whipped Mama's candy apple red Lexus IS300 into the driveway while Outkast's, "Hey Ya," blasted from the speakers. I hit the automatic window control with a freshly done, perfectly French-manicured nail.

"What's up, baby?" He greeted me, as the window slid down. He stepped forward and planted a kiss on my lips. Umm, his kisses were the bomb!

"Not much," I answered, my face lit up with a smile, showing all my pearly whites.

Dre' was the best man I'd ever had. My other relationships hadn't worked out because all they wanted was one thing and if I told them I was waiting for marriage, just to get their reactions, they'd sooner or later prove me right. I wasn't even stressin' on that though. I'd rather wait than to have some guy get what they

33

want and then run around tellin' all his homies and tryin' to dog me out. My girls went through it everyday. Not one of them was still with the first guy they'd given in to and I didn't wanna be one of those chicks who would have several partners before I settled down. I knew Dre' could have any female he wanted but I'd never heard of him doing dirt behind my back, though my home girls were convinced that all men were dogs. I mean, I'd run across a couple of envious chicks when we were out together but I never let them knock me off my square. I laughed when they tried to catch his attention, 'cause he would always play them like he didn't see them, at least when I was around. But if he did do some dirt, he'd better not let it get back to me or we were going to have some trouble.

Even though I was always complimented on my looks, I wasn't about to let people think that I was some scary chick who was gonna get dogged out because I was scared of breaking a nail or something, 'cause I wasn't. There were always jealous chicks when I was younger, trying to start stuff just because they weren't too easy on the eyes, so I had to fight, just to let them know I wasn't friendly. I guess some of them assumed I was stuck up because guys thought I was pretty, but that wasn't my problem. Ironically, those were the same chicks who would later try to be my friend, talkin' 'bout, "I used to not like you, but you're cool," and I'd be like "whatever".

Now it was a new batch of jealous chicks, all on Dre's tip 'cause he was from the ATL and for some reason, that piqued their curiosity. I never discussed our relationship with other females; that's how chicks tried to get in and then act shiesty. I knew chicks that fed off of digging up dirt on other people's men and I wasn't about to put my relationship on the bulls eye, so I left them clueless. I *had* to. The last thing I needed was for some busy body to start some drama and interfere in what I had going. So I kept our business, our business. Let the undercover haters stay frustrated. Who cared? Yeah, they said I was too secretive but that's because I'd learned my lesson the hard way by running my mouth too much. But I wasn't 'bout to fall for the okie doke twice.

"Baby, my homeboy D.J's at Club Bling and I told him about you," Dre' smiled, almost unable to contain his excitement. "He wants me to bring you by his studio and guess what?" He reminded me of a little kid with a big surprise the way he got so excited over things.

"What?" I asked impatiently, anxious to be clued in on the big news before I passed out from curiosity.

"We're gonna cut you a real demo and..." he paused, building up the suspense.

"For real," I squealed in delight, "What else?" I pleaded, hating being left dangling in suspense.

"You're gonna have a chance to perform at "The Show"," he said, giving me that "who's the man" look.

"Are you serious?" I asked. Dre', who was known for being a jokester, "The Show" was an annual music showcase that took place during the week long *Industry* Music Conference and Awards. The conference I'd just been reading about earlier. Anybody who was anybody in the music industry would be there from label heads, executives, artists, managers, producers and all the kinds of people I needed to mingle with to get my career crackin'!

"Yeah, I'm serious," he replied, "I don't play when it comes to my artists, so we gotta make sure you're prepared. We're 'bout to be on the grind and get you an album cut."

"Oh, what, you're my manager now?" I kidded.

"I could be," he was suddenly very serious with his hand propping up his chin as he mulled the idea over in his head.

"Yeah, right," I smiled, rolling my eyes and stepping out of the car.

"I'm serious," he replied. "I want you to come with your best material. Start writing everyday. I'ma book you some shows to help get you some exposure. We're 'bout to promote you and get you ready for this thing."

"You are serious, aren't you?" I laughed at the idea. "You'd do that?"

"*Girl*, I'ma do whatever I can to help you get on," He laughed. "You're my girl. I *want* you to make it so we're 'bout to do this!"

I was bursting with joy on the inside. Dre' was down for me. I knew he would help me if he said he would. With his business savvy and my talent, we could definitely get it crackin'.

"So when do I meet..." I gestured with my hands for him to fill in the blank.

"Shawn," he answered. "We can go by there now! That's why I'm here, at your service," he added jokingly, bowing before me.

"Ha, ha, real funny," I laughed. "Just let me leave my Mom a note. You know how she is." I said with an exasperated sigh. Mama was a trip, that's how she was. She acted like even though I was twenty, I was still a baby. She didn't want me to do anything.

"Yeah, I know." Dre' said, mimicking my actions and rolling his eyes.

Ringing the doorbell to Shawn's attic turned studio, we were buzzed into the soundproofed room over his garage where music blasted and a group of guys were in the sitting room flowing back and forth as the beat played in the background. Dre' introduced us and Shawn wanted to hear me sing. He put on an up tempo R&B track, causing the guys' attention to be riveted to me.

"I'm impressed, he said, nodding his head as I free-styled to the track. "You can blow. I have some more tracks that would fit you *perfectly*." he said, queuing up another track. The beat was smooth and melodic, taking me away to a place of peace and relaxation. Shawn had the skills I had been looking for in a producer.

"You like that?" he smiled, as I was sure my eyes showed how impressed I was.

"Yeah, it's tight!" He went to the next track. It made me wanna dance with it's up-tempo beat. "Ooh, that's hot. Now I can picture myself rockin' shows to this and that one, too. That's a banger," I added, as he skipped through the tracks, giving me a taste of what he could do for me.

"I told Dre' I *got* tracks. You can do your pre-production recording right here if you want to. I know another spot where we can mix and master. If you're serious, we can do this," he said, his eyes focused intently on me.

Dre' nodded from where he was standing, signaling to me that Shawn was cool and it was up to me.

"That's cool with me," I replied. "I'm ready."

"Cool, we can work on some tracks today if you have time," he said, checking his watch. "We can see how we vibe and I can burn 'em to a disc so you can start writing."

"Cool," I agreed, taking my jacket off. I wasn't expecting to start today, but the sooner the better.

He pressed a button on the board and the first track bumped through the speakers.

"*Boy, all I really want to know, are you diggin' me fa sho, 'cause I like ya style, ya drive me wild, you make me wanna oh...If I tell you how I feel, and I let you know the deal, boy 'cause what I feel is real, I'm bout to lose control*," I sang. Dre' was over in the corner, bobbin' his head like his favorite jam was playing, boosting my confidence and motivating me to keep going.

"Baby, you sound hot!" he hopped up and hugged me from behind, pulling me close as his hands wrapped around my waist, dancing with me.

"Really?" I asked, with a shy grin.

"Yeah, keep going!" he encouraged me, so I did.

"My friends, don't understand this thing with us, they don't know about this trust, so they envious, 'cause they don't know but that don't faze me; I just wanna say them words to you, but tell me do you feel the same way too, don't you know you got me goin', goin', goin' crazy? You got me, you got me, you got me, you got me, you got me, got me goin', goin', goin' crazy!"

We worked on the song, writing and arranging the track until I was ready to put myself to the test. I went into the booth to record my vocals, feeling the music in my soul as it played through the headphones while my manager and Shawn talked business.

We laid the track and I was floating on air as we left the studio with the songs burned to CD. I'd forgotten all about going to Paradise's, as I checked my phone I saw that I'd missed five calls and voice mail messages awaited me wanting to know how come I hadn't shown up at the club.

CHAPTER FIVE

"I missed open mic," I reminded Dre.

"That's alright, we did something good," he said, holding up the cd Shawn had burned with the song we'd created on it. "With your voice and these tracks...Kayla, I'm tellin' you, you're gonna blow up!" Dre' said, grabbing a hold of my hand.

"You really believe in me?"

"Girl, I've always believed in you from the first time I heard you sing and I'm gonna always believe in you." He reassured me. "You're my girl."

"I love you, Dre," slipped out before I even realized that my mouth was open. I covered my mouth as if that would retract the admission. I'd shocked myself, but at the same time it had seemed so natural to tell my man that I loved him. I looked away shyly.

"Kayla, it's alright." He laughed. "I love you, too." He confessed, showing that smile that was to die for and draping his arm around my shoulder to pull me close.

"Dang, girl, the way you looked just now would make somebody think you'd just confessed to a murder or somethin'," he started laughing.

"I just caught myself off guard."

"Oh, you *don't* love me?" he laughed.

"No, I..."

"No?" He was making fun of me.

"Dre', stop!" I laughed, playfully hitting at his arm. That's one of the reasons I was in love with him, he *always* had jokes and kept me in stitches. We laughed all the way to my house, listening to my new musical creation as we drove. Every time I tried to get serious, he'd say something silly. What took the cake was when he sang into his hand like it was a microphone.

"Dre', all I really want to know, if you diggin' me for sho, 'cause I like ya style, you drive me wild, I'm going crazy." He sang, rubbing his hands all over his body, imitating Prince or was it "the artist formerly known as…" shoot, I don't know, but it was funny. He imitated Jay Anthony Brown's routine from Tom Joyner's morning show, jacking up the lyrics to my song. I was still cracking up as we pulled into my driveway.

"Dang, she's waiting' up for me." I sighed, plopping back against the seat, as my Mama cut the porch light on. She blew my whole mood. The clock read 2:12 am. I knew I would hear an earful.

"I'll see you tomorrow, alright?" Dre' said, confirming our next date at the studio.

"Alright," I leaned over for my sugar and lost myself in Dre's sweet kiss before going off to face the warden.

"Pray for me," I said, dragging myself out of the car and up the steps to the house.

"Hey, Mama," I was trying to act nonchalant, praying that I could just make it to my room, but that would've been too good to be true.

"Hey, Mama?!" she responded. "Do you know what time it is?"

"Un, un but I sure am tired. I can't wait to hit the sack!" I tried to kiss her cheek and brush past her.

"Kayla, I have told you time and time again, if you're going to live in my house, you're going to live by my rules and the rule is to be in this house at a reasonable hour."

"But Mama," I started, still excited about how wonderful my day had turned out, "Dre' introduced me to a producer and he's so tight. He's going to help me record my music." I tried to

40

explain, still exhilarated from my studio session. "I was only at his studio and I left you a note. I don't see what the big deal is," I mumbled.

"I told you, you need to put that on the back burner and get yourself a real job." She couldn't even be happy that I started a graphic design business, designing flyers to get some dough even though I was making enough to not have to ask her for money. I got paid to lace hooks every once in awhile, too. But to Mama, that didn't count for anything.

"But I love singing, *that's* what I want to do. Why should I work somewhere that's not going to help me get to where *I* want to be in life?"

"And where is it you want to be? Hanging' out in the streets all night, trying to get you some blingy bling doing that hippity-hop?" she asked, disdain dripping from her voice.

Did she hear what she just said?

"Look, Kayla, I know you think all that hippity-hop stuff is 'cool'," she gestured with her hands, "but you need to think about your future. You *need* to go to school so you can do something productive with your life."

Was that a hint of concern I detected? If it was, it made me want to gag.

"Mama, I'm in the studio recording so I *can* get better at singing and so I can meet people in the business. Yes, I do love *hip-hop,"* I stressed the correct pronunciation of the word, "and I love to sing and I'm not going to stop until I make it!" I stated, boldly.

"Oh, really?" she said, putting her hands on her hips. "Do you know what the chances are of you making it as a singer?"

"Yes, they're as good as anyone else's and Dre' is even going to book me some shows and promote me."

"Dre' this and Dre' that," she mocked me, "That boy has got you trippin'."

I thought about the song I'd just recorded and she was right. He did have me trippin' but in a good way. I was in love.

"Dre' believes in me, how come you can't?"

"Because you need to face facts," she pounded her fist on her palm, "the chances of you making it in the music business are slim to none, that's why you need to go to school and get you a nursing degree. You can even be a doctor if you want to." she explained, "You don't even have to be in the medical field. Just get in a field where you'll be guaranteed a job."

"I'm not Kenya or you, Mama. Why would you even want me to get some corporate job with all these companies that are going bankrupt?" I countered. "There's no such thing as a guaranteed job anymore and I don't want to be a doctor or a nurse. *I'm a singer!*" I almost hollered, restraining myself out of respect, even though I was breathing hard and my nostrils flared from anger.

She'd struck a chord, trying to plant that stuff in my head that the only way I was going to make it in life was to follow her recipe.

How come she just couldn't take my career seriously? That was her problem. I could feel hot tears boiling in the corners of my eyes, threatening to spill uncontrollably and I definitely didn't want to give her the satisfaction of knowing that she'd stirred my emotions to this point. She could make me so mad sometimes with her narrow mindedness. I wanted to smack her like they did in the movies to jar her into reality. It would feel so good to give in to my emotions just this once. I balled and unballed my fists as I bit my lip angrily, my eyes slitted at her in anger.

"Well, you're not going to be hanging out at that studio and coming up in *here* at all hours of the night!" That same old song that she'd cried a million times irritated me. I was tired of hearing her down me and what I wanted to do with my life.

I took a deep breath to calm down. Ten…nine…eight… I

counted, attempting to put the reigns on my emotions.

"Mama," I spoke slowly, choosing my words carefully, "the only way I'm going to make it as a singer is to record my songs and to do that, I have to keep going to the studio." I explained to the brick wall for the hundredth time. "Would it make a difference if I went in the morning? Then would you support me?" I asked, out of curiosity, half pleading for her cooperation.

She sighed heavily and shook her head, like I was still the one trippin'.

"Ma, I love you and I respect you but I don't understand why you have *always* tried to stop me from pursuing my dreams. It seems like after Daddy almost messing up your dream that you would do anything to help me pursue mine but ever since I started really wanting this, you've been against me and I don't understand that."

No response. She just stood there like she was letting me get this off my chest before she said anything.

"I'm twenty years old and it's time for me to pursue *my* dreams, not yours."

"Really?" she started, sizing me up and giving me a *no you're not* glare.

"I'm sorry that you can't believe in me, but I'm not going to let anyone stop me, not even you, Mama."

"Is that right?" she said, sucking on her teeth and stepping all up in my personal space. "You think you can live under my roof and tell me what you are and are not going to do when I've told you the rules?"

"I'm not tryin' to disrespect you," I said in a soft voice, backing away as she tried to intimidate me, "but God gave me a voice to sing for a reason and I'm not gonna waste it." My words fell on deaf ears. "Going to the studio and performing at night is a part of this business and pretty soon that's going to include traveling, too, and I can't miss this opportunity. It's my dream," I said almost whining.

"Then you need to take your business elsewhere, 'cause you are not going to be staying out all night and chasing behind that man and getting caught up in that crazy music industry and some singing career that's a million to one long shot."

I could hardly believe my ears.

"Mama, what are you saying? What do you mean I need to take my business elsewhere?" I asked in disbelief. She was blowing things all out of proportion.

"Kayla, it's your choice, Ms. *I'm twenty now.*" She mimicked me, "Making choices is a part of growing up, so you decide if you want to live by my rules or if you want to make your own rules, it's all up to you." She stood firmly with her arms crossed as she laid out her ultimatum.

I couldn't believe she was playing her own flesh and blood this close. Either give up my singing or get out. What kind of choice was that? How was I supposed to pursue my career if I was on a short leash? This wasn't right.

"Alright, Mama," I saw her stance relax as she prepared to savor her victory, "I guess I'll have to find someplace else to stay 'cause I want to pursue my singing career."

She frowned up in surprise but quickly regained her composure but not before I saw the look of shock crease her forehead.

"Fine," she stated calmly as she turned, walked back to her bedroom and closed her door, not only shutting me out of our home but shutting the door of her heart to her own daughter.

I stood in the hallway as the reality of what was happening sank in but still not understanding how things had spiraled out of control so quickly. The whole scene had unfolded so fast. I couldn't believe that I'd come in from one of the best days of my life to end up in this mess.

How could she play me like this? I didn't understand. It

was a cold-hearted dis. Didn't I mean *anything* to her? My head throbbed as anger rose up inside me. But it was greater than anger, I was furious! Now I didn't have anything. Maybe I should've just said what she wanted, just given in to her. But if I did, she would control me for the rest of my life. She'd pulled the rug right out from under me. I knew she was trying to break me so I'd give up singing and let her control my life. If I ever needed confidence in myself, now was the time. I couldn't fall apart, not now. I had to keep it together however my head and my heart said two different things. My head said 'be strong' but my heart cried. I could hear her smirking behind her closed door, "you made your bed now lie in it."

I was going to stand by my decision, but when I made it as a singer, and I would, I would come back and let her see with her own eyes how successful I'd become and I wasn't even going to say, "I told you so." My success would say it all. I was going to treat her extra kind because I, unlike her, really believed that God doesn't like ugly and her way of doing things was horrendous.

I dragged myself into my room, feeling the torrent of hot tears welling up inside me again. I swung my clothes furiously onto my bed. Mama's behavior was unconscionable. She *needed* Jesus. I looked towards the door angrily, still breathing hard, wishing she was standing on the other side and I could burn a hole through the door with my eyes.

All I wanted was to have a good life. Why was she so against that? I'd been blessed to have opportunities to go into the studio for free, but Mama had stopped that. I had opportunities with different managers when I'd participated in talent competitions, she had shut all that down, drilling into my head that those music industry folk were a bunch of snakes and crooks. I couldn't argue with her on that point because some of them were, but I'd had opportunities to work with some pretty good people and every single time, Mama had cut my plans short without even

45

giving me a chance. I knew what was going on and that made me feel worse. My own Mama was out to sabotage me but I was convinced that singing was my purpose and I wasn't going to let even her stop me from doing what I had to do to get on. If this wasn't my purpose, I'd find out. But she didn't give me a chance to find out if I could make it; she just knocked me down every time I tried to take a step forward. A part of me was happy to be leaving. I was worn out and tired of her trying to dictate my every move.

"Control freak," I muttered under my breath.

I had been waiting to turn eighteen so I could make my own choices without the fear of her threatening to kick me out. I knew that if I wanted this, I would have to do whatever it took to make it happen, including getting out of my Mama's house. I flipped open my pink Baby Phat cell phone and pressed #2 to speed dial Dre'.

"Hey, girl, you missing me already?" he answered, laughing.

"Yeah, I miss you already, Dre'," I said, trying to keep my voice from quivering.

"Kayla," he asked, "What's wrong?"

"Dre', my Mama wants me out of her house." My voice cracked and I couldn't control the quivering in it as I tried to tell Dre' how Mama had just played me.

"Why?"

"Because, man, she's trippin' about me singing again," I explained. It was the same old song. I knew he was tired of hearing it. "Dre', I'm sorry to dump all this on you, but I couldn't take her always trying to forbid me from singing. I had to stand up for myself and she kicked me out."

"Where are you?" he asked.

"I'm in my room…" I sniffed, "packing my stuff."

"Kay, you know you can come and stay here for as long as you want to, I got you." He reassured me.

"Do you mean it?" I asked, not knowing if he was just trying to be nice or if he'd really be there for me. I know it was all of a sudden. We'd never even talked about moving in together. We both had been raised to believe that men and women shouldn't live together or have sex until after they were married. Dre' and I shared the same values and we respected each other. He was not only my boyfriend, but a cool friend as well. I loved him for that. He was just good people.

"Remember I told you that I love you today?" he asked."

"Yeah, but—"

"I meant that," he interrupted, cutting me off mid-sentence. "You mean the world to me. I'm not playin' games with you," he said convincing me that he was sincere.

"You mean the world to me, too."

"Don't even worry about it, Kay, I'm coming to scoop you right now." he assured me, before hanging up.

I felt numb not knowing what my future would hold, but I was about to find out if I had what it took to see my dreams become a reality. It was all up to me now. I snapped my bag shut and took one last look around the room that had been mine since we'd moved here five years ago. I was going to miss this room where I'd stayed up so many nights writing songs. The room where I'd had my karaoke machine, making amateur cassette recordings of myself before I'd ever even stepped foot in a real recording studio. I guess now it was a part of my past. I flipped the light switch off for the last time and dragged my bags down the hallway.

"Bye, Mama," I whispered, stepping out onto the porch to wait for Dre'. Not only was I leaving the place I'd called home for the past five years, I was stepping out of my life as a little girl and into the challenges of womanhood.

CHAPTER SIX

He checked his appearance once more to make sure he was GQ, smiling at the reflection in the mirror as he smoothed his perfectly trimmed mustache one last time. He ran his manicured hands over his face, grabbed his frames, and hopped in the jag that awaited him to make his appearance at the Industry Awards Show. He was especially intrigued by one artist's name whose presence would definitely give the other showcasing acts a run for their money. He'd been following her career for the last couple of months as she emerged out of nowhere to capture the hearts of everyone who was blessed enough to experience and be aroused by her voice.

Impressed by her curvaceous, yet petite physique, Indian bone structure and thick black mane that flowed down her back, he'd been unable to get her image out of his mind ever since he'd first laid eyes on her. He'd been captivated by the melodic sway of her hips the first time he'd witnessed her performance, so much so that he eagerly awaited the next time, and then the time after that, until he was sure that his behavior bordered on the obsessive. But he didn't care. Her beauty had to be acknowledged. And her voice…he imagined that that's what heaven's angels sounded like as they breathed supernatural life into songs.

He winked at himself in the rearview mirror as he slid into the jag, humming to himself as he pictured his arms wrapped around her small frame, kissing her sweet lips, looking into her innocent eyes as he wined her and dined her, and made promises that brought affectionate smiles to her lips.

He had to shake it off. He could feel himself slipping into a daze as he let his mind wander.

"Calm down," he told himself. "She'll be yours soon." He

48

smiled at his own reassuring words.

Her presence added an element of perfection to his plan. In his wildest dreams, he'd never dreamed that things would unfold so effortlessly and so perfectly. He caught the excitement in his eyes as he checked the rearview for traffic.

"Stay cool, man," he reminded himself as he navigated the jag down I-75 towards the arena.

He'd been waiting his entire life for this moment and it had finally arrived.

As he strode through the arena with confidence, he blended right in, drawing the uplifted eyebrows of females whose foreheads may as well have been branded by dollar figures. Flashbulbs were constantly going off as photographers snapped pimped-out rappers, displaying their bling with scantily clad females draped on their arms as they worked the red carpet and milled about the arena, milking every moment as their attire was admired and their names were yelled by their star struck fans. Microphones were held out as urban America's elite granted much sought after interviews and the room buzzed with excitement as the music industry players gathered for a night of partying hard and acknowledgement of the hard work that drove their sales past platinum status and caused their bank rolls to surpass that of the average working class urbanite's yearly income.

The atmosphere was eclectic as he smiled to himself, knowing that his plan was finally in effect.

CHAPTER SEVEN

The M.C. called out my name and the butterflies that had been fluttering about in my belly finally settled down as peace flowed through me. The positive affirmations that Tika told me to practice saying had paid off. I'd been declaring that I had confidence and it finally began to kick in. The buzzing of the crowd didn't distract me neither did I let those tormenting thoughts of not hitting each note perfectly frighten me. My mind was calm, centered and focused on doing my best.

Walking through the curtains that separated me from the stage, applause followed as my heels clicked onto the stage. Almost blinded by the intensity of the stage lights, amazingly, I found the path to the center of the stage, lifted the microphone from its stand and took a deep breath. I was oblivious to everything around me except for the sound of my own breathing.

The violins cut through the silence that had fallen upon the room, signaling the intro to my song. The tinkling cymbals were like intense electrical currents flowing through my body causing my adrenaline to rush! The rhythm took over my body traveling through my bones as I bounced to the beat of the drum.

I surveyed the audience; all eyes gazed expectantly at me. "What's up, everybody!!! Y'all ready for this!!!" I screamed, moving my hips to the music as my never shy, crowd ready, alter-ego took over.

"Yeah," they screamed back. The beat dropped, sending the signal to my brain that the moment was near. The crowd swayed hypnotically. Expectancy filled the room. My moment had arrived. I walked the stage, talking to the audience as if we were old friends.

"I've had something on my mind for quite some time now. And I think tonight's the perfect night for me to get this off my chest!" I yelled. "What y'all think?"

"Yeah!" The crowd screamed.

My hands were clasped tightly around the microphone, as I pictured Dre' and moved to the music as I delivered the verse perfectly. *"Boy, I just gotta let you know,"* the words slid off my lips as if it was second nature. Actually, it was. I'd waited my entire life for this opportunity and now as I moved, I knew in my heart that this was where I was supposed to be. Moving along with the rhythm, the powerful lyrics energized me, taking over my body as I sang. I was in a zone, manipulating the audience, mesmerizing them with my passion and my words. Dre' stood front and center of the crowd. My eyes locked with his for a moment. He smiled, admiration showing, inspiring me to give my all. The world was in the palm of my hand as I did my thing, moving in perfect sync with my dancers, emitting crazy energy as we executed the choreographed routine.

I wanted to scream 'I've arrived!' If my Mama could see me now, she would probably faint. I gave my heart and soul as the hot, sweaty room filled with the excitement that lets you know you were in the place to be.

The crowd danced as I spun my web, drawing them in just like I'd envisioned a million times. I'd never felt this kind of happiness, the kind that came from feeding off the audiences' positive reaction to me. This was that feeling I'd been waiting for my entire life, the one that confirmed that I'd found my purpose. People said that I had an awesome stage presence but being on the stage felt so natural to me, it exuded through my interaction with the crowd.

The final notes of my song played and for a moment I stood there, taking it all in, hating for it to end. The audience went wild, yelling and cheering as I stood there, chest heaving, soaking it all in. They clapped, cheered, and screamed my name and the applause continued to fill the room even after I exited the stage. I

51

knew right then, I was addicted.

"They really liked me!" I screamed.

"Baby, you were tight!" Dre' shouted as he greeted me backstage, lifting me off my feet, sweeping me up into his arms, and swinging me around.

"Everybody, give it up one more time for Kayla!" shouted the DJ, hyping the crowd up even more. The eruption of applause far exceeded my expectations.

My new family embraced me as I reappeared at the after party after my performance, hugging and congratulating me as Dre' and I navigated our way through the crowd.

A waitress appeared with a bottle of champagne. "Courtesy of K.D." she said, placing two glasses in front of us.

"Who?" I had to shout over the loud music.

"K.D.," she said, her eyebrow raised, pointing out a tall slim figure, making his way through the crowd toward us.

"Hi, Kayla, I'm Karlos Day, but everyone calls me K.D.," the stranger introduced himself, extending his hand, as his eyes traveled the length of my body. "Your performance was off the chain, you're amazing!"

"Thank you," I replied, shaking his hand. "This is my fiancée, Dre'."

"What's up, man?" He extended his hand to Dre'. "Kayla, I was blown away by your performance!" He gestured by clutching at his heart and smiling. "I love your voice, you sing like an angel."

"Well, thank you, K.D.," I blushed. I could feel Dre' giving me a disapproving look.

"Anyway, I'll get right to the point, I'm working on a project for a soundtrack that I think you'd be perfect for."

"A soundtrack?" I inquired. That definitely piqued my interest.

"Yes, we're putting together a soundtrack for an

independent film that'll be released in the spring of next year and we have more projects lined up after that..."

"Really, what do *you* do?" I inquired further.

"I produce stars," he stated, boldly. "And I can see that you're headed straight towards stardom!" I blushed again. "What I'd like to do is set up a meeting so that we can discuss the project and I can introduce you to the rest of the camp and we'll see how it goes from there." He finished.

"Well, why don't you give us your card and we'll be in touch," Dre' intervened, stepping between us.

"Sure, man," he paused, pulling a card from inside his jacket. "I look forward to hearing from you, Kayla, hopefully this can be the beginning of a mutually prosperous relationship," he said, putting his card in my hand. I had a feeling that comment was meant to agitate Dre'. "It was nice meeting you both." He extended his hand once again. "Enjoy the champagne."

"Thank you," I said. And he worked his way back through the crowd and then disappeared.

"Kayla, can I have your autograph," I heard, turning around to see a couple of *my fans* holding out copies of my CD for me to sign, which I did gladly.

"Did you hear that, baby?" I shouted to Dre'.

"Yeah, girl, I told you, you were tight!" He hugged me. He poured the Cristal and made a toast to me. "To Kayla, my rising star, may success follow you wherever you go!"

"Wherever we go," I corrected him. We clicked our glasses together and let the bubbly delight our palettes. I put Karlos Day's card in my Chanel bag.

"Baby, it's something about that cat that I don't like," he said, shaking his head. That was strange coming from Dre, he liked everybody.

"What, that he paid me attention?" I laughed.

"Naw, I saw him checking you out when we first got here,"

53

he started, "And I can understand that, I mean, you look *hot* tonight!" He said, as his eyes ran up and down my body. "But that cat was on some other stuff. I don't know what, Kay, but it's just something about that dude." He said, a slight frown creasing his forehead as if he was trying to figure out what it was about K.D. that bothered him.

"Aw, baby, it ain't nothin'," I reassured him, adding a kiss on his cheek for good measure. I could see he didn't let it go, even though he made no further comments on it.

"Girl, you were the bomb!" My cousin Tika popped up in the V.I.P. section out of nowhere exclaiming.

"Tika, I didn't know you made it!" I was so happy. Tika was my favorite cousin, the comedian in the family. We'd always been close but she was even more like a sister, since Kenya was away at college.

"Yeah, right!" she laughed. "Girl, you know I was not about to miss my favorite cousin's debut! You know how long it takes some cats to get this far?"

"I'm glad you came!"

"Girl, you did your thing, I am so proud of you!"

"Thanks, Ma," I hugged her.

"I saw your Moms today," she said, "Girl, she was happy for you when I told her you were performing here tonight."

"Um, was she?" I responded, nonchalantly.

"Girl, you need to *quit trippin'*, that's the only Mom you have."

"Well, I ain't the one kicking relatives out of the house and I don't wanna ruin my good night by talking about her," I stated but Tika was already on to something else.

"Oh, y'all over here poppin' bubbly, huh? Tryin' to come up with the big dogs?" she asked, holding up one of the champagne bottles. "Y'all done had a couple of shows and now y'all some ballers, huh?" she kidded.

54

"Girl, my baby got that one," I referred to the bottle of Cristal she held, "and some producer cat sent this one over," I responded.

"For real, who?" she asked.

"His name was Karlos Day." I answered.

"Karlos Day?!" she exclaimed, "Girl, I been hearing his name a lot lately. Isn't he that producer cat that's working on the soundtrack for that new movie coming out next summer? He's been scoutin' out local talent 'cause the movie's written by some cat from here, but OutKast is supposed to lace it, too." Tika always had the scoop on everything and everyone, especially since the guys she dealt with were mostly in the music industry or pro-ballers.

"*Word?!*" I exclaimed. "'Cause you know how cats around here be frontin' like their doing this and doing that and ain't doing jack!" We finished the last part of the sentence in unison, with a high-five.

"Girl, you know I know," she laughed. "But I heard my home girl's baby's daddy talkin' about it."

"So, then it must be true," I replied sarcastically. Tika was always talking about she heard something or she knew something because of somebody's baby's daddy's cousin's brother's friend.

"I'm serious, Kay." She began again, "My girl Vikki's baby's daddy, Roscoe, is a rapper, and he's been tryin' his hardest to get a spot on this soundtrack and he was talkin' about this cat, Karlos Day, who's producin' it. You better holla at him. Look, girl, I gotta go shake my thing on the dance floor," she giggled. "You did good, Kay," she shouted, heading towards the dance floor, shaking all the way just like she'd said.

"Did you hear that, Dre'?" I shouted above the music, "Karlos Day is legit after all."

"Yeah, baby, I heard," he said, flatly.

"Come on, Dre'," I finished sipping my champagne and

grabbed him by the hand, "Let's dance!" I pulled him onto the dance floor. As we danced, I caught a glimpse of Karlos chatting with some other guys as Dre' and I did our thing. When Karlos' eyes met mine, he winked at me and I could've sworn I saw a little wicked smile creep across his face. It happened so fast, I thought I must be trippin'! When I looked back around, he was gone.

I felt like a star! All these "producers" were swarming around introducing themselves, tryin' to holla at Dre' on my behalf for me to appear on their various projects. Suddenly, it seemed, I was in high demand. They gave Dre' their business cards, told him about artists that needed a female to bless their tracks, and inquired about getting me into the studio. Dre' was a pro at networking and making things happen.

Millionaire, the club's owner already had me locked in to open up for The Dime Figgas, the hot female rap duo who'd just signed under Triple Threat Productions which is the company headed by a trio of Dre's college friends down in the ATL. Dre' slid into the role of my manager as if it was second nature. I trusted him with my life and he'd come through on his promise to help me. We'd produced this hot record within months and the crowds were increasing at every show. I felt like I was already a star. After tonight's success, I loved him even more.

I was too high on life to be tired and could easily have partied until the sun came up. We had been partying the whole week, during the conferences, the club events, and the networking sessions. We worked in interviews as we celebrated, blinded by flashing bulbs as cameras snapped photos for the hip-hop publications that had covered "The Show". We capped the evening off with an extravagant meal at Justin's, where we popped more Crissy. It was gravy. This had to be what Biggie bragged about in his "Juicy" video about going from nate to great.

I was singing happily, like it wasn't after 3:00 a.m., as we climbed the stairs to our second floor apartment and I inserted my key into the lock. I was feeling a little tipsy, warm and bubbly from the champagne Dre' and I had shared with our friends. As we entered our cozy apartment, Dre' grabbed me from behind, wrapping his arms around me and hugging me tight.

"Baby, I had such a good time," I said, turning my head sideways to plant a juicy kiss on his luscious lips. "Thank you so much, Dre, you're the first person that ever really helped me with my music and believed in me."

"Baby, I'll do anything to help make your dreams come true." He kissed me on the back on my neck, sending a tingle down my spine.

"Well, you are a come true dream," I giggled as I twisted the words, my senses buzzed from the drinking. Though my back was against his chest, I could feel a wide grin spreading across his face. "What?" I couldn't stand not knowing what he was grinning about.

"Kay, when you introduced me to that shady cat, you said I was your fiancée."

"I know," I started, "Don't be mad, I just didn't want him pressin' up on me, especially not knowing why he sent the champagne to our table. He might've thought I was single but I knew that would stop him in his tracks if he *was* trying to holla."

"Naw, girl, I ain't mad," he said, gently turning me around so that we were face to face. "In fact, I'm glad you said it." He paused for a second. "I really love you, Kayla. I have for a long time."

"I love you, too, Dre'." I said, looking deep into his eyes, as the chocolate centers sparkled.

He paused and smiled nervously, then started slowly, "I've been thinkin' about it a lot lately. I don't want us to just live together anymore. I want to do it right. I want to spend my life with you, Kayla."

I couldn't believe what I was hearing, I know he didn't just say he wanted to spend his life with me, but he must have because he took both of my hands in his and knelt down in front of me. My eyes were beginning to well up as I realized what was happening as he looked up at me as if I was all that mattered to him in this world. He took a deep breath and flashed his dimpled smiled that melted my heart as much now as it did the first time we'd met.

"Will you marry me?" The golden words slid off his lips effortlessly, causing my heart to skip a beat as it leapt with joy.

"Yes," I screamed, pulling him up, "Yes, yes, yes!" I planted a kiss on his lips with each word. He produced a box from out of thin air and opened it. In it sat a perfect marquise shaped diamond engagement ring. He took it out and slipped it on my finger.

"Dre' it's beautiful! I love it! I love you!" I exclaimed, marveling at the rock he'd just presented me with. "This has absolutely been the best night of my life!" I squealed, unable to contain my excitement, even at 4:00 in the morning.

"Mine, too." Dre' swept me up into his arms, just like in the movies, and spun me around, kissing me and telling me how much he loved me and *I was the happiest girl in the world*!

CHAPTER EIGHT

My life was too perfect! I was finally living my dream. After the successful release of my first single "U Got Me," Dre' had hooked up with his home boys from Atlanta at Triple Threat Productions, who were looking for a female entertainer just like me. Timing had been on our side with this one.

Dre' had executive produced the album and his marketing and promotions expertise had helped me to launch the single successfully. My performances throughout the Mid-West and the south along with the heavy promoting Dre' did to build my name had my audiences anticipating the release of my album. Everywhere I went; it exhilarated me to see flyers with my face on them. From the hood to the burbs, I had it on lock. I had gigs lined up that would keep us eating good for awhile. My website was hot. My fans thought I was off the chain. I hit the studio and was writing daily. I loved it. I loved getting up early writing, doing interviews and photo shoots, blessing tracks, doing V.I.P. at the hottest parties, going to industry events, networking. To top if all off, I was engaged to the man of my dreams. I had it going on!

"I feel like I'm living somebody else's life," I sang happily to Kenya, finally able to talk to her since she had a break from her tons of school work.

"Girl, what tripped me out was when I read that article on you in Unsigned Hype!"

"I know, wasn't that a trip!"

"Yes, girl, you got these guys open, too, Kayla. I crack up when I hear people talkin' about you. And even the chicks, they think you're so cool!"

"Girl, I'm just happy. I mean it's hard work, but I love it…this is what I've been dreamin' about my whole life."

Even Mama had to admit that she had been wrong about the singing thing. It tripped me out when she called me out of the blue and congratulated me on my hard work and not giving up even when she didn't support me. For the first time in my life, I felt like I was doing exactly what I was supposed to be doing. Every time I performed the crowds flocked. Producers were coming out the woodwork, "Dawg, I need Kayla on this track," they'd tell Dre'. "You think Kayla will lace this hook?" the rappers wanted to know. And every appearance I did made the anticipation of my own album that much greater. Dre' had even hooked me up for a competition on BET's 106 & Park. The chance to meet A.J. and Free had me trippin'.

Karlos Day was persistent in his attempts to work with me. He came to all my shows. He wasn't backing down, he wanted my voice on the soundtrack, but Dre' didn't like him, so he wasn't havin' it.

"All money ain't good money, Kayla," he said, sternly, like I was trying to hook up with Karlos for some big drug deal. Pretty soon, it was more like Karlos just kept at it in an attempt to agitate Dre' since he knew Dre' didn't want me working with him. Karlos had tried to get at me on the sneak tip a couple of times, but even then, Dre' was always there to cut it short. It was like he had eyes in the back of his head. He reminded me of Mama in a way but I knew he had my best interests at heart.

Juggling my new found success had us busy all the time and it had me exhausted at times, unable to find time for myself, especially with our wedding a mere four months away. It seemed years ago that I'd been living another life, under the shelter of Mama's protectiveness, longing for the recognition that I was now getting, when in actuality, it had been less than a year.

60

I sat in Dre's office, studying the calendar filled with events that centered around me and was in a daze because of the life altering news I'd just discovered.

I held the Fact Plus pregnancy test in my quivering hand as tears rolled from my eyes into the little well where the bright red plus sign glowed, confirming that the weeks of flu-like symptoms weren't from the flu but from the embryo that had been imbedded inside my womb. After weeks of experiencing the symptoms of what I thought was stress, I finally followed Tika's orders to take the test and I'd failed.

I knew without a doubt that conception had taken place the night Dre' and I became engaged. That was the only time since Dre' and I had taken our relationship to the intimate level that we'd thrown caution to the wind. Now I was being punished for going against the rules. I sat on the edge of the bathtub for the longest time staring at the test. Tears began to well up in my eyes again at my newfound discovery. I didn't know how to feel. On one hand, this was a part of me and Dre' but on the other hand, I was just getting my career off the ground and now this.

This pregnancy put my dreams in jeopardy and I wasn't ready to let anything into my life that would do that. We'd worked too hard and I wasn't ready to give up singing, not now. Not when my name was ringing. Why did this have to happen now? Kids weren't supposed to come into the picture until I was at least thirty, not during the prime of my life as I was having fun, traveling *and* making money. People actually recognized me in the streets. They bought my music. Young girls told me they wanted to be just like me and now I'd even let them down.

Even after climbing my way up this far, there was still a lot of ground to cover before I reached that platinum dream. But it seemed within reach even without a major label backing me and I wasn't even pressed about inking a major label contract since we were the shot callers and making the doe. Who needed some label to cut me an advance and then pimp me to recoup their expenses while I played the role of the slave? It didn't appeal to me. We had a buzz going and the bigger the buzz, the more in demand I would be and when we landed a distribution deal, we would be in the position to get some real money.

I loved what we were doing and Dre' did too. My CD was selling like hotcakes. Ten dollars a pop out of the trunk, city to city, state to state.

I didn't know *how* Dre' would react to this pregnancy news. I mean, I couldn't imagine him being anything but supportive, but we'd discussed having children and it was no where in our immediate plans. This was messing with our dough and I didn't like it.

My plan was to work this business for as long as I could. Part of the allure of the music industry was its ability to catapult rising stars into the stratosphere and it was my time to shine.

Dre's father had left a musical legacy even though he'd never made it as far as Dre' and I had come. He opted to make the transition from R&B to gospel mid-career but having his life snatched away along his journey, his father's dreams had gone unfilled, fueling Dre's ambition to help me make it to the top. Being a part of the millionaire's club topped our list of to do's before having children. Having a child now threatened all of that.

I studied the pregnancy test and the bright red plus sign stood out, making the baby's presence inside of me official with its 99% accuracy rate. With one missed period and another one days late, I thought the interruption in my cycle could've been caused by the stress of performing. It wasn't uncommon for *Aunt Flow* to skip town when women were under tremendous stress.

I practiced what I was going to say to Dre' and how and when. Withholding secrets from him was definitely not one of my strengths. I was worse than an unplugged refrigerator when it came to that. I couldn't keep anything. Admiring my perfect size 6 figure, I wondered how long that would last with another human being invading my body.

My breasts were already a perfect C cup. I was content with that. I had curves in all the right places and at 5'7" I could've been *America's Next Top Model*. My smooth golden brown skin had been envied by many girls from the pretty ones to the less than perfect bunch. I'd never cut my hair and last summer, I'd had it colored a vibrant shade of auburn. It flowed down my back most days, drawing the wondering eyes of many to wonder if my hair was natural or the all too common weave. Today, I'd pulled the thick mane up into a ponytail, allowing it to flow freely as I posed in front of the mirror that separated the master bedroom from Dre's office. My new hair color was the perfect complement to my chestnut colored eyes. I was dime material, even if I had to say so myself. My almond shaped eyes twinkled back at me as I flashed a dimpled smile at myself in the mirror.

"Girl, *what are you doin'*?" Dre' asked, sneaking up on me from behind and drawing me into his arms as I squealed in surprise. I hurriedly wiped the tears from my eyes, turned to face him and planted a kiss on his luscious lips.

"Nothing, I'm just looking in the mirror."

"Oooh, Kayla, you are *sooo* fine," he squealed, mimicking my voice and blowing kisses into the mirror.

"Dre', quit," I whined, pushing him back playfully.

Dre' laughed at me. "Girl, I'm just messin' with you."

"Baby, do you think I'm getting fat?" I asked.

"Uh, uh," he replied, walking around me and eyeing me like I was a platter full of triple chocolate fudge brownies, his favorite treat.

"I'm serious," I laughed at his silliness.

He hugged me close again. "You're perfect." He reassured me. "Why are you so concerned with your body and being fat all of a sudden, anyway? You been watchin' them talk shows?" he asked, grinning, nuzzling at my neck.

"No," I laughed. "but I do have something to tell you." I began, biting at the side of my lip nervously.

"What, you're not bulimic are you?" he joked, "I don't want you getting all skinny on me."

"No, Dre', I'm pregnant," I blurted out, "I just found out today."

"Girl, quit playin'." He laughed, but I didn't crack a smile.

"I'm serious, Dre'." I stood there waiting for his reaction.

"You really *are* serious, aren't you?" he asked, all joking aside. "Dang, Kayla, how'd that happen?" was his shocked reaction.

"I don't know, it's not like I planned it," I responded.

"Come here," he grabbed me, seeing that I was scared too and hugged me tight. Then he stepped back and held me at arms length and touched my belly. "How do you feel?"

"I feel the same," I answered. "How do you feel?" I asked.

"I'm...shocked," he said, pulling me into his office, the place where the serious discussions took place. Sitting in the executive leather chair, he held on to my hand and pulled me down into his lap. "I mean, I want to have kids with you...one day but I thought we'd be married first," he said.

"And better established," I finished the sentence for him.

"Yeah, and established," he agreed. "I mean, we been doing swell...stackin' this paper. What about your singing, baby, that means the world to you?"

"Yes, it does, but so do you. And our baby is more important than that right now," I said. "What do you want to do?" I asked the inevitable question, looking into his eyes and shocking myself with my words. I could see that he was as scared as I was. I mean, neither one of us were prepared for a baby. "I can still sing. I just need to know that *you're* going to always be there for me."

64

"Kayla, you know you don't have to worry about that. I'm not goin' anywhere." And that's all I wanted to hear. His words calmed my fears. As long as I knew that Dre' supported me, I was alright. I mean, this was still so new to me, but I couldn't think of anyone I'd rather share my life and parenting with. Dre' was everything to me and I knew that a child would only strengthen our bond. I lay my head against his chest, hoping I wasn't making the biggest mistake of my life. I wanted to sing, and the thought of having a baby right now terrified me. I knew I could end it, too, but what would be the consequences and how would I feel afterwards?

I lay in our bed after talking about the baby with Dre'. I was so confused. I knew what I'd told Dre', but I didn't even believe the words. If I had this baby, not only would it ruin my career, but I may never get it back!

So many thoughts filled my mind. Why would God let this happen to me? Why now? Why not after our wedding or after we hit that million dollar mark? But at the same time, I couldn't help but to think that maybe this baby was just meant to be. This was all Dre's fault. If he wasn't so sexy, I would still be pure. I should've known that after moving in together, we wouldn't be strong enough to not get caught up and now I had proof, 'cause here I was in the prime of my life with child.

I let the news sink into my brain. Maybe it wasn't as bad as I thought. We could hire a nanny to take care of the baby while we traveled. Even if it took us a little longer to become millionaires, we could still do it. The baby didn't have to ruin everything if we didn't let it. Other entertainers had children and successful careers, so maybe, just maybe if I believed, it could happen for us too. I was sure of our love for each other and now we would share that love with our child and be the best parents any child ever had.

"You know, I used to ball back in high school," Dre' said, joining me in our room, taking an imaginary ball and shooting it into the imaginary hoop on the door. "You never know, you might be carrying the next Michael Jordan." I had to laugh. He was already making plans for our little one. I loved him so much. No matter what life threw at us, he almost always had a positive spin on it. He was more than I ever could've hoped for in a husband and I told him so.

"I love you too, Kayla, and I'm scared, Ma, but a part of me is glad you're having my baby, baby!" he joked. "Naw, seriously, I'm going to be a good Dad to our baby and the most perfect husband any woman ever had.

"Not any woman," I corrected him. "Me."

"Yeah, baby, only you." He smiled, rubbing my belly, "Only you."

Dre' had to call his Mom in Atlanta. She wanted to hop on a plane right away but Dre' persuaded her to wait until her planned arrival, two weeks prior to the wedding date. She protested, telling Dre' that she didn't know if she could wait another four months but Dre' persuaded her that we'd be okay until her planned arrival date. She was so excited, she rushed Dre' off the phone so she could inform the rest of the family.

My Mama was a little less than enthused but she managed to congratulate us. I was so happy that I wasn't going to let anything steal my joy, not even my Mama, I thought, smiling.

CHAPTER NINE

I was so nervous I couldn't help but to bite at my perfectly manicured nails.

"Girl, would you stop, you're making *me* nervous!" Kenya complained.

"Dang, sorry, I'd like to see how calm you're going to be when it's your turn." I replied. My stomach was doing little flips. I knew that part of it was from nervousness, part of it was the child that I carried inside of me. When Dre' and I had argued over finding out the baby's sex, I won and since then we'd been proudly anticipating the arrival of our daughter.

"Girls, don't fight," my Mama chimed in.

"I'm not, Mama, but I'm nervous."

Kenya hugged me from behind.

"I'm sorry, sis, go ahead and bite your nails, you're the one that's gonna be lookin' jacked up," she laughed and I gave a fake laugh.

"You just make sure that you throw that bouquet to me!" Tika chimed in from across the room.

"Girl, that bouquet has my name written all over it," my aunt Teri warned her.

"Well, all I can say is whoever is supposed to have it will catch it." And as I said that, they all made faces at each other and each of them let the other know that it was theirs. I was cracking up. At least I didn't have to worry about that.

I couldn't believe my wedding day was already here. After months of planning, this much anticipated day had arrived faster than I thought. I was about to be Dre's wife and our family would be official.

The sound of the organ playing the wedding march signaled that it was time. My Daddy waited at the bottom of the staircase, taking my arm as I prepared to take the biggest step of my life. My Mom and Dre's Mom, Mother Ross, were escorted down the isle first, followed by my bridesmaids, dressed in their strapless wine colored dresses.

"Well, this is it, sis," my sister announced as she prepared to take her place as my matron of honor.

"Yeah, I know," I breathed, trying to calm my shaking hands.

"I'll see you in a few minutes," she said, as she began down the isle. Whew! After the flower girls, it was my turn.

I took a deep breath and held onto my Daddy's arm for support.

"I know you're nervous, baby girl, but don't be. Andre's a good man and you're gonna have a good life with him." Daddy's reassurance was just what I needed before taking that walk.

The church was filled to capacity, flowers decorated the sanctuary and our guests smiled happily as I walked towards the love of my life. I couldn't have asked God for a better mate than Dre'. Our baby kicked as if she agreed with the thought and I rubbed my belly to acknowledge her existence.

Dre's eyes lit up my heart and soul with the love that I saw in them as my daddy walked me down the isle and placed my hand in my soon to be husband's hand. My heart skipped a beat as the realization that I was really getting married hit me. I silently took a deep breath and exhaled, my eyes meeting Dre's, confirming in my heart that I'd found my soulmate.

"Dearly beloved," the minister began, as the final notes of the organ played. "We are gathered here today in the sight of God to witness the joining together of this man and this woman in holy matrimony."

I squeezed Dre's hand as we looked into each others eyes, saying our vows, committing to each other as we entered into lifelong marriage covenant together.

"Kayla, do you promise to take Andre' as your husband, to have and to hold, for better or for worse, for richer or for poorer, in sickness and in health and forsaking all others for as long as you both shall live?" he asked.

"I do," I answered without hesitation. The minister asked the same of Dre' and then we slid our rings onto each others fingers as we promised to always be faithful and love each other in the name of the Father, the Son, and the Holy Spirit.

"By the authority vested in me by the state of Michigan, I now pronounce you husband and wife. You may kiss the bride," the minister concluded.

Dre' removed the veil from my face slowly as if he were branding the moment into his memory and blessed me with the sweetest kiss I'd ever tasted. I was finally Mrs. Kayla Ross.

Applause roared through the church as the minister presented us to our guests as Mr. and Mrs. Ross. We had a reception planned that was sure to entertain our guests, who poured into the ballroom by the dozens. Dancing couples, family members and congratulators filled the room with laughter. Champagne flowed like water, happy guests milled about, mingling; lights flashed as the photographer captured it all for us to reminisce over later, and Dre' and I languished in every sweet minute of it.

Dre' grabbed my hand and we slipped out of the reception to the Presidential suite that awaited us upstairs. Our ten day honeymoon in the Hawaiian Islands would begin in the morning but our celebration had already started.

Up until now, this much happiness had seemed unimaginable unless I was standing in front of a microphone with a room full of fans eagerly awaiting a performance but today had proven that theory wrong. I felt like a princess. I'd married the love of my life and soon we would have a beautiful baby girl. We were truly blessed.

After the baby's arrival, Dre' and I planned to make Atlanta our new home and work on my next project. I would continue my singing and we would gain financial stability within a couple of years. We had it all mapped out. Dre' had music connections in the ATL, the production company was there and plus his mother was going to help us with our daughter as I made the transition back into singing and performing. We had the perfect life and it was only going to get better. Everything was working out despite this baby that we finally realized was a blessing even if she was unplanned. I was so happy I could scream!

CHAPTER TEN

Dre' had a hard time sneaking away from Kayla.

"Wifey, I gotta run back to the house, I forgot our travel bag," he called out, while she was lounging in the Jacuzzi tub. "I'll be back in ten minutes." He could've kicked himself for leaving their travel documents at the house.

"We can send Uncle Jeff to grab that," she called back out, hating the fact that her new hubby was trying to sneak away on their wedding night of all nights.

"I know, baby, but I don't wanna interrupt our guests!" he responded. "I'll stop and get you some Ben & Jerry's," he promised. She was quiet for a moment before giving in.

"Alright," Kayla said in a sing-song voice, loving her Ben & Jerry's. She was willing to compromise in exchange for her favorite treat.

Kayla was relaxing happily in the tub when he left and knowing her, she could be in there for hours. A wave of relief swept over Dre' now that he held the small overnight case in his hand. He was ready to get back and make love to his new wife again. She was so beautiful, round belly and all. For Kayla's size it was definitely noticeable at six months but he'd seen women wobbling around at five months looking like they were ready to deliver like his cousin, who'd wobbled down the aisle to her seat just a few short hours earlier. But Kayla made pregnancy look beautiful. She glowed with happiness. Dre' smiled thinking about his bride waiting for him in the Presidential suite.

He made the promised stop to get her pint of Ben & Jerry's, her favorite treat and latest obsession, whistling as he parked the truck, hopped out and strode confidently into the convenience store, still dressed in his tux. He grabbed the Ben & Jerry's, paid and headed back to his Navigator, determined to meet the fifteen minute deadline he'd set. He nearly collided with another customer as he checked his watch and fumbled with the keys, almost dropping Kayla's goodies.

"My bad," the man apologized. "Hey, man, I thought that was you," the familiar face smiled. "You're looking sharp!"

"Yeah, I just got married," Dre' said happily but not stopping to engage in conversation, extremely aware that he'd surpassed his time limit by a full ten minutes.

"Married! Congratulations!" His excitement was evident even through his overly exaggerated New York accent. "That's a beautiful thing!"

"Yeah," Dre' responded nonchalantly, using the remote to unlock the truck doors.

"Alright, man, enjoy that marriage thing, you hit the jackpot with Kayla," he said, turning to walk away, then pausing mid-step as if he'd forgotten something. He scratched his head, "Yo, man, while I got your attention, what's up with me doin' some tracks on that record? You're girl is blowing up, show some love," he extended his arms in the air, his spirits soaring at the possibility of working with Kayla, especially since her name was on everyone's lips.

"Maybe next time," Dre' responded. "We've already got our production team on deck for the album."

"Aw, that's too bad," his response instantly changed from joyous to gloomy, realizing that his hopes of working with Kayla were quickly fading.

Dre's foot was perched on the runner to hop in and he noticed ole boy was still talking, he shook his head; some people couldn't take a hint when a conversation was over.

He stared at Dre' in disbelief, as Dre' turned his back on him, dismissing him like he was some nobody.

"You know, dude, you're bein' real disrespectful right now," he said, his voice sounding agitated. "Didn't your mama teach you to show respect to people when they're tryin' to help you out?" He mumbled, aggressively taking a step towards the truck.

"What!" Dre' turned around, a scowl etched into his forehead, thinking at first that he'd misunderstood, but he knew he hadn't when he saw eyes blazing with fire staring him down as he approached, nostrils flaring like he was ready for war. Dre' balled his fists, ready to throw a blow to his jaw as soon as he walked up on him. His stare turned from fire to ice as he stopped within feet of Dre', drew a four five, pulled the hammer back, and fired without warning, hitting Dre' in the shoulder, hurling his body around like a rag doll before he could even react to the gun that had been pulled on him. Dre' was stunned by the fire that had ripped into him, causing an explosion of pain to ripple throughout his body. His eyes were riveted to his burning shoulder, where his shoulder bone had been shattered, his body going into shock as he saw the thick, dark red liquid began to seep through the white tuxedo.

"What the…?" Dre's hoarse voice started in amazement, shock at what was happening quickly engulfing him as he tried to figure out if this was real or if he'd somehow been daydreaming or having some sort of nightmare. This couldn't be real, but it had to be. He couldn't make sense of the confusing scene that he'd been cast into. Death loomed around the corner as Dre' tried to rationalize what was happening and why. He tried climbing into the truck, thinking that if he could just get in, he'd be able to get to his own gun and flip the script on this lunatic. The shadowy figure neared closer, looming over Dre' smiling, as he pointed the gun at Dre's head. Dre' tried to protect his face with his hands but his attempt to save himself was futile as his attacker unleashed the fire a second time.

Dre' slid from the truck, trying to pull himself up but the ground seemed to be swirling around, making it hard for him to focus. His hand kept slipping in a sticky substance, making his attempts to raise himself from the ground pointless. He heard a woman's scream and the satisfactory smile disappeared from his attacker's face.

"Later, dawg," he chuckled, before disappearing into the night.

"He's been shot! Someone call 911!" A frantic voice yelled out.

"Mister, you're gonna be alright," He heard a lady's voice as she raised his head onto her lap and held his hand like she was comforting a loved one.

"Kayla," he coughed, knowing that she was expecting him back any minute.

"Don't talk, help's on the way," she assured him in her motherly tone.

He could see Kayla's sparkling eyes. He tried to call out to her again but his throat was blocked with thick fluid, causing him to choke on the words. He tried to catch his breath but struggled more and more with each attempt.

The sky seemed to be falling around him as he tried to regain his focus. He heard sirens blaring in the distance and hoped they were coming to help him. He had to get back to Kayla. She needed him. He was her husband. She'd be expecting him back any minute. This couldn't be real. She was pregnant. She needed him.

A tear slid down his face as he lay there helpless, thinking of his bride's smile. He tried to stay awake as the sound of the sirens grew nearer, but the darkness engulfed him. He could see Kayla's face in the darkness but it was fading, becoming blurry, as he tried to escape unconsciousness.

* * * * *

The police officer walked through the hotel with a stern expression planted on his face, stepping to the front desk to inquire about a guest named Andre' Ross. He was instructed to the ballroom where happy guests celebrated the nuptials with dancing, champagne, and laughter after getting no answer at the suite. This was the worst part of the job. He hated to interrupt such a happy occasion with bad news.

Kayla stepped out of the elevator in her gown, searching the ballroom for Dre', who'd been gone way past his promised fifteen minutes, just as the police officer was entering the ballroom inquiring about her.

"I'm Kayla Ross," she stated, looking at the police officer with a quizzical look on her face as she overheard him ask for her by name. "Is there a problem officer?"

"Mrs. Ross, we're sorry to have to tell you this," he shifted feet, "but there's been an accident."

"An accident?" she shook her head as if there'd been some sort of misunderstanding. "What kind of accident, is it Dre'?" she asked, panic settling into her voice, tears already in her eyes, knowing that something wasn't right when Dre' hadn't called or returned to their suite. "Is it Dre?!" she repeated. "Is Dre' alright?" she demanded. She caught the scowl that crossed the officer's face, confirming her fear.

He shook his head. "I'm sorry Mrs. Ross. Your husband's been shot." The news caused her to hurl over in pain.

"Shot! What do you mean shot? What happened?" she screamed, losing it, holding her pregnant belly as if it would give her support. The officer's lips were moving but she couldn't hear. The buzz was still going on around her but her world had stopped and in the blink of an eye her world had shattered.

"Dre'!" The ear piercing scream silenced the ballroom and every head turned to witness Kayla's frantic cry as she fell to her knees, her world spiraling out of control as darkness overtook her.

CHAPTER ELEVEN

The rumbling thunder and the thud of the raindrops pounding against the windows only served to intensify the sadness in the hearts of those who loved Dre'. I couldn't feel. I was numb, except for the burning sensation nagging at my eyes from the endless stream of tears that overflowed from their rims. I tried making sense of what had happened but I couldn't. The news of Dre' being shot on our wedding night had come like a swift blow to my chest knocking the wind from me. It didn't make sense. I couldn't grasp the reality of what was happening. I didn't even want to.

I looked at Dre's lifeless body, dressed in his new Armani suit, a gift from himself for the endless work he put in to drive my single to success. He called it his "power suit". How ironic; he lay there powerless over death, a victim of another man's hateful desires. His chocolate complexion was still as smooth as a baby's cheek as I stroked it with my finger. He looked as if he were asleep in the satin lined casket. I wanted to crawl in and curl up beside him, tell him to wake up. If I couldn't do that, I wished someone would put me into a box and lower me into the ground.

Dre' didn't deserve this. He was the best person I knew. I kept expecting him to look up and wink, "Gotcha!" But this wasn't one of his pranks. It was the realest, most cruel reality that a woman could face. My husband had been murdered.

My tears fell onto his black silk suit like the rain pounding against the church's windows, in nonstop torrents. I felt my legs weaken as I began to collapse.

"Dre', baby, I'm so sorry," I sobbed, my apologies unfelt by the lifeless corpse. If only I'd stopped him from going out that night. If only he hadn't stopped at the store to get my favorite ice cream, he would still be here. Didn't God know that I needed him? Didn't He care that my baby needed her father?

"Why?" I heard, not even realizing at first that the low-pitched moan was coming from me. My Mama's arms wrapped around my waist, offering me the support I needed. Daddy came too, lifting me before I crumbled to the floor and helping me to my seat on the front pew, with its perfect view of the casket. A wave of nausea swept over me. This was the last place I wanted to be. I didn't want to see Dre' like that. But then again, I didn't want to take my eyes off him.

The sharp pain in my chest was unbearable. My heart cried, seeing Dre' in that coffin. He was really gone. He was never coming back and no amount of crying, or praying, or begging would change the facts. After today, I would never see him again. I wanted to curl up and die. My soul-mate, best friend, and husband had been stolen. Our futures had been altered forever, and for what?

The police were flabbergasted. No leads! All witnesses had seen was Dre' talking to another black male and as he got into his truck, the suspect opened fire. No argument, no tussle, no robbery, just a cold-hearted execution style murder.

I couldn't figure out why anyone would take away *my* husband. He'd never hurt anyone. What motive was there for killing a man on his wedding night? We hadn't even started our new life together. The unfulfilled dreams that would never be realized played themselves in my mind. Dre' and I would never honeymoon in Hawaii. I'd never hear his laugh again. And our daughter would never know her father.

I shook with grief and Mama tried to comfort me. Kenya cried uncontrollably, too. It was she that had introduced me to the man that would become my husband and the father of my child.

I ran up to the casket as I saw the funeral director approaching.

"Dre', I'm going to get whoever did this to you," I whispered against his ear, knowing that he was no longer in the lifeless body but hoping that his spirit was there. "I promise, if it's the last thing I do, I'm going to get the person who ruined our lives." I kissed his cheek for the last time.

The funeral director approached the casket while the soloist sang, "... *constant friend is He. His eye is on the sparrow and I know, He watches me.*"

Moans of sadness filled the sanctuary as the director closed the casket. Mother Ross rocked back and forth, too filled with grief to cry; she just stared at the casket with expressionless, red swollen eyes. I couldn't watch. It was too much. I tried fighting the temptation to run as far away from the church as possible. I couldn't take this whole grief stricken ceremony, with the organ music imprinting the sadness into my spirit.

My feet were like putty as I stood to run. Daddy caught me struggling to escape and eased me back onto the pew, laying my head on his shoulder and stroking my hair like he used to do when I was a little girl. The baby inside me kicked and, instinctively, I rubbed my swollen belly. Overwhelming grief struck me at the realization that my unborn daughter would never see Dre's smile or laugh as he chased her in our backyard.

I zoned out of the service. There was nothing anyone could say that would ease the pain. Is this how God treated good people? Dre' had never hurt anyone in his life. Is this what people got for trying to do the right thing?

All this time, I thought that if I just lived right then everything would turn our right. I thought God loved me. But now, I felt abandoned. Not only had Dre' been taken away, my happiness had been murdered. I'd believed in God to bless me with a singing career, a husband, and a family and this is what I'd gotten—temporary bliss and a life filled with pain.

Life as I knew it had been drastically altered and now I was lost. How could a loving God give me a taste of everything I'd ask for and then snatch it all away in an instant. I was the object of a cruel, cruel joke that I couldn't escape no matter how I tried. My dreams had been shattered, replaced by a never-ending nightmare.

"God, why have You forsaken me?" I cried, watching as the pallbearers carried Dre's casket away so he could be committed to the ground. It may as well have been me, my life was over.

CHAPTER TWELVE

Destiny Nicole Ross made her entrance into the world at 2:55 a.m. on Friday, January 31st in the middle of a blizzard. My Mama and Tika were there to witness her birth as the intense contractions squeezed her through the birth canal and into my life. Her head was full of black wavy hair and she looked at me through squinted eyes as if she recognized my voice.

"Hi Destiny," I smiled, wrapping her tiny hand around my finger.

"Oh Kayla, she's perfect," Tika said, admiring the precious child whose presence in my belly had saved me from losing my mind after Dre's death. I wanted to be with my husband, but Destiny was the next best thing.

"She sure is," my Mama added. "She's beautiful, Kayla."

My eyes welled up as I looked at the miracle in my arms. Labor was nothing like I'd expected. The five hours of excruciating cramps I'd experienced before finally begging for the epidural had been worth it though. Destiny was the product of the love that Dre' and I had shared. I kissed her tiny cheek and told her how much I loved her before the nurse removed her from my arms to take her APGAR score and place her under the heated lamp. Just to think, I'd actually thought she would ruin my life but she was the only thing that had kept me hanging on.

Mother Ross beamed, having witnessed the birth of her first and only grandchild. She admired Destiny, lying peacefully under the heating lamp.

"She looks just like her Daddy," she smiled. We'd both been through so much since Dre's death, but Destiny was a part of Dre' that would never fade away. Not like the scent in his shirts or the memory of his laugh. She was real and her presence eased the pain a little.

I thanked God for the miracle that was my daughter but I was still angry at Him for taking Dre' away.

After Dre's murder, I retreated from the prying eyes of the industry and took the time to grieve over my shattered dreams. Now staying home to nurture my daughter for the first three months of her life was my priority. The music industry, my dreams, the money, all seemed a part of another life. I'd always said I was living a dream and I'd been right.

The insurance policy Dre' had left us enabled me to live comfortably, but I'd trade it all just to have him back. He deserved the same opportunities I had to develop a bond with our daughter, to be there to witness her first smile, her curious eyes and be the one to nurture and care for her the way only a Daddy could.

Even though I doubted that I would ever be truly happy again, Destiny was the reason I breathed. She was the only slice of happiness in my sky, the only reason I thought about the future and how I could give her a wonderful life even if mine had been stolen. She was everything to me now.

The first taste of warm air that breezed through our quiet Oakland county community prompted me to take Kayla on her first official shopping spree and stroller ride through Piedmont Park. Somerset Mall held all the treats that could make girls of all ages, especially mine, swoon from excitement. It was a beautiful spring day as the valet returned our truck after the much needed girls' day out.

We headed towards the city next, browsing shop windows as we strolled through downtown.

"Kayla?" a semi-familiar voice called as I walked past, turning to see who'd recognized me. It had been a long time since I'd had contact with the public or my fans.

"Hey, how are you?" I responded, recognizing the stranger as Karlos Day.

"I'm good, how are you?" he asked, his eyes filled with concern. He'd no doubt heard about my loss.

"I'm blessed," I replied, looking down at my daughter, the reason that I felt blessed. But then I wanted to say, "I'm cursed," remembering how God had abandoned me like damaged goods.

"Does this beauty belong to you?" he asked, smiling.

"She sure does," I answered proudly, bending to stroke her smooth cheek.

"Wow, she's gorgeous," he said, admiring Destiny, while directing his next question at me, "So, have you been okay, I haven't seen you in awhile."

"I'm makin' it," was all I could manage, as his question pulled the memories of Dre' to the forefront of my mind.

"That's good, it's good to see you out," he commented, stuffing his hands into his coat as a breeze blew by. There was an awkward pause. "Hey, I was just about to grab a bite to eat. Are you hungry?" he inquired. "I'd love to buy you lunch."

"Well—"

"Come on, Kayla," he pleaded.

"I'm really not that hungry," I answered, content to enjoy the day alone with my daughter.

"Come on, just lunch, okay?" he pleaded for me to reconsider.

"I guess that'd be okay," I responded reluctantly.

"Cool," he said, walking in stride with me as I stored my packages in the truck. "Do you like seafood?"

"Sure, I love it." Dre' and I both did.

"How about Pappadeaux?"

"That sounds good. I'll meet you there." Conversation was easy as we ate our lunch in the city's newest restaurant. I had fried chicken fingers and shrimp as he devoured the buffet.

"So Kayla, have you thought about getting back into your music?" he asked casually. There was still a void there that Dre' had left. He'd always managed my career, hooked me up with the right people, made sure that I was taken care of and I felt lost without him. I hadn't given much thought to pursuing my music without Dre'.

"Nah, I've just been focusing on my daughter," I replied.

"I know your fans miss you," he smiled.

"What fans? I've been out of commission for so long."

"Yeah, but you were building quite a buzz. You were like a breath of fresh air to the music industry." His words were flattering.

"I haven't written in so long, I don't even know if I still have it in me." I confessed. It was true. I'd been driven to write by my Mama's cruel and unusual punishment and then my passion had been fueled by my love for Dre'.

After my reconciliation with Mama and the realization that her over-protectiveness had been her way of expressing her love, I'd been able to heal from the pain she'd caused me, where at one time, music had been my way of healing. And now Dre' was gone. I was in love with Destiny now, but I'm sure no one wanted to hear me sing lullabies.

"Kayla, don't under-estimate yourself," Karlos said, taking a bite of his shrimp salad. "You're a very talented artist. You shouldn't let that talent go to waste. I'd still love to work with you."

"I'm sorry," I said, scooting my chair from the table. He'd hit an open wound. The music belonged to me and Dre, that was our thing and I wasn't about to let Karlos Day intrude on it. This was too much and too soon.

"Kayla, I'm sorry, did I say something wrong?" he said, instantly standing to his feet.

"I just...I have to go," I explained, bundling Destiny up in her crocheted blanket.

"I'll walk you to your car." He said, throwing a fifty spot on the table.

I walked briskly from the restaurant, desperately needing some air. I could feel the tears welling up in my eyes as I thought about Dre' and how he'd been so passionate about helping me accomplish my dreams.

"I'm really sorry, Kayla, I didn't mean—"

"Don't apologize," I turned to face him. "I just...I don't even know if I'm ever going to sing again. If I do, it's going to take some time."

"I understand." He said. But he couldn't. He wasn't the one who'd lost his partner on his wedding night or who'd had to go through childbirth to deliver a baby girl who'd never know her father. He couldn't possibly know what it was like.

I went home and cried. I cried for myself, I cried for Destiny and most of all I cried for Dre'.

* * * * *

"Hello," I answered to stop the phone's irritating jingle.

"Kayla, it's Karlos."

How'd he get my number?

"I just wanted to apologize for yesterday. I didn't mean to try to push you into getting back into the music, it's just that, I always thought you were talented and I hadn't seen you in so long...it was just stupid, I'm sorry."

"I accept your apology," I said, anxious to get back to my nap, where I'd been happily married to Dre' and we were on our first family vacation in Disneyworld.

"Look, I know this is a hard time for you and I'd just like to extend my friendship, if you ever need anything, please...just call me."

"Thanks, Karlos."

"You're welcome," he said before hanging up.

Maybe I did need a friend. Jealousy had ruined a lot of my friendships, revealing some who'd been friends from way back as haters, when the fame began to come as a result of my hit single. Others, I had pushed away, too stricken with grief to be bothered with anyone. I didn't want their sympathy or their pity, I just wanted to be.

Mama begged and pleaded for me to go to church with her, realizing that God was that missing ingredient from her life all those years she'd allowed unforgiveness towards Daddy to poison her relationships; but that was the last place I wanted to be. I just wanted the pain to stop, but I felt like God had caused my pain, so why should I go to church.

I trotted to the kitchen, grabbing my New York Fudge Chunk Ben & Jerry's from the freezer, topping it with walnuts and a huge scoop of whipped cream, before settling back into bed. I'd started watching "How Stella Got Her Groove Back," and pretty soon was crying along with her as she cried over the death of her best friend.

I couldn't watch any longer, drowning in a sea of sadness over my own loss; my once favorite movie had become depressing. I flipped through the channels, desperate for some comedy, anything to lift my spirits and make me laugh. I stopped at BET. A preacher was on teaching about discovering God's destiny for my life. Not my style but what he said made perfect sense. I wanted to turn the channel but even as I tried, I couldn't unglue myself from the sermon. He was talking to me.

Who was this man? I'd never heard anyone teaching the way he taught. His mesmerizing message made me hunger for more. I listened and recorded the scriptures in my journal and for the first time since my husband's death, I picked up my Bible. The pastor said it was the word that could save me; it was the armor to fight every trick and fiery dart of the devil. Lord knows I'd been shot with more fiery darts than I could stand.

I fell asleep reading my Bible and thinking of this charismatic new preacher I'd discovered. Maybe if I tuned in again, I'd find out what I'd done to make God abandon me. Maybe I'd be able to get my life back.

Okay God, what is it You're trying to tell me? I asked, before letting sweet sleep lure me into dreamland.

CHAPTER THIRTEEN

I felt totally new as I awoke, anxiously searching my digital cable line-up to find that new preacher I'd discovered last night. My sleep had been so sweet as I dreamed about the words he spoke. A long awaited peace had come with anticipation, the kind that comes when you're on the verge of something new, and emerged as my spirit longed to be fed by the powerful words.

At first unaware of the impact it was having on me, I noticed that watching Dr. Dollar's broadcast had become a habit, just as waking up feeding Destiny and having my morning Cappuccino with crème had become habits. Weeks had passed since that lonely night when I'd discovered Dr. Dollar, the man who had more impact on me than any pastor I'd encountered in my twenty-two years. I'd been watching this broadcast like an addict and found myself saying the prayer of salvation as I closed my eyes and repeated after the preacher, accepting God's gift of salvation.

I didn't know what to expect after saying that prayer but I believed the preacher when he said that God was about to do a new thing in my life. I longed for something new, especially after the tragedy I'd experienced. I needed healing. He'd said to stop being offended at God because that was the Devil trying to keep me in that place, the place where I couldn't receive what I needed to move on and he was so right.

I have to tell someone, I thought, singing along with my Mary Mary CD as the phone rang.

"Hello," I answered, still filled with joy at the decision I'd made and out of breath from singing along with Mary Mary.

"Hey, Kayla, it's K.D." said the masculine voice on the other end.

"Hi, what's up?" I asked happily, shocking myself with this joyful spirit that had arisen in me.

"Nothin' much, you sound happy," he commented.

"Oh, my God, I am, I am! I was watching this broadcast on T.V. and I know it sounds crazy to you, but I just got saved!" I gushed.

"Kayla, that's wonderful," Karlos said, his response catching me by surprise. "You know, I used to be a preacher."

My jaw nearly dropped at his admission.

"Are you for real?"

"Yeah," he said, then reluctantly, "It's just that…this music thing was pulling at me and it just got to be confusing, so I took a break to get my head straight, you know?"

"I just feel…" I paused, searching for the perfect word, "…better," I finally said.

"Yeah, God has a way of doing that," he laughed.

"So true, but what were you calling for? I just got to going on and on about me, I nearly forgot to ask."

"I was just calling to see how you were doing," he replied, "but I see everything's cool with you."

"Yeah, I even took your advice," I admitted, "I've been writing a little here and there."

"That's good, that's good," he said, "You know, I know the last time I brought this up, you weren't really open to talking about it but, Kayla, I only keep asking because you're so talented," he began. "I mean, you wouldn't even have to do anything that you're not ready for but I've got these cats in the studio that *really* need your touch. I've told them all about you. People miss you," he paused, "…the streets, Kayla, we miss you."

"I don't know, K.D. I haven't been in the studio in so long."

"It doesn't hurt to try," he went on. "You have this amazing voice, this amazing look and this amazing talent that…" he searched for words, "the world is missing. Don't you miss singing?" he asked, prompting me to explore my feelings on the subject.

"I do, but that was me and Dre's thing. You don't understand," I tried explaining. "He's the reason I was so successful, he's the one who made me what I was."

"Kayla, no matter how much you love a person, he's not what made you who you are or the star you're meant to be. Come on, Kayla, please just..." he paused. "I'm just asking you to not give up on your dream." He said.

"That was another life," I responded, unable to make him see that singing was in the past.

"Then start a new life!"

Silence.

"Okay, I'll do it," I answered, surprising myself by giving in on impulse. "When?"

"Tomorrow at three o'clock." He answered and gave me directions to the studio.

"I'll be there." I said, hanging up wondering, what have I gotten myself into? I turned up the volume on my Mary Mary CD. "Take the shackles off my feet so I can dance..." I sang along, happier than I'd been in a long time.

*   *   *   *   *

The recording session had gone well. This new group that K.D. was producing sounded tight! I didn't realize how much I'd missed the environment until I was in the booth, singing my heart out again. It felt right.

Working with Hustle Hard, the musically gifted rappers that K.D. was producing, was a new opportunity for me to start rebuilding my life. One session had turned into two and before I knew it, I was on stage with Hustle Hard, wooing crowds like I'd done in my other life with Dre'.

* * * * *

I greeted K.D. as he slid into the seat next to me. We listened as the Anointed One's, the trio of brothers who were gospel's newest rising stars, sang, *"Tomorrow is not promised, won't you choose the Lord today,"* moving the entire church to stand to their feet. The words were so true. I was glad I'd made my decision before it was too late. I had peace in my life for the first time since Dre's death. I felt like there was hope for me, especially after listening to the minister's sermon about letting God be our guide in this life.

"Wow, that was a wonderful sermon," K.D. said.

"It was, wasn't it," I agreed, as we walked the isle towards the exit.

"Do you have plans for dinner," K.D. asked before I could get away.

"Actually, I do." I replied. "My Mom's making some big announcement today and the whole family is expected at her house."

"Oh?" I saw a glimmer of hope in his eyes.

"Yeah, I don't know what it is. Maybe she hit the lottery or something!" I said jokingly.

"Hey, you never know." He replied, standing there with an expectant smile.

I extended my hand, not wanting to give the wrong impression. Inviting him to church was one thing but I wasn't about to be parading him around my family. It was strictly business.

"I'm really glad you enjoyed the service."

"Yeah, it was cool. Thanks for inviting me." He responded as we said our goodbyes and went in our separate directions.

"Oh, before I forget," he said, pulling a CD from his Bible and handing it to me. "I made this track the other night. Let me know what you think about it."

"Okay, I will." I took the CD that was imprinted with his name and number. "Thanks."

I slid the CD in and turned up the volume after snapping Destiny into her car seat and heading for Mama's. The music was rich and soulful as I free-styled to it.

"That's hot, *Mami*, isn't it?" I asked, peering over the seat at Destiny cooing at me and displaying her dimple indented cheeks.

I thought about K.D. as we made the drive to Mama's. He'd certainly surprised me by going to church with me and extending his friendship. I couldn't understand how someone could profess to have been a preacher and then just turn away from God just to pursue music. I was doing both. Why couldn't he?

It was a challenge being in the studio around all the things that never used to bother me, the rappers were always firing up blunts, drinking, cursing, it was like…anything goes. I felt out of my element since I'd given my life to Christ.

"Karlos even flipped the script on me." I complained to Tika during one of our late night chat sessions. "I mean, sometimes he can be so cool. We both love the music, you know, he's always talking about God. I never would've guessed he was so into the Bible."

"The Bible?" she asked, quizzically, "K.D?"

"Yeah, he said he used to be a minister."

"Hmm, that's interesting." Tika was forever the skeptic. "So what happened?"

"He said he just didn't want to be judged by the church folk because of his music."

"Well, hey, I never would've guessed it," she said, "but I guess you can't tell if a person is on God's team just by lookin' at 'em."

"That's true. I guess what bothers me is how he's always talking about God when we're alone or on the phone, but when we're in the studio and people are around, he's totally different, cursing, drinking, smoking hydro…goin' with the flow. And then when I said something, he was like I shouldn't be judging him unless I want to be judged, so I left it alone."

"What?" she asked, shocked.

"Well, he said he's not pursuing ministry so I guess he does what he does. Who am I to judge? At least he's not doin' that and trying to minister to others."

"I guess," she sighed. "Girl, I'm gonna get off this phone, it's after midnight," I yawned.

"Yeah, girl, and Kayla, don't worry about K.D. I mean, you're already doing the right thing," she started. "Don't just listen to what he says. Watch what he does and you'll be cool."

"You're right, as usual." I laughed. "Alright cuz, love you." I said before hanging up.

Her words stayed on my mind. As if to re-enforce the knowledge Tika had just dropped, Dr. Dollar's broadcast was on as I flipped through the channels. He was talking about women getting married to men they barely knew, only to discover their true colors after the wedding. What if K.D. was just faking, trying to get me to trust him? After hearing that message, I knew it wasn't by coincidence that every time I needed answers Dr. Dollar was addressing the issues I faced. Both tonight and that first night I'd tuned in, it was like his messages were answers to my prayers. After observing this, I knew that my stumbling upon this man of God was a divine connection. I was going to take heed to Dr. Dollar and Tika. I was on high alert.

CHAPTER FOURTEEN

"Kayla, I'd like to go over some things we learned about in Bible study," Karlos said as we finished our recording session with Hustle Hard.

"Okay, that's cool," I said, looking at my watch, "just let me call my mom and make sure it's alright if Destiny stays a little longer." I said, before confirming with K.D. "She's all set." I smiled, flipping my cell phone shut.

"Do you mind going back to my place, I took some notes but I forgot them at the crib," he looked at me expectantly.

"I guess I could come over for a little while."

I followed K.D. to his house, listening to my Dr. Dollar CD that had arrived in my mailbox earlier.

"Make yourself comfortable," K.D. said, inviting me into his cozy condo.

"This is nice," I commented, noticing that he was looking at me differently, admiring me, while I pretended not to notice.

"Um, you smell so good," he said, sliding onto the sofa next to me.

"Thank you," I replied, scooting closer to the edge. "Dre' gave me this…" I stopped, the memory of Dre' bringing tears to my eyes.

"Kayla, I'm so sorry," he said, reaching for my hand. "I know it's painful to lose someone you love."

I could only shake my head as the knot appeared in my throat. K.D. wiped a tear from my face as I sniffled, trying to hold in the torrent that threatened to spill.

"It's okay to let it out," he said, as the tears began. I felt like such a baby.

K.D. comforted me as I cried away the pain from the past, releasing some of the pent up grief that still caused me to stay in bed some days snuggled up with Destiny, the most tangible reminder of my love for Dre'.

I was grateful for the comfort K.D. extended to me as he gave his shoulder for me to cry on. It felt good to release the hurt that had been clogging my heart for so long.

He held me tight, rubbing my back, soothing the pain into submission. "It's okay," he whispered, smoothing my hair with his hands. "Just get it out."

After what seemed like hours of crying in K.D.'s arms, my tears finally subsided and the rest that I had been seeking filled my tired bones. K.D. continued to soothe me, offering his comfort.

He stretched out on the sofa as my body relaxed, allowing me to rest my head on his chest.

"Your so beautiful, Kayla," he spoke softly. "I've hated seeing you in all this pain. "I've been waiting a long time to see you happy again."

"I really appreciate your friendship, too," I responded.

He kissed my hair lightly.

"That's what friends are for," he spoke softly as he began kissing my neck, moving my hair aside to bury his face in my neck. I wanted to move away but my hands were rendered useless by the warmth of his breath on my skin. I froze as soon as I felt his hands fumbling with the button on my jeans.

"What are you doin'?" I gasped in surprise, instantly drawn back into reality by his wandering hands touching me in off limit places.

"I'm about to make you my wife," he breathed into my ear, sounding off sirens in my head.

"Your wife?" I asked, horrified by his statement, pushing against his chest with all my might, which pinned me against the leather sofa and was the only thing separating me from freedom.

"Yeah, the Bible says that after we make love you'll be my wife."

"What? That's crazy and I know that is not in the Bible!" I could feel the heat rising inside my chest. The nerve of him, trying to play me like some dummy.

"Then how do you think they got married in the olden days?" he asked, not even giving me a chance to respond. "A man slept with the women and when they came from the tent, she was his wife," he said in a persuasive tone, but I wasn't going for that.

"Well, we're not in the olden days!" I snapped, pushing at his chest. "Get up!"

"Kayla, come on, I just want to do what's right," he pleaded, relaxing his grip on me.

"But this isn't right..." I'd sprang to my feet, straightening my clothes, as soon as he offered the leeway.

"I know you're scared, you got hurt before," he looked up at me with pleading eyes, "but I'm not gonna leave you like Dre' did," he said.

I was even angrier at the mention of my deceased husband's name, "This isn't about Dre'," I spat the words at him, trying unsuccessfully to control my simmering anger. "This is about me and what *I* want!"

"But I thought you wanted a good man!"

"I did and I had one," I stammered.

"But he's gone," he said as if he was frustrated by this but I was the one who should be frustrated at his trying to take advantage of me. "Now I'm the man that God's sent to take care of you and your daughter."

"No," I said bluntly, "that's not what I want with you."

He looked shocked at my admission.

"Not what you want?" he asked in disbelief. "But I love you."

"But I don't love you like that," I tried to explain without making things worse.

"But, Kayla, if you asked God for a good man and I'm a good man and I love you, we can make it work."

"You're right," I spoke slowly, hoping that it would help him to realize that we were not on the same page and I didn't want to be with him at all. "If I felt that way about you, we could make it work, but I don't, so we can't," I stood with my hands on my hips.

"Kayla," he stood, reaching for my hand but I snatched it away quickly, refusing to give any signal that this is what I wanted. "I love you enough for the both of us, if you just give it some time, you'll learn to love me, too. We can wait on the marriage thing and once you see how much I love you, I know you'll love me too."

"No…" I started but he silenced me with his finger to his lips.

"Kayla, it's okay to be scared," he began.

"That's not it," I began, cut off again as he talked over me.

"And it's okay, you don't have to thank me for understanding. I know it's hard to find a good man like me," he said as if congratulating me for being a lucky winner.

"Uh, uh," I said, backing away, "I am not feelin' this," I shook my head, "And I definitely don't want to get married and wait for the love to kick in." I grabbed my jacket and slung my Gucci bag over my shoulder. "I don't even want a good man right now."

"See, that's the problem with females," he muttered. "Maybe this isn't about you."

No he didn't have the nerve to raise his voice. He tried to switch back to being calm again, continuing the conversation even as I gathered my belongings. "How do you know God doesn't want us to be together? Your daughter needs a father and you need a good man to take care of you, to commit to you." His gazed drifted away from me as he looked past me into the distance before bringing his eyes back to mine, speaking in a low tone, "I know

96

this may seem kind of like a fairytale, but I love you and I want to give you everything you ever wanted," he smiled tenderly.

"Well, obviously God didn't want me to have that because I had it and it was taken away!" I looked him square in the eye and spoke sternly. "If I led you on, I'm sorry, I really am. I thought we both were happy just being friends, but I guess not. I don't know how else to say it, I just don't want a relationship like that. You can do what you want with the music, I can't even handle this," I said, as I opened the door and was out before he had time to respond.

Hitting the lock on my truck, I hopped in, started it and sped up the street to get as far away as I could from K.D.'s house.

I turned into a nearby sub-division, pulled the Navigator to the side of the road and held my hand to my chest to quiet my pulsating heart. Letting my head fall to the steering wheel, this time I allowed the hot tears to spring from my eyes. I needed to release the pent up anger and frustration I'd felt ever since Dre' had been taken away from me. I missed him and was mad at him at the same time for leaving me. He was supposed to protect me for life, not get killed.

"Dre'!" I cried out, longing for my husband's comfort. I cried until all my tears were spent for the second time that night, pulled myself together, wiped the wetness from my eyes with my already tear-soaked sleeves and drove the short distance to my mama's house.

I picked Destiny up from my mom's, longing for my own bed and a good night's sleep.

My cell phone buzzed, jarring me from my restless slumber. I was tempted to not answer but wanted to get this over with.

"Hello," I mumbled groggily.

"Kayla, I just wanted to apologize for earlier," K.D. said.

I was silent.

"It was partly the alcohol and I smoked some dro at the studio. I'm just sorry for making you uncomfortable. I've been praying since you left and God told me that you need time to heal and I need to just be patient and help you with your music right now. I don't want to be the cause of you giving up on your music again so please give me another chance and just let me help you get back on.

"Yeah, I think that would be best if we just keep it business."

"That's cool," he readily agreed. "It shouldn't take too much longer anyway to get these last few tracks outta the way. I reserved a block of time for next week and we can get everything squared away within the next month. Is that cool with you?" He asked.

"Yeah, I guess that's cool," I replied, feeling a little uneasy about going forth with my music with him involved, but I ignored the feeling as I agreed, especially since now he knew it was just business.

"Alright, Kayla, I'll talk to you later," he said, hanging up.

"Alright," I agreed, turning my ringer off as I snapped the phone shut.

He sure was taking it well for someone whose profession of love had been met with rejection. I plopped my head back against my fluffy down pillows and closed my eyes.

"Lord, just help me get my album finished, so I can get back on," I prayed. "It's the least you can do." I added, before allowing the much needed sleep to overtake me.

CHAPTER FIFTEEN

"Girl, I don't know what to tell you," Tika said, as I recounted my dilemma with K.D. to her over lunch.

After the night that K.D. tried to "make me his wife", I knew something wasn't right with him but I just couldn't put my finger on it. I kept thinking about what Dre' had said the first time we'd encountered K.D., the night he'd proposed to me. "Baby, it's something about that cat that I don't like," he'd said. At the time, I'd brushed it off as a little jealousy on Dre's part and tried to reassure him that it was nothing but now I was beginning to agree with Dre's observation and I was wondering what it was about K.D. that wasn't quite right.

"I mean, he acts like he's on the up and up but that's just it. It's like he's trying *too* hard," I sighed, "you know what I mean?"

"Yeah, girl, like he's trying to *convince* you," she replied, taking another bite of her shrimp scampi.

"Yeah, it's just crazy. I don't know if he's hiding something or what and it's just... buggin' me."

"So, what are you gonna do?" she asked.

"I don't know," I put my head in my hands, "I just wish Dre' was here. If Dre' was here, I wouldn't even be goin' through this crazy mess."

I was questioning everything about K.D. now. Was he ever really a preacher? Was he going to stick to his word and keep it business? It made me question if anything about him was real or just a front. I missed Dre'. He'd always had my back. I'd never had to question his motives. I trusted him, something that was lacking in my relationship with Karlos.

"I mean, if you jump ship now, what about your music?" Tika posed the question that I'd been asking myself ever since I first began to feel funny about K.D.

"That's what I'm sayin'. I didn't even want to start back singing, but now that I have, I have to make it. I gotta go platinum for me and Destiny. How else am I gonna make sure that we're straight?"

"Why you actin' like you need him to go platinum?" Tika asked, frowning like I had lost my mind. "You were on your way before Dre' was killed." She reminded me. "And besides that, you got enough money to be straight for awhile unless you plan on just splurgin' everyday."

"I know, but since Dre', Karlos is one of the only people who's believed in me."

A hurt expression crossed her face.

"I been believing in you since day one," she stated, tilting her head for emphasis.

"I just mean, when I hooked up with Karlos, I started writing again, going to the studio, doing shows, you know. I been doing my thing again."

We'd even had a photo shoot a couple of weeks ago for Urban Elite magazine's emerging entertainers' column, promoting the soundtrack and that's really when I begin to feel the first twinges of doubt about K.D.

All the artists on the compilation had a chance to shine during the photo spread. It had gone perfectly up until K.D. tried to invade my personal space as we took promotional photos. The first shots were innocent enough, while it seemed that with each snap of the camera, K.D. tried to invade my boundaries. Each explosion of the flashing lights brought K.D. more into my personal space. It made me uncomfortable, especially since the charm and the mystery from our earlier meetings was fading into oblivion as the reality of the situation was revealing itself. The mask covering K.D.'s true motives was slowly starting to slide away.

I had a feeling in the pit of my stomach that there was more to K.D. than what I could see with my natural eye. My keen intuition was heightened and I had to trust what I was feeling. He slid his hands around my waste and that's when I had to remind him that he was supposed to be keepin' it business, even as he tried to persuade me that it was just for publicity.

"People love to see this kind of stuff, it boosts sales, baby," he'd laughed.

His masquerade gave me an ice cold chill, making it difficult to maintain my composure, but at the same time, I didn't want to throw away my hard work. So I sucked it up and tried to keep my cool, thanking God that he didn't try me anymore doing the shoot.

Tika listened attentively as I unloaded about K.D. to her.

"Then, when we're at the studio he's always making little comments like we're together or something, it just irks me." I put my head in my hands, taking a deep breath. "Girl, I'm tellin' you, if I wasn't saved, I would end up snappin' on him, for real!"

The more I began to think about it, the more it bothered me. I just couldn't shake this feeling that there was something about him that wasn't right.

"Kayla, if he's got you that stressed out, why don't you just find another producer and drop him," she advised. "Later for all that drama."

"I know," I told her, "you're right. I'm just thinkin' 'bout all the work I put in. You know, he's got my masters. Do you know how valuable that is?"

"Yeah," she said, her dealings with the industry cats put her on top of her game in music, too. "I'm just sayin', it's not like your album is done. You can drop hits Kayla. It's not like you don't have what it takes, you do not need K.D." she said convincingly. "I know cats in the industry and then there's your management team."

"I don't know. I hadn't even been in contact with them since right after Dre' died."

"Girlfriend, you need to get on your p's and q's," she advised.

"You're right again," I smiled. "I was just trying to wait until I had something to bring to the table. I figured I could at least get my stuff together with K.D. before I approached them." I told her.

"I can see where you're coming from but how much is that gonna cost you? Are you gonna be able to put up with him 'til then? I mean, yeah, I know you put in a lot of work since you've been working with K.D. but think about what's best for you. It's not like you're just anybody. You were comin' up. I'm sure you have connections that you can reach out to."

"Alright, alright!" I laughed at Tika's positive persistence. "I'm just gonna go tonight and get some of my stuff I already recorded so I can at least have something to show. Plus, I have this ASCAP showcase coming up, there'll be some people there that I need to connect with." I said, mostly thinking out loud. "You're right, girl, I don't need K.D. to do my thing. After tonight, I'm out!" She gave me a high-five.

"Now that's what I'm talkin' 'bout," she laughed as we continued our lunch date, less weighed down by my drama than when we'd first arrived.

I met K.D. at the studio later that night for our last session. Though he didn't know it yet, my plan was to get my masters and by the time K.D. knew he wasn't about to get paid off me, it would be too late. I knew it was a dangerous move, but it was a risk I was willing to take.

Everything went smoothly. I took my opportunity to download my music and get my masters when K.D. made a food run, relieved that this was the last time I'd have to deal with him.

The session ended and I walked out to my truck with a smile of victory on my face. I'd won! I drove the short distance to my house, relieved when I saw K.D. drive past as I turned into my apartment complex. I'd had K.D. follow me home on occasion to make sure I made it in safely and even as the relationship was souring on my end, he continued the tradition. I grabbed my bag with the masters in it and headed upstairs. I was free of K.D and was on my way to stardom. My lunch with Tika had boosted my confidence and I was ready to step back out and make my mark. I sang as I bounced up the stairs to my apartment, taking two at a time. "Watch out world, cuz I'm 'bout to take y'all by storm!" I said, spreading my arms as my words echoed throughout the hallway. "I'm back!"

CHAPTER SIXTEEN

My cozy second floor apartment awaited as I arrived from another late night at the studio. I still loved the place that Dre' and I made our home after Mama went on her power trip, forcing me to choose my dreams over hers. Dre's love had sustained me as I made the transition from living under my mama's roof to running a home of my own. Not only did Dre' provide the emotional support I so desperately longed for, he provided the amenities that made our home comfortable. From the Italian leather furniture and plasma television set to the elegant maple dining ensemble and massive king-sized bed framed with overstuffed pillows. He'd more than come through for me when I needed him. Together we'd created a safe haven, a place where we could relax from the stress of our demanding careers.

Heading straight for the safe in my bedroom closet, I spun the safe open to deposit the music that was the key to my new start in life.

With the key to my future tucked securely away and my ties to K.D. severed, I could relax. A cup of chamomile tea was the perfect solution for my weary body. Besides its calming effect, the smooth, hot liquid helped to relax my throat. My body needed a deep sleep to replenish my energy after the stress K.D. had brought into my life and sleep always came readily after consuming the steamy concoction. I hummed along with the soft jazz flowing from the Bose music system while it soothed my soul as I prepared my magic potion.

Swift rapping at the door startled me from my task.

"Who in the heck could be at my door this late?" I wondered aloud, squinting at the clock to discover it was past midnight as I tipped to the door and peered through the peep hole.

Dang! I leaned against the door with a hard sigh. It was K.D. What in the world could he want?

"Yes?" I responded to his knocking, ignoring my instinct to leave him hanging.

"Kayla, my car stalled out down the street, can I use your phone?" He asked with his voice full of urgency.

"Dang, didn't he have a cell phone?" I wondered. My first thought was to deny his request, go back to my kitchen, and finish preparing my tea. I opted to let him in, let him make his call, and get him out as quickly as possible instead, reluctantly sliding the chain off the door. I turned the deadbolt with a disgusted sigh, allowing him entrance into my abode.

"I don't know what happened," he said, rubbing his hands together and blowing into them, trying to warm them up. "I can call AAA. It shouldn't take that long."

"The phone's right over there," I said pointing to the phone over on the cocktail table. Pulling his AAA card from his wallet, he proceeded to dial the number. I was tempted to watch every number he dialed, but the whistling tea kettle demanded my attention in the kitchen. Dropping the tea bag into my mug and adding crème and a wedge of lemon, my relaxing ritual was cut short by my need to make sure K.D. wasn't getting too comfortable.

"That sure smells good," he commented from the living room. "Mind if I have a cup?" he asked as I perched on the chair opposite him. I sat my cup on the coffee table, sighed, and went back in the kitchen to prepare K.D.'s tea. I was so exhausted, not even caring if he could feel the coldness I was projecting. But if he was affected by it, he acted as if he wasn't.

He was finishing his call as I came back with his tea. "They said it's going to be at least an hour and a half. They had a lot of calls because of the weather." He explained. "People driving crazy, sliding into each other," he finished, laughing at the mishaps of the other drivers. "You don't mind if I wait here, do you, Kayla? I gave them your number to contact me when they get to the car."

"I guess it's alright," I said, looking towards the clock. Dang, that would be nearly 2:00 in the morning. I really wasn't trying to be bothered with him, especially not for that long and besides that, I needed some sleep!

"Is everything cool, Kayla?" he asked, a hint of concern in his voice. "You seem a little agitated." He sipped the tea, eyeing me over the top of the cup. *Better make sure to bleach that cup good*, I thought. I realized with that thought just how truly disgusted I'd become with him. After tonight, this "playing cool" stuff with him would be *over*.

"I'm fine, but it's late and I'm tired." I replied instead, sipping my tea.

"I can understand that, if you want, go ahead and go to bed. I'll wait for AAA and be on my way when they get here."

I didn't trust him alone out here in my apartment. I didn't even want him here while I was in my jammies, but I *was* tired.

It was as if he was reading my mind, "Kayla, I promise," he gave a hint at a laugh, "I'll be good. I won't bother any of your stuff and I'll lock up on my way out."

I felt drowsiness conquering my body like a strong sedative. I looked in my teacup, whose image became a blur as I studied it, and it was nearly empty. I must be tired, I thought, trying to shake it off. "I'm even more tired than I thought," I yawned.

"Go ahead, go to bed" he said gently, his eyes smiling, trying to persuade me as a wicked grin appeared on his lips.

I felt my mind screaming, 'No! No! No!' But my body yearned for sweet sleep. I stood and stretched, amazed at how quickly the tiredness had crept up into my body. "I'll be right back," I said, walking the short distance down the hallway that led to my bedroom. I didn't feel right.

"*The masters!*" my mind screamed, as my heart rate increased. Remembering that they were tucked safely away in the safe, I breathed a heavy sigh of relief.

The tea, which usually had a gentle, calming effect, affected my consciousness like a sedative, making me drowsy. I longed for my soft down pillows to cradle my head. My bedroom seemed further down the hall than I'd remembered. My feet dragged along slowly, feeling as if weights held them to the floor, causing me to have to lean against the wall for support just to make it the few steps to my room. Climbing into my bed was paramount to climbing Mount Everest as the oxygen seemed to seep from the room with every labored breath I took.

Wow! I thought, sinking into my mattress. My bed had never felt so good. I decided not to change into my pajamas since K.D. was in the other room. I didn't feel like it anyway. I just wanted to rest. The soothing lull of sleep was taking over my entire body, working its way towards the center of my body, relaxing my muscles like an erotic massage.

My bedroom was dark, except for a tiny glimpse of light peeking through my blinds from the street lamp outside my window. The door squeaked as it opened slightly. I squinted, observed a man's shadowy figure hovering above me, and blinked twice, realizing I was imagining things. What I thought I was seeing was impossible. I tried sitting up but my body felt like dead weight. Trying again, I failed. My body was just too heavy to pull up especially in the midst of the wonderful massage soothing away my anxiety.

"Dre'," I breathed, "Is that you?"

"Um, Kayla, I love you so much," he said. "I've wanted to be with you for so long."

"I love you, too, Dre'," I said, smiling. I couldn't believe he was actually here. This must be some sort of wonderful dream.

"It's not Dre', baby, *it's Karlos*," he whispered, coming closer, bending down over my limp body and kissing me softly.

"Karlos?" I asked, confused. Why would Karlos be here? What was he doing in my bedroom telling me he loved me?

"Kayla," he said, sliding into my bed beside me, "I just want to be with you."

Confused by what was going on, I tried to resist, but the more I tried to sit up, move, or do anything, the more sedated my body felt. What was happening to me!

"Baby, don't fight it," he whispered, kissing my lips, then my neck, and beginning to unbutton my blouse.

"But," I started, trying to tell him that I didn't want him here. He slid his fingers to my lips, shushing me, and continued unbuttoning my top.

"I'm going to show you how much I love you," and with each button he opened, the kisses followed.

CHAPTER SEVENTEEN

I awoke with a startle, feeling like a Mack truck had plowed into me. A familiar aroma drifted through the air tickling my senses through the fuzzy cobwebs clouding my mind. It was the smell of freshly cooked bacon. I looked around through squinted eyes, forcing my eyes to adjust to the sunshine streaming through my half open blinds. I was at home, in my own bed, but I felt strange. The bedside clock read eleven fifty-three. I had slept right through the alarm.

I thought I heard something coming from the living room, but was unable to make out what it was. Maybe, I'd left the T.V. on last night. As the faint sound of whistling traveled through the air, my body stiffened. What the heck? It couldn't be Dre', 'cause Dre' was gone, though the wonderful dream about him last night had almost convinced me that the events of the past year hadn't really occurred.

Oh my God! Horrible thoughts rushed through my head, flooding my mind and clouding my ability to think rationally. If last night was a dream and Dre' really was dead, that meant there was an intruder in my house! My heart began beating wildly as I searched the room for the phone but it wasn't in its cradle. Dre's gun was still up in the closet but would I have time to get it before the whistler got to me? Not likely, my legs felt like lead.

"Kayla," a man's voice called out in a sing-song tone, stopping me in my tracks. "Baby, I made you breakfast."

Oh no, this was crazy. Was that...nah, it couldn't be who it sounded like but my eyes confirmed my suspicions as Karlos Day entered my bedroom carrying a perfectly arranged tray with pancakes, bacon and a glass of orange juice on it. He had a big self-congratulatory smile on his face, wearing nothing but a towel around his waist and Dre's favorite slippers on his feet.

"Girl, last night was the bomb!" he exclaimed, smiling, approaching me with the tray. "I had to get up and make my baby breakfast!"

I could feel my forehead creasing into a frown. Now I was really confused, unable to respond to this...whatever *this* was...that was happening to me. Last night? I tried to come up with an explanation that could result in Karlos Day standing in my bedroom half naked like we were the new Bobby and Whitney. *Uggh*, I was trapped in the twilight zone!

"Umm, umm, umm," he said, licking his lips like he was L.L. or somebody, as he set the tray on my bedside table. "Girl, you taste better than the whipped cream on those flap jacks!" he said, biting at my shoulder playfully. I drew back, pushing him away.

"K.D., what are you doing in my house?" I shouted, hopping out of my bed and edging into the corner. "And what in the world are you talking about?" I screamed, pulling the covers up around me to keep my body sheltered from his prying eyes. "Are you high or something?"

He cocked his head to the side, challenging my look of shock with one of his own. "What am I talking about?" he exclaimed. "I'm talking about the best night of your life, girl!"

This fool was trippin'!

"I don't know what you're talking about, but *you* need to get out of my house right now," I pointed to the door, as I spat the words out. Oh, my God. I'd gotten tangled up with a mad man. My hands trembled behind the covers but I fought to keep the fear from my voice.

"What, now you're gonna put me out?" he asked in a high-pitched voice, a surprised look frowning up his features. "We make love last night and you say it was the best night of your life, and now you want to put me out?" he asked again unbelievingly.

I tried thinking back to last night but it was fuzzy. The studio session was still fresh in my mind and afterwards, I'd come home. I'd taken my masters and put them away. Then, as I tried remembering more details, all I could see was K.D. showing up at my door talking about his car. That caused a light bulb to flash in my brain as I recalled him calling AAA about his car.

"What happened to your car?" I asked suspiciously.

"Don't you remember?" he asked, innocently.

"Obviously not!" I almost screamed at him sensing he was trying to push my buttons.

"Kayla, my car stopped down the road and you let me call AAA from here. While I was waiting, we started talking and we finally admitted to each other how we really feel," he said, looking into my eyes for some sign of recognition. "Do you remember now?" he asked sympathetically.

"No!" I shouted. "I let you call, but that's it. We didn't have any conversation like that."

"No, Kayla," he shook his head. "It happened. Then we made love and you told me that you loved me and I was the best thing that ever happened to you!"

I knew that something was terribly wrong, but I didn't know what; all I knew is that I felt like my whole life was depending on what I said to this man. I was so confused, but I had to put up a strong front. I didn't know what had happened the night before or what he might do. I wished desperately that someone would just knock at the door or call.

"Look, K.D., I don't remember exactly what happened last night," I chose my words carefully and tried to keep the agitation from coming through my voice, "but if I said anything to lead you on, I'm sorry. The only man I've ever loved is Dre'!"

He was shaking his head in unbelief. "Nah, baby, you said you love *me*!" He was beginning to lose his composure, "I know you meant it. You can't just take something like that back. You can't play games with me like that."

I was bewildered at this bizarre scene that was unraveling before me. Was this really even happening or was it a figment of my imagination like seeing Dre' again had been? He was trippin' if he thought I said I loved him. I didn't even *like* him. This was crazy! He was crazy. I could see it so clearly now. Pursuing my music wasn't important enough to put my life in danger. I wanted success for the sake of my daughter. I wanted that platinum dream to come true more than anything, but not with Karlos. Now I was really regretting ignoring my intuition. There was no one else to blame. I'd put myself in this situation. Now my body tensed at the thought of what he might do to me. This crazy stuff was scaring me. I had to get him out of here.

"Karlos, I don't know what to tell you. I don't know *why* last night is a blur. I *really* can't remember. I don't know why you think I would say I love you when I don't feel that way," I said softly, attempting to get my message across without provoking him. "I still love Dre'. I apologize for this…misunderstanding and whatever you think that happened but you have to leave."

"Kayla," he pleaded as his voice quivered and he actually broke down and started crying. I couldn't believe this was actually happening. This *Loony Tune* actually thought I loved him. What kind of game was he playing? His crying became hysterical as he fought desperately to regain his composure. If he wanted me to hold him or something, maybe tell him that I did love him, it wasn't going to happen. Not today. I wanted him and his disgusting lies out of my house.

I stood in the corner, stunned and disbelieving. This had to be the craziest thing that ever happened to me. He swore up and down that we made love and that I'd professed my love for him and I couldn't even remember what happened. It was frustrating, to say the least.

He wiped his eyes with the back of his hand, "Kayla, I'm sorry," he stammered. "I'm not trying to upset you."

He began gathering his clothes from the floor. "Once you have some time alone to think, you'll realize that what happened between us was real. I know you couldn't make love to me like that if you didn't love me." He came towards me as if to kiss me, but I turned my head, putting my hand up to stop him.

"You're right, I do need time to think. I'm not gonna be able to come to the studio for a couple of days, this is just trippin' me out right now." I said, not alerting him that it was over. I would never go to that studio again. He would never see me again if I could help it.

"Baby, I understand," he said, wiping at the tears rolling freely from his eyes. "I just hope you don't throw this away. I'm a good man and I can love you and our daughter better than anyone ever will, even Dre'." He added.

I couldn't believe he just called Destiny our daughter. He was more far gone than I realized. What had I gotten myself involved in?

"Don't even mention Dre'. You can't take his place." I stated bluntly, momentarily forgetting that I was supposed to be agreeing with him and doing whatever it took to get him out. "Just leave…please." I pleaded.

"You're making a big mistake," he said, pulling his shirt over his head and then pulling his jeans on before he turned to leave.

"Uggg!" I screamed into the covers at the top of my lungs, sinking onto the floor.

This was the worst day of my life. I'd attracted a true to life nutcase! Now I had to figure out how to get rid of him. I heard the door shut and dragged myself from my room to make sure he was gone because after today, he would just be a bad memory.

I had a bad feeling that I'd come upon one of the wolves in sheep's clothing that Mama and G had warned us about back in the day. If I ever needed God's help, this was one of those times. I dropped to my knees right in the corner and began praying like never before.

CHAPTER EIGHTEEN

He walked into the hallway and wiped the tears from his eyes. Who did she think she was? Did she really think that she was going to get rid of him that easily? She'd been willing to do whatever it took to get into the recording studio, but now that he was in love with her, she thought she could disregard his feelings and discard him like yesterday's trash. She was sorely mistaken. "I need time to think, I won't be at the studio for a couple of days." He mimicked her. He was never going to let her go. She was much too special, even more fascinating than Nicole had been.

Kayla was the most stunning woman he'd ever laid eyes on, with her golden, honey kissed skin, silky auburn hair and fiery chestnut colored eyes. She was by far, the most talented of them all. Her voice sang to his heart, making it beat erratically every time he heard it. He'd imagined what her soft skin would taste like, how her curvaceous body would feel beneath his and how his hands would delight in the pleasure of caressing her beautiful body.

Last night, she'd far exceeded his expectations and he loved her even more. He was never going to let her go. She would be his most prized possession, his best discovery yet. They were going to be a family, even if it killed her.

Dre' had thought he could stop him from creating a family with Kayla but he'd cut him down like a blade of grass. It was still fresh in his mind. He let a wicked smile slide into place at the mere thought of snuffing out the life of the one person Kayla might let come between them.

He'd been watching them for weeks. The first time he'd heard her, she'd reminded him of his own mother. As he slid into his car, which he'd parked down the street from Kayla's apartment last night, he allowed himself to drift back in time.

*   *   *   *   *

His mother was always singing around the house, that is when her lips weren't wrapped around her crack pipe or she wasn't drowning in a sea of cheap wine. He'd seen pictures of her before she'd had him and she was so pretty, a far cry from the skeleton of a woman she'd become since she became addicted to crack. Her voice had been so angelic, sweet and melodic, yet strong. She would have been famous, too, if his father wouldn't have ruined it. He'd been the perfect candidate to lead "The Strokers" the group he'd put together to launch his singing career. With his muscular physique, standing at six feet two inches tall, chocolate skin, smiling eyes, and dressed to impress style that emitted sex appeal, he was the ladies' delight and his mother had instantly fallen in love with Anthony Stokes.

Brenda Baker loved to sing and one night after performing at a local bar, Anthony had sweet talked her so good that by the end of the night, she was head over heels in love with him. He didn't think she was all that pretty, but she had the curvaceous body of a centerfold model and the voice of an angel.

Even though he was married, she didn't mind as long as he gave her a few dollars every now and then and fulfilled her desires in the bedroom. But then he'd flipped the script on her and he wanted her to be the bread winner. He figured she was so in love with him, she would do anything; so one night, he put her to the test.

They'd been partying, drinking, and playing poker with a couple of the cats he hung out with at the bar and he told Brenda to come back in her fanciest dress. She arrived, barely able to contain herself, thinking he was going to take her out for a fancy night on the town. Instead, he told her they could make some quick, easy dough if she'd do his main man a favor and perform her best song for him as a birthday gift. She was to dress up like when she performed at the club, sing her heart out and do whatever else he wanted. She'd protested at first, but Anthony knew she had a soft spot for him and would eventually do whatever he asked if he asked nice enough.

He kept her glass full until she began to loosen up and cajoled her into singing in front of all of them. He even introduced her as his main squeeze, *B.B.* They applauded for her like she was the star of her own Broadway show. Anthony had her to stand up under a light so she could really feel like the spotlight was on her. And she did, too. She felt like a star. She looked out into the room and Anthony's smile gave her the confidence she needed to go on. She sang with all her heart. She loved making Anthony happy. If he was happy, she was happy. He was the only man who'd ever really loved her or done anything nice for her, like buying her dinner and admiring her singing the way he did. He made her feel special, something she'd longed for all her life and she never wanted to be without that feeling. It felt good.

It didn't matter that Anthony had a wife, he loved him some Brenda. She made him feel good which was something his wife couldn't do. She must not've been on her job if Anthony was laid up under her half the time. But it was her loss and Brenda's gain. She couldn't remember a time when she'd ever felt this happy and satisfied. And tonight, as Anthony allowed her to put on a private show, would be the best night of her life.

After the song was over, his friend, who'd been drooling over her performance during the entire show, took her by the hand and led her towards a room in the back. She tried to resist without making a scene but his grip on her arm was tight. She looked to Anthony to do something to save her, to rescue her from this tall, lanky, alcohol induced stranger, but he nodded his head in approval as his friend tightened his grip and pulled her along. The smell of Hennessey permeated the room as he breathed heavily down her neck and groped at her body. She couldn't believe that Anthony was so eager to share her with his friends.

She'd cried at first, humiliated that he would even want her to do it, ashamed of herself for what she'd just done. Anthony told her how much he loved her, how no woman could ever compare to her, and how her voice and her body were much too beautiful to let go to waste. He told her that he was so proud of her for proving that she really loved him and was on his team. If she'd do it just a few more times, they could save enough money for him to leave his greedy wife. *They* could be together, just the two of them.

Brenda hated being with any other man but she knew that once they had the money, they could be together and she wouldn't have to subject herself to this kind of humiliation any longer. Besides, she liked the singing part so she did what she had to do to secure their future together.

Brenda was always bugging him to leave his wife but he kept telling her they didn't have enough money saved, even though she'd been doing these favors for his friends for months now. His excuse was they had to get far away because his wife was so crazy that if she ever found out about them, she'd kill them both. So he wanted to buy them a bad crib. He didn't want to move from one ghetto to another, he wanted them to do it big, move way out, buy a nice ride and a suburban crib.

He'd buy her some nice clothes to perform in to keep her pacified and she'd get off his back, for a while anyhow. But it all came to a screeching halt one day when she busted him walking downtown, hand in hand, carrying shopping bags with his pregnant wife.

She'd been devastated. He was always acting like he hated his wife so much but they looked like two people in love to her. She was even wearing a fur coat. He'd never bought *her* a fur coat. And later that evening, after he dropped off a new outfit for her to perform in, she questioned him about it.

"Anthony, I thought you said you weren't sleeping with her," she'd cried and he went off, telling her she didn't have any business questioning him about that as long as he was being good to her. He told her she shouldn't even worry about that, knowing they were just months away from getting a crib together. He *had* to act like he loved his wife so she wouldn't catch on that he was dating Brenda on the side. So Brenda acted like everything was cool when underneath her calm exterior, she was seething at the thought of her man having a baby with someone else, even if she was his wife.

The next time they were together, she fixed it so that she could have his baby, too. She knew that if she gave him a son, he'd leave his wife sooner and then they could be together. Plus, she'd be able to stop doing favors for his friends. So she waited until she was sure her plan had worked before she told him about their baby. It had been three weeks since she first suspected that she was pregnant and she'd even taken one of those home pregnancy tests.

Brenda prepared his favorite dinner and set the mood with candles, soft music and her best perfume that she wore only for him. She wore one of the sexy dresses he bought her and was nearly bubbling over with the news, almost barely able to keep from spilling the secret during dinner.

From somewhere, she found the patience to wait until after dinner when he was nice and relaxed before she sprang the good news on him. Surprisingly, his reaction wasn't what she'd expected. He almost tore the roof off her little one room apartment. She'd never seen him that angry before. She couldn't help but to shrink away every time he came near her. She wasn't sure what he'd do. She thought he would be ecstatic at the thought of them being a family. She'd made a way for him to finally leave his wife. Surely she wouldn't want to fight the divorce when she found out he'd been playing her for a fool all along and Brenda was having his baby. But Brenda was in for a rude awakening. Anthony demanded that she terminate the pregnancy and when she refused, he smacked her so hard that she felt her lip split and tasted blood in her mouth.

She rose up to deal him a blow but was cut down with a sharp blow to her stomach. He kept telling her that she would ruin everything by having the baby. Her singing career and any hopes of them getting their own crib would be out the window. And how was she supposed to perform for his friends if she was big and pregnant, he demanded? But Brenda was curled up on the floor crying as she realized that she'd been the one getting played all along. He'd never meant to leave his wife, she was his jewel and Brenda was just his money maker.

Anthony was in a rage as he went about the tiny apartment breaking up everything that meant anything to her. He demanded that she get rid of the baby and if she didn't, he threatened, she would regret it for the rest of her life. But Brenda was determined to have her baby. If she couldn't have Anthony, she would have the next best thing to him, his son.

He left and came back a little while later. Brenda was on the floor, rocking back and forth with grief, distraught over the fact that the man she thought loved her really hated her and wanted her to kill their child.

"You still gone have that baby?" he asked, his voice filled with a rage she'd never heard before. She could only nod her head.

He pulled something out of his pocket. It was one of those pipes that people smoked crack from. There was a little white rock in it. He lit a fire under the pipe and told her to put her mouth on the pipe. She kept turning her head from side to side, but he was relentless. She tried to knock it out of his hands, but that infuriated him more. He grabbed the back of her head trying to force it into her mouth.

"You're going to hurt our baby!" she cried, and he smiled wickedly, as he forced it into her mouth.

* * * * *

K.D. had heard this story so much from his mother growing up; it didn't even faze him to think about it anymore. He didn't even know if he could believe that Anthony was the one who got her strung out on crack. He didn't even think it was around at the time he was conceived. He believed she'd turned to it for an escape from the reality that he'd left her and their son. He knew the truth was somewhere in there. He'd heard that Anthony shot her up with heroine and that led her down the road to everything else.

She'd always blamed him for Anthony not being in her life. Even after all he'd done to her, getting her strung out on drugs and abandoning her while she was pregnant, she still loved him. She always hoped he would come back and be a family with them but he never did. And now, he never would. K.D. had made sure of that; before Anthony knew what hit him, K.D. had cut him down, just like he'd done Kayla's precious Dre'. But one thing he knew for sure, *he* was going to have a perfect family.

He took the key he'd stolen from Kayla's apartment from his pocket and dangled it in front of his eyes like an exquisitely cut diamond. He wasn't going to be like Anthony and run out on his responsibility. In fact, he would do whatever it took to make sure his family never left him, ever.

CHAPTER NINETEEN

I couldn't believe K.D. actually thought I would sleep with him. That liar! The disgust I felt for him, especially at this moment, wouldn't allow me to commit such an unthinkable crime. Plus, I knew I would remember sleeping with him, even if everything else seemed out of whack. Not knowing was driving me nuts! The question of what had *really* happened and *why* I couldn't remember consumed my thoughts. All I knew was that I wouldn't sleep with him if he was the last man on the planet.

K.D. had done a good job of disguising himself, turning on the charm during our first encounter, but as I began to get to know and observe him, his true motives had been revealed.

My instincts had been eating away at me for weeks, I felt stupid for ignoring the warning signals that flashed before me, screaming to my subconscious that something wasn't right, especially after that night he'd invited me to his condo under false pretenses. It was as frustrating as discovering halfway through a novel that the most important pages were missing, the pages that held the key to the story. There was a missing page in the story of K.D. This mystery loomed ominously over my head giving me an eerie feeling in the pit of my stomach because there was no way of finding those missing pages.

G had always told me to follow my first mind, "…'cause that's God, honey," she'd said. "That's his way of directin' us."

I was so intent on tasting the sweet success of fame and platinum status that I'd ignored my first mind, time after time, where K.D. was concerned. I had been taking his word at face value, a dangerous move for a woman to make, especially in the music game. I'd foolishly let him persuade me to work with him. When it seemed my dreams had died with Dre', I let K.D. prey on my fears until I was convinced I had something to prove. I'd allowed myself to be deceived, not wanting to look like a quitter or a failure.

Doors had opened effortlessly as Dre' and I set out to pursue our dreams, but it was different with K.D. I shook my head, recalling the times I'd forced myself to deal with him. I kept hearing Dre's voice saying, *"there's something that just ain't right about that cat."*

"I don't care if I have to start from scratch. I'm never going to his studio or calling that whacko again." I promised myself out loud. I felt stupid for letting him into my home.

"Oh, God, please forgive me for getting myself in this situation and not listening to you." I apologized, hoping for forgiveness for my disobedience. I had put my confidence in K.D. instead of God and now I was back to square one after losing valuable time. "I know you have a good plan for me to be successful and have the life I've been dreamin' about. I don't know where to go from here, but I'm asking you to please help me get to where I need to be." I cried, tears streaming down my face. From now on I'd put God first, even if it meant sacrificing my own wants.

My legs wobbled as I climbed slowly up from the floor using the corner of my bed for support. Thank God for caller I.D. I could avoid K.D.'s call, which was sure to come. The thought reminded me that I'd forgotten to call Tika. She'd babysat for Destiny while I made that fateful trip to the studio the night before. She should be out of church by now, it was after one o'clock. I called Tika's cell phone.

"Hey, girl, I'm just leaving the church. I was just about to call you!" She said sounding rushed.

"Oh, how's Destiny?" I was anxious to know. Destiny was my heart. I loved her more than life itself; she was a gift from Dre' that no one could take away. A deep twinge of pain ran through my heart at the thought of my little girl never knowing her Daddy. My daddy's absence had given me a taste of how it felt to not have a father around and that was a pain I never wanted her to feel, but when Dre's life had been cut short, it had brought one of my worse fears to pass. My daughter would be fatherless.

"She misses her mommy," Tika replied.

"I know I was supposed to come and pick her up, but do you think you could bring her home?"

"Girl, that's not a problem. Are you alright?" The last thing I wanted to do was cause her to worry. She was almost as bad as Mama, being protective over me at times.

"Yeah, I'm sure I will be. I just have a headache. I'm going to hop in the shower," I answered, trying my best to calm her fears that I'd inadvertently aroused. I *wanted* to spill the whole K.D. incident to her but not over the phone.

"'Cuz, what's *really* wrong?" she asked with concern. "Did something happen at the studio last night?"

"Tika, I promise, everything is okay now," I paused, feeling my emotions welling up, especially at her concern and her ability to peep me out even through my attempt to masquerade the truth. She was usually so upbeat and silly, but when I needed her, she was the best friend a person could hope for. "I'm okay, I just don't feel good so I'm going to hop in the shower and I should be out by the time you get here, okay?"

"Alright, but we're going to talk when I get there," she stated firmly.

"Okay, I'll see you in a little while." I clicked the phone off and started towards the bathroom, but I was stopped in my tracks by the lingering smell of bacon in my apartment. I made a detour to the kitchen to dispose of the plate and the food that K.D. had prepared. I didn't want any trace of him in my house. Resisting the urge to slam the plate against the wall and watch it shatter into a million pieces like I wished K.D. would do, I dropped it into the sink with a loud *clang!*

Starting the shower, I undressed and stepped into the hot water, letting the jets pound away at my body extra hard to dispel all traces of Karlos Day. Ughh! I felt nasty as I tried to scrub my skin clean with the soapy loofah. It was frustrating trying to recall details and make sense of the foggy details from last night. I needed to know if he'd touched me. Thinking about it made me gag. My skin felt contaminated and it was all K.D.'s fault. What if he'd slept in my bed when I was asleep? I mean, he obviously wasn't working with a full deck. To try and convince me we'd "professed our love for each other" was at the very least absurd. I refused to believe it, though I couldn't get his words out of my head. The image of him standing in my room with Dre's slippers on and knowing that he may have touched me caused me to lurch forward in the shower. My stomach reeled from convulsions as I released the pain that he'd caused.

I scrubbed even harder causing red streaks to erupt from my skin, taking my fury with K.D. out on my delicate skin.

"What did he do to me?" I screamed, watching my tears mix with the soapy water and disappear down the drain like my memories had done.

CHAPTER TWENTY

The knocker pounded persistently against the wood door as I stepped from the shower, wiped my face, and threw on my silk robe to greet Destiny and Tika. I sprinted to the door, taking a deep breath before facing Tika face to face.

"Hey, Tika," I greeted her.

"You look horrible," Tika said, entering the apartment with Destiny's car seat carrier perched on her arm, looking expectantly at me for clues to my strange behavior earlier.

"Hey, you look beautiful yourself," I replied sarcastically, with a half smile. "Hi, baby," I greeted Destiny with a kiss on her forehead, as I reached for her car seat.

Her hazel eyes lit up and her cheeks produced a dimpled smile as she cooed back at me.

"What is that on your neck," Tika asked, nosily, lifting her sunglasses from her eyes, "a passion mark?" She peered at me as if it were the strangest thing she'd ever seen. She walked past me, placed Destiny's diaper bag on the floor, threw her Louis Vuitton tote on the sofa, and proceeded to check my neck out with her nose frowned up.

I went to the hallway to check out the mark for myself. She was right. The mark of the beast had been implanted on me by Karlos. It was dark and purple, the blood pulsating just beneath the surface of my skin. I ran my hand over the mark in disgust, wishing I could rip it off. "*Ughh*, I'm going to kill him!" I screamed, startling Destiny. Her tiny lip curled as she cried at the sharp outburst I displayed. "I'm sorry, Destiny, Mommy's sorry." I rocked her carrier back and forth to calm her.

"Kayla, what happened?" Tika was standing behind me searching for answers.

"Let me put Destiny in her swing," I said, my voice quivering. I didn't want my daughter to witness my upset. I plopped down in the sofa, shaking my head, trying to make some sense of what was going on. "Tika, I'm really trippin'. I can't even make sense of this mess in my head." If I was confused, I could only imagine how strange my behavior seemed from Tika's viewpoint.

"Look, I'll fix us some tea and you calm down and try to get your head together." She got up to walk into the kitchen, striking a familiar chord from the night before. I remembered fixing myself tea last night. But almost everything else about K.D. being here was still a fog.

"Tika, something strange happened and I feel so stupid and embarrassed. I don't even know where to start," I began.

"Just tell me what's goin' on," she started. "I've never seen you act so...strange before."

"I know," I said softly. "K.D. was here last night." I blurted out.

"Here! Why?" she asked, knowing that I'd planned to get the masters and make a split from him.

"After I left the studio, he followed me home to make sure I'd made it safely, as usual." I started. "But then he showed up at my door, talking about his car had stalled or something."

"And you let him in?" she asked in amazement. "Dang, Kayla," she said slapping her forehead. "Why you let him in knowing you don't feel right about him?" She asked the same question I asked myself, rubbing in how stupid I had been.

"I didn't want to clue him in to the fact that I was splitting." I said, realizing with hind site that I should've just called AAA for him or better yet I should've ignored him and let that be the end of it.

"I was just tryin' to keep it social, especially since I knew I had those masters."

"Well, what'd he show up here for anyway? Doesn't he have a cell phone?"

"I think so but now I remember he said he'd lost it earlier in the day. I'm tellin' you, Tika, he's always got excuses to cover everything."

"Dang," she breathed a disgusted sigh, "so what happened?"

I buried my face in my hands unable to answer.

"Kayla," she said, moving to the sofa where I sat. "...it's okay. What happened?" she asked sympathetically.

"I don't know," was all I could say.

"I'm not here to judge you," she said, looking at me with understanding eyes. "I just want to help you through whatever you're going through but you can't shut me out." Trust wasn't the issue here. I knew Tika wouldn't judge me because of my involvement with Karlos or my lack of good judgment.

"I promise, T, I'm not tryin' to shut you out but I really don't remember what happened. It's crazy, it's like trying to piece together a puzzle with missing pieces. K.D. was here, he made a call, I fixed him tea and the next thing I knew..." my voice trailed off not wanting to think about what might have happened next.

"The next thing you knew, what?" she pleaded.

I tried to shake off everything else he'd said to me. "He's got this delusion that I'm in love with him."

She almost spit her tea out. "In love with him? Why would he think that?"

"He claims that's what I told him."

"Yeah, right," she looked at me with disbelief. "What is *he* trippin' on?"

I avoided her eyes as I whispered my secret. "He says we slept together."

128

"Whoa, whoa, whoa!" her eyes got so big I thought they were going to pop right out of her head. "Back this way up. What do you mean, he said you *slept together?*"

I was stammering. "I mean, he was here this morning, he said we made love and now I'm trippin' because I can't even remember what happened last night!" I poured out in one gigantic breath.

"That's how this big hickey got on you're neck?" she frowned, "You got busy with K.D.?" she spoke the unspeakable. The room fell so silent you could hear a pin drop.

CHAPTER TWENTY-ONE

I put my hand to my neck, wishing I could rip out the contaminated portion, the evidence from Karlos' twisted version of last night.

"I did not get busy with him." I almost screamed.

"Calm down, Kayla." She said in an almost whisper, motioning towards Destiny, who was content in her automatic swing. She swayed back and forth as her eyelids drifted between sleep and what was going on across the room on the sofa as her mother sat wanting to scream out in frustrated anger at her foolish decisions that had led her to cross paths with the likes of Karlos Day again. A pang of regret coursed through my veins at the mere thought of his name.

"Tika, all I really know for sure is that after he made his call, he asked to wait here until his car club sent a tow truck."

"Kayla, what else do you remember?" she asked slowly, as if she were a detective working on the case to find the missing details that would magically make everything fall into place. "Just try to remember as much as you can."

I closed my eyes, willing the recollection of the events of last night to produce an image of the truth in my mind.

"Just take your time." Tika urged softly.

I began to recall as much of the previous night as I could remember up until this morning when he stood there with a breakfast tray wearing a towel and Dre's slippers. The words came out in a whisper. "He started lying, tellin' me we made love and that I told him I loved him. I was really scared and I was trippin'. I tried to act like I wasn't scared, 'cause I didn't know what he was going to do."

"Dang, Kayla," she said, hugging me. "I'm so glad you're alright, there's no tellin' what was goin' through his mind."

She was right. He could have done something to really hurt me and I'd been a dummy to let him in. I felt like stupid red riding hood. I'd been right in the room with a big bad wolf trying to disguise himself in sheep's clothing. My own selfish desires had caused me to put myself in danger. I was so thankful to God for watching over me. No matter what had happened, I was still alive. I looked over at Destiny. I couldn't believe I had been so gullible and stupid to put myself at a risk of never seeing her sweet little face again. Even if I hadn't thought about my own safety, I should have taken my daughter into consideration.

"Wait a minute," Tika said, "You said you remember having tea with him?" she asked as if a light bulb had come on her mind.

"Well, yeah, I mean no, it wasn't like I was entertaining him." I tried to explain.

"That's not what I meant, Kayla. I just asked because," she paused, mid sentence, "maybe he gave you something. How come you can't remember everything from last night? You never had that problem before?" she said as if putting the pieces together. "I wouldn't put it past him from what you've told me about him. I mean, come on, you let this guy in here in the middle of the night, he comes up with some story about a broken down car and then on top of that he's trying to make you believe that you said something you know you didn't say. It just doesn't sound right."

"You know what, you could be right, Tika," I said, contemplating on everything she'd said. As I thought about it, I could see how he would've had the chance to slip me something when I went back into the kitchen to get him a cup of tea. That was the only time I left him alone that I could remember.

"I'm tellin' you, this sounds like something I heard on a talk show," she said, shaking her head.

"Basically," I agreed. "Now do you see why I'm trippin'?"

"Yeah and I see that he's sick!" she said angrily. "All of that's not a coincidence. Who does he think he is? Are you really supposed to just say, duh, okay, I love you, whatever you say?" she said, mimicking her best dumb look. "Come on now!"

"I can't even believe I wanted to get my music done so bad that I just got caught slippin' like that."

"I know but, I mean, nobody's perfect." She said. "It never occurred to you that he might've set you up?"

"Set me up?"

"Come on now, think about it. I know you. Once you get fed up with somebody, you start givin' off them body signals. He probably peeped it and figured you were gonna ditch him, so he figured he was gonna get what he wanted regardless." She said, reaching for the cordless phone on the table behind her. "And you say he used the phone?" she asked.

"Yeah," I responded.

"Then let's see who he called. She clicked the redial button.

"265-6600," she called out the number. "Whose number is that?" she asked.

"That's his cell number."

"Look through the numbers on your redial and see if you see an 800 number for his so called auto club that he called," she said.

As I clicked through the list of familiar numbers, Tika's theory had proven correct. K.D. hadn't called AAA like he'd pretended. He had set me up. The cold, hard reality sunk in.

"Dang," was all I could whisper.

"Now I see why you felt the way you did. He thinks he's so slick." She said. "I bet he really thought that you were going to just accept whatever he told you, even that you love him."

"I don't care what he said, that doesn't make it true."

"I'm not saying it does, but you know how men are, especially them outta town cats. They think they can get over and we ain't supposed to be up on game."

"He did catch me slippin' but I don't care what he thinks, me and him ain't happenin'. Not now and not ever."

"You and I know that but he probably thought if he could get you to believe that junk, he could tell you whatever else he wanted you to think and you would fall for it."

Tika was right but I didn't want to let any of this sink in because I felt like everything was my fault. Agreeing meant that he'd been right to think that he could get over on me. To believe would mean that I'd invited him into my home and he'd drugged me, invaded my home, and maybe even my body. It would mean that a part of me that I couldn't get back was lost and he could've done any of a thousand disgusting, unthinkable things to me and I would never know the truth. I'd let this stranger into my home and he may have even raped me and not just my physical body but my hopes and my dreams. I would never know all the answers.

I couldn't stop the tears from spilling over the rims of my eyelids. Tika held me in her arms, but I wanted to shrink away. She wanted to comfort me but I wanted to die.

"It's okay, Kayla, it's going to be alright." She spoke softly, barely audible as if I were a little baby crying in its mother's arms. "Shhh, don't cry, it's going to be okay."

"How is it going to be alright?" I asked, looking into her eyes hoping to find an answer, any answer. "I feel so stupid."

"That's what he wants you to feel but don't give him that. Don't give him that power over you."

"But I feel dirty, I don't even know what he did to me." I cried.

"Do you want to call the police?" She asked gently. Embarrassment, shame and anger boiled inside me. I wasn't going to let him get away with this. I had a plan for him.

133

"I don't need the police for what I gotta do," I said, almost under my breath. In fact, I hoped they stayed far, far away, so when he came up missing, they wouldn't even think to suspect Kayla Ross.

"I'ma kill him, just like he's tryin' to do me." Tika followed behind me as I stomped into the bedroom that K.D. had violated, the bedroom I'd shared with the real love of my life. The gun was tucked away in the closet. What good would that do if a stranger tried to come in? Last night had proven that it hadn't done any good. I should have had it right next to my bed, that way, I could have put a nice big hole in Karlos Day when he least expected it, when he first came into my private sanctuary or when he stood there in Dre's slippers acting like this was his house.

"Kayla, don't do that, you don't want to ruin your life!" Tika grabbed my arm.

"My life!" I shouted, "Do you realize what he's done to my life!" I checked the clip. No bullets. I grabbed Dre's ammo and began to fill the empty magazine.

"Kaaayla," her pleading voice was hoarse, "don't let him do this to you, he's not even worth it."

I cocked the gun.

"How can you defend what he did to me?" Outrage boiled inside of me. I just wanted all memories of K.D. gone so I could resume my life. How did she expect me to move on knowing that he thought he'd won and was somewhere probably fantasizing about what he'd done to me? How was I supposed to have a life as long as he was out there somewhere? Was I just supposed to let him continue to play me for the rest of my life? 'Cause that wasn't how I operated. Somebody had stolen Dre's life and he didn't have a chance to fight back. K.D. was trying to steal my life right out from under me but I wasn't going to let him. He was about to see what it felt like to have someone come into your world and take what was yours, 'cause I was about to show him that he couldn't

134

take my life. I would get to him first! He must've thought that because I didn't live in the city I was going to let him get over but he was about to see what I was made of. He was going to feel all the pain I had built up inside me. I let the hate settle into my heart so I could kill him with no regrets and feel good about it.

"Kayla, please, you're not thinking, you have a beautiful little girl out there. What's going to happen to her if you go out and kill that fool?"

"I don't care," I screamed.

"You're not thinking. Listen to yourself. Don't you care about what'll happen to Destiny?"

"What do you mean, what'll happen to her?" I couldn't think. All I could see was red as the tears streamed down my cheeks. "I'm doin' this *for* her. He brought this on himself."

"Kayla, I know you're hurting but, please, you have everything to live for. Destiny has already lost Dre' and if you go out and kill K.D. you never know how it's going to go down." She pleaded with me not to do it. "You said you gave your life to God but now you're tryin' to run out and solve your own problem instead of puttin' it into His hands."

"What am I supposed to do, just let him get away with it?" I cried.

"No, you're supposed to wait on God. You always talk about how God is going to work your life out for good. Believe that now, Kayla." She pleaded with me. "Please, believe that now," she hugged me tight whispering, "just believe in God" until my spirit calmed down. I loosened my grip on the gun as I slid to the floor unable to control the sobs that rose up inside me. I was hurting really bad. As much as I wanted to hunt down K.D. and serve him up a bitter dish of revenge, I wanted a life with my daughter more. And I knew that Tika was right, I needed now, more than ever, to believe in God. But I knew that God was love and just in case He decided to spare K.D., I was going to keep that

135

.45 loaded by my bed and if K.D. ever showed his face around here again, I was going to lay him down.

CHAPTER TWENTY-TWO

I sat in Dre's office wondering who in the world could have written the letter that had shown up in my mailbox this morning. It had a Newark, New Jersey postmark and had been mailed out last Wednesday. Whoever had written it had seen the exposé of me and K.D. in Urban Elite Magazine. I felt dirty all over again just thinking about the photo shoot and how he'd been trying to press up on me. Knowing he'd been in my apartment still sickened me. I had to find out what was going on. I knew one place to start: the Internet. I was going to find out all there was to know about Karlos Day. Who exactly was he?

The letter, which simply stated: "*Karlos Day is not who you think he is. Be careful!*" only confirmed that my intuition about him had been on point. That's why I'd been getting all those strange vibes. God had been warning me all along. I could hear Him deep down in my spirit telling me not to trust Karlos' words, warning me that he was trying to deceive me. But my hard headed self wouldn't listen, too busy chasing that platinum dream and trying to reclaim the fame that had awaited me before Dre' had been killed.

I searched New Jersey's phonebook for a listing under Karlos Day's name, but there was none. The letter left so many questions wide open. Did it mean that Karlos Day was pretending to be something he wasn't or did it mean that he was pretending to be *someone* he wasn't?

My search through New Jersey newspapers for possible leads landed me in the Star-Ledger's obituary section. If this guy was real, maybe he'd done something newsworthy. But what came up in my search sent a shiver down my spine. He'd generated some press alright. "Producer, Karlos Day, was found stabbed to death in his recording studio Monday morning. R&B singer Nicole Banks, Day's protégée and the newest addition to Day's stable of artists is missing..." the article read. There was a photo of Karlos Day and, one thing was for sure, the photo of the slain producer was definitely not the man that I knew to be Karlos Day. I felt sick to my stomach reading the story and even sicker as I read his obituary.

Doing a search for information about Nicole Banks turned up a similar story. "Nicole Banks," it read, "the 22 year old Newark, New Jersey native who was feared kidnapped from her fiancé's recording studio was found dead." The date was three months after Karlos Day's death. One suspect in the case, Mark Shepard, is wanted for questioning in connection to the murders by the New Jersey police.

Oh, my God! This was crazy! I thought as more pieces to the puzzle became apparent. This producer and his girlfriend had come up dead within three months of each other and now this Karlos Day impersonator was here...terrorizing my life! The connection was clearly laid out in black and white and this was no coincidence. Whoever had murdered Karlos Day had also kidnapped Nicole Banks and murdered her too. My gut was telling me that if K.D. was impersonating this dead producer Karlos Day, then he must be Mark Shepard. Why else would someone impersonate a dead man? A million questions raced through my mind. This was too much to digest. I felt a migraine pounding against my temples. Something told me that if I continued to dig, I would find even more shocking discoveries. And with a couple of strokes on my keypad, my suspicions were confirmed. I hoped for anything but that and as the truth unfolded it became clear. The man I knew as Karlos Day was really Mark Shepard, the producer's murder suspect. Now the question was, what was he doing here and how did I fit into the equation? Out of all the people in the world, how did I become entangled in this web? I

138

probed deeper for more answers about Mark Shepard wanting to know who would send me this letter and why. Was Mark Shepard even his real name?

The postmark was the only clue I had to go on as far as finding the person who was trying to warn me. Dang, I knew something was up with this cat! Why couldn't I have listened to Dre'? He'd known from the beginning that K.D., Mark Shepard, or whoever he was, was up to something, but me and my ego. I had played my baby off like he was just jealous when he'd been on point. I needed time to calm down after reading the disturbing articles.

"Get a grip, Kayla. Get a grip!" I told myself over and over.

I searched as much information as possible and one name kept popping up in the stories about Nicole Banks and Mark Shepard. *Monica Banks.* As I read the articles, her name appeared in both. She'd been the one trying to get the police to do something about her sister's disappearance and her murder. She'd been desperate to find the man who had been stalking her sister and had eventually killed her boyfriend, Karlos Day and kidnapped her sister, Nicole, after months of terrorizing her.

The article stated that although no one had been arrested in the murder of Karlos Day, Monica always believed that it was Mark Shepard who murdered him and later her sister. Nicole had subpoenaed a restraining order against him. After it was served, Karlos had been found murdered in his studio, where he'd last been seen alive in a recording session with his girlfriend, singer, Nicole Banks.

"Monica Banks," I said aloud. I wanted to remember the name. She could link everything together. Was she the one who'd written the note? It would make sense. If her sister had been murdered by this Mark Shepard, it was very likely that she or someone else he'd hurt had sent the warning.

This was too much to consume, especially after that episode the other day. Even after not hearing from him since then, I had a feeling that I hadn't heard the last of him, especially after reading these chilling stories. I felt like my whole life had become an episode of *Tales from the Darkside*.

I wrote down Monica Banks' name and tried to think of how I would contact her and more importantly what I would say. I had to know if she'd written that letter and, if so, what else there was to know about Mark Shepard.

I called New Jersey information to get the number but as a female voice answered, I realized how strange it was to be calling this woman about this lunatic man who, in all probability, had killed her sister. But if she'd written the letter, then she already knew about me and wanted me to know about him.

"Hello?" the woman said a second time, sounding irritated from a lack of response at the other end.

My voice caught in my throat. "Hello, may I speak with Monica Banks?"

"*This is Monica.*" She replied, a hint of agitation in her voice. "May I ask who *I'm* speaking with?"

"Monica, you don't know me." I started in what seemed to be a small voice. I cleared my throat. "My name is Kayla Ross."

I heard her breath catch on the other end, followed by what sounded like a sigh of relief.

"So you got the letter, huh?" she asked. "I hoped you were intelligent enough to start piecing things together."

This was too strange.

"Monica, I have to admit, this is too weird. I still don't know everything that's going on here. It's confusing and if this person that I've been dealing with is who I think he is, I could be in danger. This is really scaring me."

"Kayla, I don't want to scare you any more than you already are, but if you're dealing with Mark Shepard," she paused as if remembering something. "Are you okay?"

"Yes, I'm okay." At least I was okay as I could be. This kind of stuff wasn't supposed to happen to real people. This was surreal.

"Does he know anything?" she probed, "Have you confronted him?"

"No, I just finished reading your letter and trying to figure out who sent it and how to locate you and…"

"Burn it!" she demanded.

"Monica, I don't think he'll be coming back," I started to explain that I'd cut him off.

"Kayla, you really have no idea of what he's capable of," she paused. "Mark Shepard *killed* my sister."

I let what she said sink in. I felt so sorry for her. Losing a sister had to be terrible. I couldn't imagine how I'd feel if someone took Kenya away from me. I knew how Dre's loss felt and I knew that this woman was hurting over her sister's murder just as I was torn up about Dre's murder. Knowing who'd killed her sister and that he was still out there seemed that it would make matters worse. I still didn't have any closure about Dre's death. His killer was still out there somewhere. I felt sick knowing that Karlos Day, or whoever he was, was a cold blooded murderer and even worse, he'd been in my home.

"I am so sorry about your sister." I said, sympathetically. I'll burn the letter." I promised.

"Kayla, I've been restless ever since my sister's murder and I know this is a lot to ask," she began, "but the only way that Mark Shepard is ever going to pay for my sister's death is if the police catch up with him. Do you know where he is?"

"He could be at the studio but I cut him off a couple of days ago and I haven't spoken to him since, so I don't know for sure. I could call for you." I offered.

"No, if you cut him off, that's good." She said. I could hear the relief in her voice. "Can you give me the number?" I rattled off his number to her.

"Monica, now I have something to ask you." I garnered up the strength to ask her for what I knew would stir up awful memories, but I had to know. "I really need to know everything about this man. I still don't know why he's been perpetrating to be this Karlos Day person or what he wanted with me, can you tell me anything?"

"Kayla, I've been praying that I would be able to help you. Even before I wrote the letter, after I saw that picture, I'd hoped he hadn't charmed you into something you would regret." She said. "But I saw something in your eyes, the same look my sister had in her eyes when he was around and that's what made me reach out to you, so to answer you're question, of course I'll tell you everything you want to know and probably some things you don't want to know, but believe me, you'll be happy you cut *him* off. I don't think I should come there, just in case he might be lurking around somewhere. But Kayla, the police here have been after him for a long time, if you could help them or talk to them and tell them anything to help them catch him, I would be so grateful."

I was instantly creeped out by her suggestion that he may be lurking. I knew if someone had information on Dre's killer, I would want them to come forth. I decided to help her.

"I could come there, as soon as tomorrow. I want to get him off the streets, too."

"Tomorrow would be wonderful." She agreed and gave me her address. "I need you to bring any information that will lead the police to him. I can't believe he was stupid enough to pose in a magazine."

142

"Well, I can, he acts like he's God's gift."

"Then he hasn't changed," she laughed but I could hear the sadness in her voice behind the laugh. "Kayla, be safe." She warned. "It might even be a good idea for you to spend the night somewhere else before you come here, just in case he's watching and tries to follow you."

"You think he's watching me?" I asked, disgusted by the idea.

"Kayla, you never know with him. He stalked my sister for months, so don't take him lightly, especially if you cut him off." She said. "Just watch your back.."

"I'll call my cousin right now and ask her to ride with me. We'll leave from there."

"I hate that we have to meet under such peculiar circumstances, but I don't want anyone else to go through what he put my sister through."

"I just appreciate that everything is coming to light," I responded. "I know this has to be hard for you and I just thank you for giving me some answers."

We made plans for me to drive to Jersey tomorrow afternoon. Together we were about to shut Karlos or Mark Shepard or whoever he was, down. I burned the letter as I'd promised and flushed the ashes down the toilet. Then I called Tika and asked her to come pick us up. I had a lot to tell her. I snatched the paper off my little notepad and printed directions to Monica's home in Jersey from map quest.

I only hoped Mama would agree to take care of Destiny and Tika would agree to accompany me on this trip to discover what the missing pieces to the Mark Shepard puzzle were.

143

CHAPTER TWENTY-THREE

She'd had some nerve staying out all night. She never stayed out all night, rarely past two a.m. And that was when she had been in the studio with him. She'd better not be trying to hook-up with someone else. That would be a violation. He'd made her and he wasn't going to let anyone take that away from him.

He'd been watching and waiting since the last time they'd seen each other. After he'd spent the night, he'd convinced her that they'd made love but they hadn't. He wanted her to enjoy it, not be thinking that he was that weakling, Dre'. After all Dre' couldn't even protect her. He didn't want any part of their first time to bring Dre' to her remembrance. That's another reason he hadn't made love to her. She'd given him a headache talking about Dre', hoping and wishing he'd come back from the grave to spend one night with her. Even though he kept telling her he wasn't Dre'. She thought she was seeing him in her room that night. No, he had anticipated making love to her and when it happened, it was going to be perfect. She was going to say and feel everything he'd told her. She was going to love him so much, tell him he was the best thing that ever happened to her and confirm how long she'd been waiting for a good man like him. She was going to admit that she wanted him to be a family with her and Destiny and even have their own child, a son, to make it complete.

He couldn't wait. He was going to have the life his father had denied him and his mother. He was going to have a perfect family.

Where was Kayla? He should have followed her but he knew there weren't too many places she could be, probably at one of her family member's homes. Either Tika, her dime piece cousin with the Coca-Cola shaped figure, bronze skin, slanted eyes and long wavy hair who, if he'd met before Kayla, may have diverted him from the plan. Or maybe she's at her mother's, the forty-something, over-protective diva that had given him a disapproving look when he'd been Kayla's guest at her church.

Kayla better not be with some other man because if she was there would be hell to pay he thought, scowling. Kayla could be so inconsiderate at times. Didn't she know that there were dangerous people out there and the best place for her and Destiny was at home? If she didn't know, that would be one of the first lessons he'd teach her. He would make sure that once they were married, she'd limit her activities so she could be home more. He'd make sure that they were always together so that he could always protect her.

He fiddled around with the key in his pocket. Taking the key out, he eyed it, smiling, before deciding to check things out.

The door swung open easily as he unlocked it, welcoming him in.

"Kayla?" he called out. No response. He flipped the light switch and plopped down on the plush leather sofa. He felt right at home. He couldn't wait to move in. But this would be temporary. He was going to make her a star and then buy them a mansion in Virginia. Right on the ocean, so every morning they could wake up with a view of the ocean. They would stroll along the beach together while he listened to her tell him how he was her king and she was going to worship him for the rest of her life. He allowed himself to drift off into his fantasy of their perfect life.

He let a wicked grin slide onto his face as he imagined their new life together. He almost drifted off to sleep right there on her sofa, savoring in the pleasurable feeling that consumed his body whenever he thought about Kayla. But he couldn't let sleep pervade his body, he had to find out where she was.

He looked for clues as to her whereabouts. Her luggage was still in her closet but her toothbrush was missing. Was she spending the night with someone? He wondered, jealousy clouding his irrational thoughts. He'd punish her good if she was.

Her cousin, Tika had stayed with her three nights in a row after the night he'd spent with Kayla. He still couldn't believe she'd acted so foul the next morning. He'd enjoyed holding her that night, tasting her soft skin, even preparing breakfast for her the next morning. He'd wanted to surprise her with something special, something he was sure Dre' had never done but she reacted like she'd been violated. She'd started trippin' and demanded that he leave. He restrained himself from smackin' her, lettin' her know who the man of the house was. He'd teach her some respect later. He'd left but he'd been coming back to check on her. It was a good thing he'd taken her extra key. It came in handy on nights like tonight.

He checked her caller I.D. but he didn't recognize any strange numbers. He pressed the redial button to see who she'd been calling. When he came to the third number on the list, he could feel the red cloud passing over his eyes at the discovery of the 973 area code. What was she doing calling Jersey and who had she contacted there? He pressed *67 and the redial button to block Kayla's number from showing up as he traced the call. A female voice came over the answering machine. He could feel the heat began to rise inside his body. The sound of her voice was like a flame that made his temper reach its boiling point.

All he'd wanted to do was make Kayla happy and now she was going behind his back, being nosey. Just like a female! He shook his head in disgust, ripping the phone line from the jack and threw the phone into the wall. He needed to calm down. But all he could see was red. He was furious. Kayla was going to be sorry she'd ever made that call.

CHAPTER TWENTY-FOUR

I called Monica's number to let her know we were almost to her house but as we drove up the street we were met by a fleet of police cars. What had happened?

"Hello?" A man's voice answered.

"Hello…" I began slowly, distracted by the scene before me, "is Monica in?"

"Who may I ask is calling?" he inquired.

"This is…" my voice caught in my throat as we approached Monica Banks' house and I realized that the police cars were surrounding her house. I jumped out and ran towards her house.

"What's going on?" I screamed, dropping my cell phone as I ran up to the lawn.

"Miss, you can't go in there." An officer demanded standing there all big and cocky, looking like a defensive player for the NFL and I wasn't about to get through.

"But I was supposed to be meeting Monica Banks," I explained, "What's happened?"

"And you are?" he questioned me, looking dead into my eyes.

"I'm Kayla Ross. I just drove here from Detroit to meet with her!"

"We found your name on a piece of notepaper in Ms. Banks' home." He stated. "What was the nature of your relationship with Ms. Banks?"

"Was?" It was too much. "What do you mean, *was?*"

"Ms. Banks is dead."

"Dead?" I shouted, not caring that the yard was full of officers. "I just spoke with her this morning!" I was near screaming.

"What were you supposed to be meeting Ms. Banks about?"

"She wanted to warn me about the man she suspected of killing her sister."

"And this man's name?"

"Mark Shepard!" I screamed, vaguely aware of my surroundings. My legs almost gave out as I realized he'd been here. I could barely hear the barrage of questions that followed, neither those asked while I stood in Monica Banks' yard in disbelief nor those asked at the police station. I couldn't believe this was happening. Would I survive this horror flick?

* * * * *

He sat down the street observing the scene. He'd never liked Monica. It had been a pleasure eliminating her and her big mouth. He'd let her slide for too long, but her mouth had gotten her into trouble as usual. If she could've only learned how to mind her own business and stay out of other people's relationships, then maybe she'd be enjoying her life right now. But some people just had to learn the hard way and she was one of them.

He couldn't believe she had the nerve to try and come between him and Kayla. It's a good thing he had that key to Kayla's. Otherwise, he might not have known that she was coming here. Who did she think she was? And Monica, that home wrecker never gave up trying to act like Robocop. She hadn't been so big and bad a little while ago. Acting all surprised to see him. What did she expect? Did she actually think he was just going to sit by and let her wreck his new life? She must've been off her rocker if she thought her tactics would work against him.

He'd wanted her for months and she'd provided the perfect opportunity. He had to laugh at her stupidity. She'd wanted to warn Kayla but she was no match for him. He enjoyed watching her struggle against him though, it gave him a rush. He really couldn't understand why she was trying to preserve her useless

148

life. She'd wanted to be with her sister again so bad; instead of screaming, she should have been thanking him for making it a reality. She should've learned her lesson from seeing what happened to Nicole. Sweet Nicky. She had been hard headed too, all the way up until the end.

Why couldn't these girls just realize when something was meant to be and give in? Why couldn't they recognize a good man when they saw one? They were always crying about how they wanted someone to love them for who they were but then they would hook up with guys that would dog them out. Then when someone came along that would treat them right, "He's not my type." They whined. "He's too nice," they complained. "I just ain't feelin' him." They were so confused; they didn't know what they wanted.

He knew what they needed. They needed a good man, like him. All they had to do was submit to him, even the Bible said that. And they all claimed they believed in the Bible but when he would tell them that, oh, they weren't trying to hear that. They all prayed for a good man but then when he showed up to answer their prayers…they acted like they couldn't recognize. He became disgusted just thinking about those silly women. He just wanted to focus on Kayla now. Forget all those other chicken heads. He was going to make it work with her no matter what. He even had a letter all prepared for her mother when she came searching. It read:

Dear Mama,
I'm sorry I have to leave like this. I feel like I'm responsible for that woman's death and I can't live with that right now. Everyone that tries to help me ends up dying and I don't want that to happen to anyone else, especially you or Destiny.

Mama, please take care of my daughter and let her know that no matter what, I love her.

Love,

Kayla

CHAPTER TWENTY-FIVE

I rubbed my head, trying to recall what had happened.

"Hey, you're up," came Karlos, I mean, Mark Shepard's voice.

"Tonight's going to be the best night of our lives," he said as he informed me of his plans for us to conceive a son together, but I had other plans. I prayed silently, not daring to let him know that I was talking to God.

Now I remembered. I'd gone back to my West Bloomfield apartment after leaving Jersey and answering all the questions about Monica Banks' murder. I'd dropped Tika off and stopped back by to pack some stuff for me and Destiny to stay with Mama for a couple of days. When I'd walked in, something was funny. I saw a brief flash of light, heard footsteps, turned to see who it was and had been struck in the face. Now I was bound and gagged, awakening to the chilling sound of the maniac's voice. Oh my God, I'd been kidnapped.

I screamed and then cried through the bandana that was stuffed in my mouth, only to realize that would do no good. I was dealing with a madman and he probably planned to kill me just like he'd done the real Karlos Day, Nicole and her sister, Monica Banks. "God will never leave me or forsake me," I mumbled, recalling the scriptures that I'd confessed to help me receive healing while I grieved for Dre'. I had to walk by faith and believe that God would help me. It was the only way out. I believed that God was with me no matter how my situation looked. He was going to help me out of this situation. I refused to let anything convince me otherwise. No matter what, I was going to see my daughter again and I was not going to allow Mark Shepard to force me into having his child. Tears streamed down my face in torrents.

I knew God was with me, but what would I have to go through before he came to my rescue.

"I just need you to love me," he pleaded desperately. "I need you to be my friend and my wife," he went on, as he drove deep into the woods, checking the rearview window every so often. He was now under the impression that this musty old abandoned house that he'd dragged me into, bumping my head on the low ceiling as he forced me down the old raggedy staircase, would be the backdrop for his sordid fairytale to unfold. He'd sworn, as we drove along in the darkness to the abandoned hideout. We traveled through the house until we ended up in what seemed like a hidden room sheltered from light by boarded up windows. I was doomed as he confessed that he was going to prove his love and trust in me by telling me things he'd never told anyone and true to his word, he'd polluted my soul with sordid stories that made my stomach turn.

I was shocked to discover that he'd stolen my spare key, let himself into my home as if it were his castle, and put together the puzzle pieces that enlightened him about my meeting with Monica and how he'd driven all night to beat me to her house, to torture her with his confession of Nicole's murder and then deal her the same fate.

He laughed as he recounted the details, "It was so satisfying, Kayla, strangling her and watching her body twitch and jerk. I thought her purse straps would break from me pulling them so hard, but they were sturdy," he laughed. "So I kept pulling 'til she finally shut up." He said through gritted teeth. "You should have seen how she was throwing her arms everywhere," he demonstrated, "and then in that one instant "they just fell to the side," he said. He recalled how her neighbor must've heard her screams from her backyard because she ran into her own house, probably to call the police, but he'd held on to the straps until he heard the sirens. I listened in fear at his chillingly detailed description of how he'd watched from his car as the police arrived on the scene and kicked the door in only to find that they could save Monica no more than they were able to save her sister.

"I mean, Kayla, you should've seen those stupid cops." He laughed, getting a kick out of recounting the details of the events to me. "Every time, baby," he used his hands to describe their stupidity. "They were right here…I was right there…and I never got caught." He laughed as if this whole thing was hilarious to him. "I left them cops flabbergasted at every scene," he bragged.

He'd outsmarted the police alright.

"And, awww man, you should've seen how scared you looked," he laughed. "I mean, you actually had this look of horror pasted on your face when you came rolling down the street." He was holding his stomach to control his laughter.

I felt stupid, knowing that he got off on the fact that he'd beat me to Monica.

"Why would you want to meet her?" He questioned me. "That broad was deranged, runnin' around blamin' everybody that knew Nicky for her murder," he nodded. "She was always trying to run her sister's life and she would've tried to come between us too if I wouldn't have stopped her." He went on and on without pausing. "Kayla, you should've seen her, I'm tellin' you…" He was laughing hysterically about how she'd tried to play the hero, thinking she was going to stop him from being with me.

"You shouldn't have done that, Kayla," he said, scratching at his head, all of a sudden serious, reminding me of one of those mad men that up until now, I'd only seen in the movies. "What am I supposed to think when you go around looking for trouble?"

"I wasn't, I didn't even believe all the lies she was telling me about you." I lied. "I just wanted to tell her that she was wrong about you."

"What do you mean she was wrong about me, about what?"

"She wanted me to believe that you didn't really love me and that you were going from woman to woman and it didn't matter if it was me, her sister, or whoever. You just wanted any woman who could sing so that you could get rich quick."

"Get rich quick?" he shouted. "Do you think this is about getting rich quick?" He yelled furiously, his voice carrying through the house.

"No, that's why I was going to see her," I had to think fast in order to convince him that I was on his side. "She mailed me a letter the other day and she wanted me to believe all these lies about you, but I knew that you couldn't be the person she was describing."

"Tell me everything she told you." He demanded.

"She told me about seeing our pictures in Urban Elite," I started. "She was trying to convince me that you were weren't who you said you were and she wanted me to come there so she could prove it to me but I was going to talk to her and show her the music we made together to prove her wrong." I cried. "I was only trying to protect you. I was going to call you when I got back."

"Yeah, but all this time, you been saying you don't love me and you never could because of Dre'. So what happened? Why would you try to protect me from her?" he wanted to know.

It took all my might to lie about my feelings for Dre'. I wanted to take his hands in mine to maximize the effect of my coming admission.

"Dre' is gone now and you're here." I answered. "At first, I was mad because you said we made love and I couldn't remember, but then I realized that you were right. If we made love, then it had to be because I do love you." I began, willing myself to cry, but he had a confession of his own.

"Kayla, Kayla, Kayla," he shook his head slowly, "we didn't really make love that night," he admitted. "Not the way you think."

"What do you mean, not the way I think? I don't understand."

"Do you really think I wanted you like that?" he asked. "You kept callin' me Dre'." He started. "Our first time, I want you to call my name. I wanted you to know it was me, not that weak nigga," he continued. "I had to tell you we did so you'd believe that we'd been together so you would forget about Dre'."

"But we can be together," I cried. "You didn't have to trick me."

"Oh, *now* we can be together, since when?" he demanded. "You expect me to believe that after the way you been treatin' me?"

I nodded innocently. I know he wanted to believe me. I just had to be convincing enough to give him a reason. I was scared for my life and I realized that every word I said had an impact on whether or not I would make it out of here alive.

"I never said I was perfect." I answered. "I realize now that no matter what I do, Dre' isn't coming' back and I have to move on. Besides, no other man has ever loved me enough to go through this much trouble for me... to risk going to jail, that says alot."

"Jail?" he laughed. "You think I'm going to jail?" He found it so hilarious. "I'm too smart. They don't even know where we are and they're never going to find us," he promised.

"I don't want them to," I lied. He stepped close to me and hugged me.

"I was hoping you'd say that. Now, I have a surprise," he smiled wickedly. "Put this on," he said, throwing a yellow dress at me. "You're going to entertain me. This is your first lesson on how to treat your king. And I hope you do good, Kayla, 'cause if you don't," he paused. "I'm going to have to punish you."

*　　*　　*　　*　　*

He sat there becoming aroused at the sight of her. She was a portrait of beauty, standing there nervously, preparing to

155

perform. Her tight silk dress clung to her perfect hourglass shaped figure like a second skin. Her shoulders, dusted lightly with glitter, sparkled against the bright lights. Her lip gloss made her lips look as if she'd just run her wet tongue over them, letting him know that she'd anticipated this moment just as much as, if not more than, he had. He rejoiced silently at the miracle that was all for him. He knew she would give him everything she had because she was all his tonight.

He blew out a few candles, as if he was dimming the lights, and all that existed was her. She owned the stage. She was a single star radiating throughout the whole galaxy. He couldn't help but smile wickedly. It began down in the innermost parts of his stomach and traveled through his entire body until he could no longer contain the joy that radiated from within him. He bit his lip hard in his struggle to control his excitement. The anticipation of her performance was overwhelming.

As the music began to drift softly from the portable karaoke system, his palms began to sweat. She slowly slid her delicate fingers around the large microphone, silently praying for the strength to perform perfectly. Her life depended on this. She had to make a perfect impression. He had to feel that she really loved him or it was over.

*   *   *   *   *

I sang with all of my heart. Not for myself and certainly not for Mark Shepard but because I wanted to see my daughter again. She'd already been left fatherless. I refused to allow him to make my daughter an orphan. He was so twisted; I wouldn't put it past him to try and kidnap Destiny from Mama and raise her as his own. He'd already said over and over that we were going to be this perfect family. God only knows what else was on his twisted agenda.

CHAPTER TWENTY-SIX

"You really are special, that's why I love you so much," he said after I'd given a heart wrenching performance. "I'm about to show you just how much I love you."

"Oh, my God!" My mind screamed. What had I gotten myself into, admitting that I wanted to be with him was supposed to gain me some leverage so I could get away. Not so he could humiliate me more and suck me further into this nightmare.

"What do you mean?" I asked, unable to keep my voice from quivering.

"We're going to get married and then we're really going to consummate our marriage so we can have that son we want so much and make our family complete." He ran his fingers through my hair and leaned down to kiss me. I wanted to vomit but I couldn't show how repulsed I was by his touch. I had to gain his trust so that I could somehow get away.

"Baby, how are we supposed to be this perfect family when you don't even trust me?" I asked.

"I do trust you," he said defensively. "Do you honestly think I would have told you all those things if I didn't?"

"I don't know but if you really did, I wouldn't be locked up in here like a caged animal. I mean, can't you at least take these handcuffs off." I whined, miserably. *They hurt.*"

"I can't do that, Kayla," he scowled, as if it was hurting him that he wouldn't do it.

"I knew I was right." I said, giving my disgust a voice. I slumped sideways, letting the sadness I felt take over my body. I was going to use whatever ploy I could to get him to feel like I really loved him and he was lying about his love for me.

"That's not fair," he said tenderly. "You *know* I love you and I do trust you, but I just don't want anyone else to come between us."

"There's no one else here, just us," I pleaded tenderly. "We've been through so much. I didn't know all this stuff you had been holding inside. Everyone needs someone to care about them and you haven't had that. Just let me hold you," I offered, holding my handcuffed arms out to him. He moved close, resting his head on my shoulder but made no efforts to uncuff me.

"You break into my house and you take me God knows where..." I cried. "How am I supposed to know you're not going to kill me or something?" I pled my case before him, not knowing if he would have some semblance of compassion in his cruel heart. It was part acting, but mostly for real. He'd killed people. He was telling me that he wasn't going to hurt me but how was I to know that whatever sanity remained wouldn't snap at any moment. I had to get through to him. The tears welled up in my eyes, threatening to spill over at any second.

"Kayla, I'm not going to kill you," he promised. "You're not like the others, we're really meant to be. We're soul mates and God has a special plan for us. Just trust me." He begged.

"I want to but how can I? Trust works both ways but I guess in our relationship it doesn't." I said, dropping my head in resignation.

He studied me carefully, sighing heavily, as he pondered the possibilities of what I would do if he took the cuffs off. He leaned forward to kiss my cheek, breathing heavily and to my surprise, he produced a key.

"Kayla, I'm telling you now so you won't be surprised at my reaction. Don't cross me," he stated very solemnly, his face so close to mine as he breathed the threat into my ear, "because if you do, I'll be forced to do you like I did the others."

"I promise I won't." I whispered, jumping for joy on the inside. I leaned forward to kiss him, solidifying my promise, all the time wanting to vomit. He slid the key into the tiny lock and loosened the first cuff. Freedom felt wonderful as I shook my fingers to circulate the blood through my limbs. Exhilaration passed through me as he removed the second cuff. "Thank you, Mark! Thank you!" I cried.

"Don't call me that. Call me K.D.!" he demanded.

"I'm sorry, K.D." I hurriedly apologized. "Thank you." I added gratefully. My mind was spinning trying to formulate a plan now that I had gotten him to trust me a little. I had to take it a step further. He wasn't going to let me just walk out of here. I had to get him in a vulnerable position and fast. The idea came to me like a light bulb had flashed on.

"I'm beginning to see you in a new way. After we're married, there's all sorts of things that I want to do with you," I said. I knew he was full of lust and I had to use that against him.

"Like what?" he asked, closing his eyes a little, taking the bait.

"Like using these sexy handcuffs that tried to break the trust between us to establish the trust between us." I breathed, trying to sound sexy in spite of the fear coursing through my body. "Let me see them."

"Uh, uhhh," he breathed. "What are you up to?"

"Nothing', I'm just exploring this trust thing. I want to believe you won't hurt me but we've got to trust each other, especially if we're going to be together."

"So, what's that got to do with you wanting to cuff me?" he asked, baited by the idea. I could see his curiosity clouding his judgment.

"The only other man I've ever had a real relationship with was Dre'." I explained. His face twisted in anger over the name but in a bold move, I put my fingers to his lips to shush him. "Just hear me out." I added. "You say you want to be my man but I haven't been with anyone in so long, I don't want you to hurt me. I just asked if I could put one on to establish the trust, if you really meant that." I questioned his sincerity in trusting me. "Just let me put one on," I pleaded. "I always wanted to cuff my man, but I never had that kind of trust with anyone."

"Not even Dre'?" He asked with a raised brow.

"Not even Dre'," I smiled bashfully. He smiled at the idea.

"Yeah, I'll let you do it but we're going to have our ceremony first.

"What ceremony?" I asked, drawing back from him.

"If we're going to do this, we're going to do it right. We're going to get married first."

Thoughts fear and desperation bombarded my mind. Should I make my get a way now or wait for a more opportune time? Was he going to take me somewhere else to have this so-called wedding? I surveyed the room. There was the stage and a small door that led out to a crawl space under the house. I would have to crawl through there to get out of here because that's the only exit I could locate in this room. I had no idea where we were because he'd blindfolded me most of the ride here and then again as he'd brought into this strange room. He'd had to have been here recently because there was food here even though he hadn't left me alone for more than a few minutes since we'd arrived. He pressed a button on a small remote control and the Wedding March began to play.

"Come on," he said. "I'll be down there waiting on you."

I looked down at the dress I was wearing. Not only had he wanted me to wear the dress for his private performance, he expected to marry me. He had lost his marbles. Waiting at the other end of the room with a smile plastered on his face, he beckoned for me to come to him.

"Come on," he motioned for me to walk down the pretend isle. I started walking towards him, surveying these cramped quarters every step of the way. It was dark, except for the candles he kept burning to illuminate the otherwise dark space. There was a pole on the far side of the room. If I could get him over there, then maybe I could distract him and get away. I began to let my plan formulate in my mind as I met him at the "altar".

"Dearly beloved, we are gathered here today to witness the marriage of Kayla Marie and Karlos Day," he began, smiling. "Kayla, do you take me to be your lawful wedded husband, to have and to hold, for better or for worse, for richer or for poorer, in sickness and in health and forsaking all others until death do us part."

I nodded in agreement.

"Good enough!" he said. "And K.D., do you take Kayla to be your lawful wedded wife, to have and to hold for better or for worse, for richer or for poorer, in sickness and in health and forsaking all others until death do us part?"

"I do!" he yelped, answering himself.

"The rings please!" he said, as if continuing in the part of the minister. He produced two boxes from his pocket. "Kayla, I know you didn't have time to shop for me a ring, so I took the liberty of picking one out for you," he said, putting the box in my hand. "Say these words," he commanded me, handing me a piece of paper.

I read the note. "I, Kayla, give you, Karlos, this ring as a symbol of my love and all that I am and all that I have." The paper then stated that I was to slide the ring on his finger, which I did. Mark took the ring he'd gotten for me and placed it on my finger, saying the same words to me.

"With the exchanging of vows and the giving and receiving of rings, I now pronounce you man and wife," he announced. "You may kiss the bride!"

He leaned over to kiss me but I turned my head slightly so he missed my lips. He grabbed my hands and began to spin me around the room. "We're married, we're married!" he sang happily. He led me over to a table where a candle had been burning and a small cake sat with a miniature bride and groom figurine adorning the top. He sliced the cake and sat a piece in front of me. "This is the best day of my life!" he shouted out happily.

I can't believe he did all of this: the cake, the dress, the wedding. He'd told me the whole story about his mother and father and how he was going to have everything his father had denied his mother and he was going to make things right. But his sickness had caused him to go about it in the wrong way. How could he expect someone to make a life with him built on lies, deceit, kidnappings, and murders?

"Come on, Kayla," he said, taking my hand and leading me onto the stage. He pushed a button on the remote control again, and wanted me to dance with him. When the song finished, he whispered. "Are you ready to make our baby?" I nodded. Now was my chance. If I didn't make my getaway, there was no telling what he would do to me.

"Let's go over there." I suggested, guiding him to the farthest corner of the room, near the pole. He followed willingly, a smile fixed on his face, thinking he was about to have me, but I would never let that happen.

"Lay down," I demanded, my voice filled with passion, as I poked his chest with my finger, commanding him to follow my instructions.

"Calm down, baby," he smiled. "Let's enjoy each other."

"I'm sorry,' I knelt down in front of him. I had to make sure he was relaxed. I kissed his neck and allowed him to nuzzle mine. Each time his lips touched me, I had to force myself not to show my repulsion. I ran my hands up and down his arms, trying to get him in a position where I could carry out my plan.

I tested the waters by seeing if he'd protest to me slipping a handcuff around his wrist. He didn't. I continued to plant light kisses on him. Seeing that he was caught up in the kisses and professions of my love, I took my chance, snapping the cuffs around the pole with a quick click as I hopped up and turned to flee.

"What the..." He stopped mid-sentence, realizing I'd secured him to the pole. He kicked at me in anger, tripping me as I turned to run. "Get back over here!" he demanded, as I lost my balance and he wrapped his legs around me and held me down. I started kicking wildly.

"Let me go!" I screamed, but I could barely move; only one arm was free because of the way he had me bound with his legs. This cat had supernatural strength! I hurriedly snatched off one of my high heeled shoes and slammed it into his face as hard as I could, creating a gash beneath his eye, which caused him to scream out in pain as blood gushed from it. I struggled to get from beneath his muscular legs as I kicked violently. He kicked me back and connected with my face. I swung the shoe again with all of my might, aiming for his eyes. I got my leg free and kicked him in the jewels, causing him to draw up in pain and whimper like a puppy.

This was my opportunity. I slid from beneath him as quickly as I could and ran over to the exit. It was rigged like a trap door, but I pushed with all my might until it gave way allowing me to push through it. I looked back to make sure he was still cuffed as I made my exit. He was, though he was reaching desperately for the key. Fear prevented me from going back over there and kicking it out of his reach. Later for that, I had to get away from that sick freak.

The crawlspace was dark. I hated dark, cramped spaces where creepy crawlers camped out. I could imagine thousands of them running around me, searching for the smallest hint of food, but I crawled through anyway, feeling for my way out. There was a staircase at the end that led to the rest of the house. The obvious exits, the front and back doors, were both locked in a way that prevented me from making my escape easily. Every window had bars on them.

I ran up the stairs to the second story, taking two steps at a time, checking the windows in each room but they had bars too. If there was an attic, I had to find it; maybe that was the only escape.

Wandering from room to room, I checked the closets and ceilings for an escape, unable to find one. Frustration caused my hope of getting away to diminish as I realized that each room was a dead end with the windows barred. Discovering that there was no attic solidified the realization that even though I'd escaped Mark's clutches, I was still trapped inside this house.

The last undiscovered room was a bathroom located at the end of the hall and I secretly hoped that it would be the one or else I might curl up and die. There, but for the grace of God, was a tiny window that had no bars on it. I ran to it, grabbing the handles to open it, but it apparently had been nailed shut. Hot tears descended down my cheeks. The frustration caused by these dire circumstances chased away almost all hope I had of escaping.

"God, help me." I prayed. "I know you didn't bring me this far to let me be recaptured. You said you'd *never* leave or forsake me." I cried, sinking down to the floor in despair.

My head throbbed as I tried to think. With no escape, I had to find some kind of weapon to defend myself against the monster. I recalled seeing some fireplace utensils on my way up the stairs, but they were on the first floor and that could mean a confrontation if Mark had freed himself. If he captured me, he'd kill me. Going back downstairs posed too much of a risk, not knowing if he had freed himself or where he might be. I searched the room for something, anything, that could be used against him as my eyes came to rest on the toilet.

"Thank you, God," I whispered as I grabbed the top from the toilet and hurled it at the window with as much force as I could muster. Shards of glass flew as the top crashed into it.

I looked out of the window but all I could see was trees; there wasn't a light in sight. I couldn't even tell how far down the drop would be, but I would rather risk breaking some bones than allowing myself to be recaptured.

I tried to clear away as much of the glass as I could. I ripped a piece of my dress off to protect my hands from the glass. I was able to squeeze my legs through the window and I began to pray desperately for the Lord to soften my fall. I wished a mattress could magically appear for me to land on, but being able to get out of this window alive was enough of a miracle for me.

As the thought of being recaptured flashed through my mind, I loosened my grip, closed my eyes and prepared to take the fall. God had been with me so far. I just had to continue to trust him to get me out of here. There was no mattress waiting for me beneath the window, but just as good, was a pile of leaves awaiting as I plunged into them with a loud "swish".

I crawled out of the leaves slowly and surveyed my body for injuries. Although my hand throbbed from scraping jagged pieces of glass as I held onto the ledge. I was okay! No one could tell me after this that God wasn't with me. Now if I could just find my way out of here. I had no clue as to my whereabouts. All I could see were trees surrounding this secluded old house out here in the middle of no where. Mark Shepard's car was parked not far from the house, but after a desperate attempt to find the keys turned up nothing, I flattened the tires with a shard of glass, smiling to myself with the satisfaction that at least he wouldn't catch up with me in this car.

I began the walk away from the prison, not even turning back. I *never* wanted to see it again. After walking for what seemed like several miles, I tried to gain some sense of direction.

The trees weren't as dense as they had been closer to the old rickety house, so I kept on moving. There was no telling where Mark Shepard might be. For all I knew he could be close behind. The very thought caused me to pick up my pace.

I heard a noise from the distance. I stopped for a minute to focus on exactly what it was. Relief passed through my body as I realized that the engine belonged to a plane flying above and not Mark Shepard's disabled vehicle. How I wished I was on that plane as I trudged through the dark woods. I heard all kinds of hissing and flapping and howling, but none of it was as scary as what I'd just left. I heard another plane above and this one seemed to be dropping in altitude as the red light flashed from it.

I began to follow the path the last two planes had taken. The last one dropped out of sight, but another one came and it, too, seemed to be dropping lower and lower, the engines becoming louder and the planes more visible as I continued my ascent through the dark forest. My instincts were telling me an airport was nearby and if that was true, I knew God had my back.

I ran in the direction the plane had flown, not able to move my legs fast enough, especially having used my shoe as a weapon against Mark Shepard. I guess high heels wouldn't have aided me in sprinting any faster, but at least my feet would've been protected. Right now, that was the least of my worries. I had to find some help, and fast. I had no idea if Mark was still handcuffed to that pole. He had ways of getting out of difficult situations that would seem impossible to a regular person, like when he'd escaped from the police after he'd murdered Monica and then watched as they arrived at the scene.

I couldn't stop running. It seemed like I'd been going for miles and I knew that God had supplied me a supernatural dose of adrenaline to keep going. Cold drops of rain dropped from the sky and it was becoming increasingly foggy, a mixture that hampered my get away efforts by limiting my visibility.

Another plane flew overhead and I followed the sound of its engine and the red and white lights as far as I could. There was a slope up ahead, but I couldn't tell where it lead. Hopefully, there wasn't a river at the bottom. As I neared the embankment, I saw a road and ran towards it with everything I had. The airport, if there was one, couldn't be too much further. As far as I'd come, I was exhausted. I felt like curling up on the side of the road to take a couple of breaths, but resisted, knowing that would be unwise considering there was a mad man on the loose.

The miracle I needed became apparent to me as dimly lit headlights approached through the fog. My heart skipped a beat at what could be my only chance to get help. Running into the road, the thought crossed my mind that it could be Mark. I froze. The car skidded across the road to avoid me as I attempted to protect myself from the impact with my arms shielding my face.

"Thank you, Lord!" I shouted, realizing that it wasn't Mark behind the wheel of the automobile. The man behind the wheel of the Benz stared at me in disbelief, as the tinted window slid down. He backed up slowly from the muddy patch he'd slid into. I was in awe that he just happened to be driving out here in the middle of nowhere at the exact time that I needed a miracle. "God, thank you for sending him," I cried. My breathing was still labored as the stranger stared at me with confusion in his eyes. I'd almost caused him to run me down, running out in front of him like that. Instinctively, I knew God had divinely arranged for this man to rescue me.

My eyes followed another plane as it began its descent. I was thankful for my ears, my eyes, the planes, the airport, and the stranger. He continued straightening his car, still unaware of what he'd intruded on. As I tried to regain my composure so that I could alert him to the danger I faced, I stared behind him as a figure appeared from out of the foggy darkness, running down the road towards me. My fight or flight response kicked in, screaming at me to run for my life. It was Mark Shepard and this time he had a gun!

CHAPTER TWENTY-SEVEN

Kevin Swift was a go-getter! He set goals and once his eyes were on the prize, there was no stopping him. He'd been that way ever since he was a kid. Whatever he wanted, he got. This applied to the latest video games, good grades, and money. He wanted the prettiest girls in school and he got them, too. Back then, he was the boy that every girl wanted to be *her* boyfriend. He always had the prettiest girls chasing after him. They thought he was so cute with his curly hair, dimples and smooth golden brown skin. He was fly!

From elementary through high school, Kevin enjoyed the benefits of the opposite sex drooling over him. Girls just couldn't get enough of him. He had a gift with the ladies and he capitalized on it. They did whatever he wanted and he liked it.

Some people called him K-Swift, but most people called him Swift. It was fitting, too. He'd always been athletically inclined, signing up for the basketball team in the third grade and being the star player that attracted more family members than any of the other players. In the fourth grade, he'd joined the track team, solidifying his position as a multi-talented sportsman. Every sport he played, whether it was football, basketball, baseball, or track, he was always swift, his movements as smooth, precise and slick as a panther. His last name truly fit him. He couldn't have picked a better name for himself.

Besides his athletic prowess, he dressed, walked and talked jazzy. It drove the ladies crazy. He was so sexy and so fly. He was the type of guy who could talk people into doing whatever he wanted, especially girls. He had game. Swift made things happen and people were drawn to that. He was a winner. His muscular build, good looks and confident swagger had attracted many admirers over the years, but none had managed to settle him down, though many had tried, unsuccessfully. He had to laugh at the fact.

It wasn't that he was totally against being with one girl, actually, *quiet as it was kept, he would like to settle down one day, but only with the right woman.*

When he decided to settle down, he wanted it to last. Most people got married for all the wrong reasons, which is one reason why he hadn't gotten married yet. Pretty, smart women were a dime a dozen, but he wanted someone special, he needed a challenge. Actually, he craved it and although some females were challenging in the beginning, he became bored easily. This was especially true when they started trying to trap him and once he became bored, he was in pursuit of the next challenge and he would leave them frustrated, wondering what they'd done wrong. It was all a game and he always made sure he positioned himself to win.

There was no doubt that Swift had sex appeal and talent, but he was also intelligent. For the past four years, he'd been making his mark in the music industry. He'd started dabbling in it at first when his homeboy wanted to partner with him to open a recording studio. Swift loved music and had since he was a young cat. He listened to all kinds of music but he'd grown up in the era when hip-hop began as an escape for young black men who wanted to do something productive and who found rap music as an outlet to be creative, to change their lives and to touch and influence the world around them.

Swift was no singer or rapper but he had an ear for music and he could spot talent. He knew that one day he would be big in the music industry so he started dabbling in music and producing hot tracks as his partner taught him the art of musical engineering. He fell in love with music, sometimes staying in the studio for days, foregoing sleep, just to make sure his tracks were on point. He not only demanded perfection from himself but from every artist he worked with. If his name was going to be on the credits, then it was going to be done right. No exceptions!

Swift eventually stepped into the role of executive producer and artist manager and from there he began to build his own label. It was his baby and like a caring mother, he worked hard to make sure his label was successful. After all, he'd been there from its conception, laboring to educate himself on the music business, all the while dealing with the drama that being in the entertainment business brought; and now *finally*, he'd birthed success.

Tonight was the culmination of all his hard work. His talent, intelligence and business savvy had earned him a nomination for producer of the year at the annual Industry Awards, the most respected Awards show honoring hip-hop creators. Swift had turned out three of the hottest acts to hit the R&B, rap and pop charts. All three artists had been nominated best artist in their respective categories with hits that he'd produced. He was definitely the man behind the magic. Even though he didn't cameo in all of his artists' videos trying to steal their shine or making sure the general public knew his face, he was definitely well-known in the industry.

He loved mingling with people. He was respected and loved and had friends from coast to coast, from up north to down south, and it didn't stop there. He was internationally known.

Aside from all that industry hype, he was a private cat which was one of the main reasons he avoided being in the limelight. Even so, privacy was something he hadn't enjoyed a lot of, especially as his label enjoyed more and more success. He was beginning to think privacy was a thing of the past. The cost of success was high and his right to privacy was just part of the expense.

Tonight was one of the first times in ages he was driving himself to the airport. Most of the time, one of his chicks would see him off but this time, he'd rented a car just to have some time to himself instead of partying and celebrating all night long.

171

Although he knew he was getting older and his desires were changing, it shocked even him that tonight he was actually thinking about it seriously and exploring in his mind what he really wanted. This was one of the best nights of his life and he wanted someone to celebrate with. It wasn't that he didn't have plenty of friends but he was thinking about sharing it with someone special, someone he loved. That seemed strange even thinking that because he had plenty of girls but that's all they were to him, just girls. They did this and that for him, trying to win his affection but they all had crooked motives as far as he was concerned. Most of them wanted money, and he didn't mind spending, but when they expected it, they got played, or rather, they played themselves. Some of them were so beautiful, dime pieces, but it seemed the more beautiful they were, the more problems there were and the majority of *them* were insecure. Then there were those who were beautiful and successful and yet, with them, they were so focused on their careers or on themselves and they didn't know the first thing about making a man like him happy. What he wanted was a woman that loved him, not for money, not for his success, but for *him* and that was hard to find. Most of these chicks didn't even know how to love themselves but expected him to love them. The majority of them didn't know what real love was, they thought it was some kind of fairytale. It was just depressing sometimes. So he went from one to another, never getting too involved. But he was getting older now and he didn't even find the thrill of kickin' it with chick after chick as appealing as he had in his not so distant past. It was an empty existence and he wanted more.

Cartier, the female artist he'd discovered and recently released, was betting on the fact that she would win his love and become his Mrs. She'd put it out in the industry that they were dating but Swift had already peeped her. She thought he was diggin' her because her beauty and talent and marketability had gained her a spot in his stable. The fact that he'd worked overtime

172

insuring that her album release was a success had further convinced her that she was "the one" but he didn't even really like her. He'd let her join him on a couple of trips to industry events, but she didn't have what it took to win his affection so, of course, she couldn't be his Mrs. She talked too much, for one, and she was one of those bossy chicks. He'd never had to hit a woman, but she was the type who might press her luck. So he played with her mind and had fun with her body when he felt like it but she wasn't going to get a ring, no matter how slick she talked. He knew she didn't love him, she just wanted a life on Easy Street but he wasn't offering her that kind of ride.

He drove towards the airport, clasping his award in one hand and gripping the steering wheel of the Benz with the other, barely able to see as the rain thudded against the car's windshield. The lightning lit up the sky and the thunder crashed angrily. He followed the directives of the navigation system, wondering at its accuracy as he turned onto a side street that was supposed to guide him towards the airport entrance.

Out of nowhere, Swift saw a woman dart out into the road. She wore a muddy yellow dress, her long hair hung limply around her face and her face was stained with tears. She stopped momentarily, like a deer caught in blaring headlights. The stretch of road was dark and visibility was low. She froze, staring into the headlights, her eyes big with fear and her chest heaving up and down like she'd been running for miles. Her dress was torn and there was blood streaming from a gash in her face. Swift slammed the brakes and the car skidded, the smell of burning rubber filling the automobile as it slid sideways off the road into a grassy patch, barely missing the woman.

Where had she come from? There were woods on either side of the road. Swift looked around but there was no other car visible. He began to back the car up back onto the road. The woman was still standing there, gulping for air, frozen to that same spot where Swift had first spotted her in the road. She began to walk backwards, the fright in her eyes becoming more pronounced with each step. She looked past Swift's car into the eyes of the Grim Reaper. Swift turned around to see a tall figure running up the road towards the woman. Although it was still raining slightly and the figure was now about 3oo yards away, Swift could see that he had reached into his jacket as he sprinted up the road and was pointing a gun towards them. The woman screamed as she turned to run. Swift's mind was racing. He put the car into drive and raced the short distance towards the running woman. Stopping abruptly, he fidgeted with the automatic control to get the window down, "Get in!" he yelled. But she was running for her life. "Get in!" he yelled again, cutting her off with the front end of the car and throwing the passenger door open. Just then he heard a shot and the glass casing of one of the back lights on the car burst into a million pieces. The woman dived into the car and Swift slammed his foot to the pedal, speeding off into the night. The dark scary figure ran behind them as if with supernatural speed. He let off another shot! Swift drove the Benz like he was on the NASCAR speedway manipulating the car along the winding, dark stretch of road until they were far away from the gun wielding freak.

The rain began to subside as they drove along. The woman was sobbing frantically, gasping for air. They were well out of range of the shooter as Swift glided the car to a halt in the parking lot of a mall complex.

"Are you okay?" he asked, turning for the first time to face the woman he'd just rescued. It was plain to see that she was anything but okay. He flipped open his cell phone to dial 911. "Are you hit?"

She wrapped her arms around herself, fanning her hands up and down her sides as she surveyed her body for wounds. "I'm...I'm alive!" she stammered. "I'm not hit." She sobbed even more violently.

"It's okay, you're safe now." He consoled her. "You're safe."

She looked up at him, the fear diminishing from her eyes and being replaced by a look of gratitude. She was still in shock, unable to believe that she'd really escaped and that she was free! "Thank you, thank you so much," she cried. "You saved my life!" She broke down, crying, her whole body shaking violently. Swift flipped his phone closed, unable to resist the urge to comfort this woman. She'd obviously just escaped some sort of horrendous nightmare.

"What's your name?" he asked, gently.

"Kayla," she barely managed to say in a small childlike voice.

"It's okay, Kayla," he soothed her, wrapping his strong muscular arms around the stranger. He didn't even care that her blood was staining his $3000 suit. "It's going to be okay, you're safe now." She let him console her, crying into his chest.

Kayla actually believed the words. She was so thankful to be alive. God had to be on her side to send someone down that dark deserted road where she thought the only thing she'd meet was the end of her life. She sobbed harder, thinking about escaping Mark Shepard's deranged idea of blissful romance. It seemed like they sat there in the mall parking lot for hours, Kayla crying, thankful to be alive and Swift holding and comforting her.

Kevin finally pulled away from Kayla just enough to flip his phone open and called 911, reporting what had just happened. Kayla kept looking back, so afraid that Mark would catch up with them and carry her back off into his warped world of darkness, pain, and torture. The mall parking lot was deserted.

"Please, can we wait for the police somewhere else," Kayla pleaded with the stranger. She looked so scared and helpless; her voice was shaking as she pleaded with him. He took her hand.

"Kayla, I promise you, you're safe." He reassured her. Just then two police cruisers raced towards them, their red and blue lights blaring. Kayla's whole body was flooded with relief at the sight of the two uniformed police officers approaching the car and the other two surveying the scene for signs of the psychotic kidnapper. The nightmare was finally over.

CHAPTER TWENTY-EIGHT

The phone rang incessantly as I grabbed my towel, hopped out of the shower and raced to my room to see who could be ringing the phone off the cradle. I checked the caller I.D. before pushing the talk button. The area code was 310. Who could be calling me from California?

"Hello," I answered, breathlessly.

"Hey, what's crackin'," the voice on the other end asked.

I hadn't heard the voice many times but I would recognize his voice anywhere. It was Kevin Swift.

"Not much, I was just getting out of the shower," I replied.

"Hmmm," he paused as if to let that sink in. "So how have you been?"

"I've been good. I'm just happy to be back home and tryin' to get my life back to normal."

"Yeah, baby, you *have* been through a lot, huh? Talk about made for TV."

"Well I guess that's one way to look at it," I agreed. "I'm still trippin' tryin' to comprehend the fact that the last few months actually happened. I mean, you hear about stuff like that on talk shows or see it on some movie and it's like…not really real, you know? But then it happens and you realize that bad things really do happen," I sighed, shaking my head.

A chill came over me just thinking about it. As I talked to Kevin about it, it dawned on me that I hadn't been able to open up about this to anyone. I mean, everyone had heard what happened but it was hard to explain to someone who hadn't been there. Maybe that was why it was so easy to talk to Kevin. He'd witnessed some of the terror that Mark Shepard inflicted on people's lives. He'd been there that night of my escape as Mark

Shepard tried to hunt me down like a mad dog and kill me. Kevin had rescued me and I would forever be indebted to him.

When I'd seen those lights on that dark road, I knew that whoever was in that car held the key to my survival. I'd just prayed that it wasn't Mark Shepard. And somehow, God had heard me. Those woods had been so dark and scary. It was still hard to believe that I'd gotten away. Mark Shepard had plotted every detail of his twisted plan, from the wedding dress, to the rings, to that hidden cellar in that old, musty house.

It was scary to think that someone with such a sick mind was out there watching and waiting, calculating his next move. A chill ran down my spine as I tried to block the memories.

"Kayla, are you there?" Kevin asked, jarring me back to reality from that far off place where my mind had traveled.

"Kevin, I'm so sorry." I apologized. "I'm here."

"Are you sure you're doing alright?" Concern filled his voice, warming my heart.

"To be honest, I'm just taking it one day at a time." I searched for the words to explain. "I mean, everything is just so…different now."

"Kayla, that's understandable. You've been through hell," he started, sincerity in his voice, "You're a strong woman. I think the average person would've broken down but look at you. You're getting your life back together and moving forward."

"Yeah, Kevin but I don't feel strong." I sighed. "I mean, I have to be for my daughter. Otherwise I might lose my sanity—" I inhaled deeply. "I may seem strong to you, but I'm always afraid," I admitted. "My sense of security has basically been stolen."

He was the only person I'd told that. Of course, I tried to put up a front for everybody else. I didn't want to go through life looking like some wounded animal, but on the inside I was hurting so bad that it took every ounce of strength I could muster to keep from screaming, pulling out my hair, or just balling up in a corner

178

and letting myself slip away from reality. The worse part was...*no one* understood. And even though my physical body had been freed from the prison that Mark Shepard had thrust me into, the memories continued to haunt me and there was nothing I could do about it, especially when the nightmares began.

The only thing that had kept me from completely losing it was my faith in God. It had kept me when I lost Dre' and I'd held tight as I'd prayed to God the night I'd escaped. He came through then, sending Kevin Swift down that lonely deserted road in the nick of time. The mere fact that I'd escaped was a miracle; and for God to do that, to deliver me from the hands of death, made me believe that He had a purpose for me. Mark Shepard had killed so many people on his sick mission to become his father and re-create his mother; it was only by God's grace that I'd survived.

What really terrified me, though, was that he was still out there somewhere and the thought frightened me to the point that I couldn't be alone. I'd given up my apartment and moved back in with my Mama; but sometimes, I didn't even feel safe here. It was crazy. Mark Shepard didn't have me physically captive but now he had me mentally captive and at times, that was worse.

Kevin interrupted my thoughts once again. "Kayla, I really hate that you're going through this alone."

"I'm not alone, my mom, her husband, and my family are here for me."

"Well, obviously, that's not enough if you still don't feel safe." He stated. "You know what you need?"

"No, but I wish I did," I attempted to laugh.

"You need to get away from there." He said. "I'd love to see you and make sure you're okay. Why don't you come out here for a few days?" he asked. "It'll be a change of scenery and you can relax and try to get your mind off things.

"Kevin, I can't."

"Why not?" he asked.

"For one, I have a daughter." I started. "For two, we barely know each other."

"That's true, but this would be the perfect time for us to get to know each other."

"Kevin, I really appreciate everything you did for me. I owe you my life, but—"

He interrupted my refusal. "Bring your daughter with you, bring your mom, bring whoever you need to bring but at least think about it before you reject the idea," he pleaded. "You even said you don't feel safe there, but if you come here, I promise, I'll protect you with my own life!" he stated, adamantly.

For some reason, I believed him. He'd certainly put his life on the line for me before, even as a complete stranger. When Mark Shepard had taken those shots at me, he hadn't abandoned me out there; he'd put his own life on the line to get me away from there and to safety.

"Okay, I'll think about it," I conceded.

"Good, I'm going to check into some arrangements and I'll call you back with the details!" he said, excitedly.

"Kevin, I just said, I'll *think* about it," I laughed.

"Alright, Mami, I'll hold off on the arrangements, but when I call back, I expect an answer."

"Okay, Mr. Swift, I'll talk to you later." I laughed before setting the phone back in its cradle.

I'm going out to Cali my heart sang. I digested the thought. Kevin was right. It would be good for me to get away from here. Mark Shepard wouldn't have a clue and I would be safe. Now I just had to tell Mama. I knew she would have a fit and as much as I loved and respected her, the decision was mine to make and I truly believed that going away for a few days would be good for Destiny and me.

CHAPTER TWENTY-NINE

Kevin was standing at the gate waiting with open arms as we disembarked the plane. "Hey, Mami. You look nice, how was your flight?" Kevin asked, sliding his eyes down my body. His cologne was mesmerizing as he scooped me up in a big hug. I peeped him out; he was looking fly from head to toe, perfectly groomed, wearing Polo attire with a diamond encrusted cross hanging from his platinum chain. Seeing him made me quiver on the inside. He was *fine.*

"It was good," I answered with a smile.

"That's cool, come on, let's go get your luggage." He said, taking my hand in his and leading the way as if it were the most natural thing in the world.

We speed walked through LAX; I was anxious, yet intrigued by my new surroundings. Destiny gazed curiously at the man who'd hugged us and planted kisses on our cheeks.

His smile made my heart beat triple time as he looked at me approvingly. My hair was pulled up in a ponytail and my Chanel frames protected my eyes from the beaming sun while providing the disguise I needed for my tired eyes. How could he see beauty through my rumpled, fresh off a cross-country flight, appearance?

"I'm just happy to be here, I feel better already." I took in my surroundings, observing the busyness of this new environment. My spirit had released some of the stress that had fatigued my body the minute I'd felt the plane begin its descent from Detroit Metro Airport. Now my body felt rejuvenated by this West Coast energy.

We made small talk as we picked up my luggage, waited for his driver to load my luggage, and began the drive towards his Los Angeles home.

*   *   *   *   *   *

L.A. was just the change of scenery that I needed and Swift's home was immaculate with its six bedrooms, personal gym, Olympic sized swimming pool and state of the art recording studio. Being here with him gave me the extra security I craved. I thanked God for him daily.

Kevin made me feel more than welcome and I let my worries melt away as I focused on the future for the first time in months. Being here opened my mind to new possibilities. After Swift heard me singing in the shower, he'd almost dragged me into the studio, talking about I was going to be his next artist. I did need to channel my energy into something positive and my music was the perfect prescription to heal my punctured spirit.

Kevin's studio was unlike any I'd ever worked in, definitely hi-tech. He allowed me to preview his upcoming artists' projects and observe as he put together tracks that had brought him success in the music industry.

"Swift, do you ever think about God?" I asked, as we sat in the studio creating a track.

"Yeah, Ma, all the time." His answer surprised me. "Don't look so shocked," he laughed.

"I'm sorry. I just never figured you for the type," I commented.

He raised an eyebrow. "Oh, what type is that?" he asked, still bobbing his head to the music.

"I been hearing all the phone calls from the different women, I just figured a guy like you..." my voice trailed off. "Let's just say, you don't seem like the type to put God first in his life."

"Nah, baby girl, that's not true. And all them females, that's getting played out. I been doing that most of my life. I'm like," he searched for words, "bored with that. If I found the right woman, I might make her my wife."

"Oh, really?" I asked, laughing.

"Yes, really," he laughed. "If I had someone I really loved, yeah, I could see that."

I went back to writing in my songbook.

"How do you feel about hip-hop gospel music?" I asked.

"It's cool. Why? Is that what you're over there writing?" He asked, leaving his board to peek over my shoulder.

I nodded. "I don't wanna do the same music I did before. Not that I was doing explicit music or anything but I just want everybody to know what God has done for me. And I want to express that through my music."

"That's a cool mission, Kayla," he started. "Come here," he pulled me up, hugging me. "However you wanna do it, I got you. Okay?" he asked, looking down into my eyes.

"Okay," I replied.

At that moment, I realized there was something special about Swift and I really appreciated him for it. It wasn't just that he'd rescued me from the woes of Mark Shepard or that he'd invited me out here and into his home to give me a safe haven and time to recuperate, but he wanted to help me resume where I'd left off with my music. He reminded me of Dre', how he'd taken me by the hand and guided my career. He'd believed in me and I saw that same excitement in Swift's eyes.

With Swift on my team, everything was easy. I was in the studio everyday with him and sometimes all night. His grandmother was sweet enough to tend to Destiny while Kevin assisted in rejuvenating my spirit, taking me out, and giving me a taste of a new life. He introduced me to his friends *and* the artists on his label. I met all kinds of people when I was with Swift from actors, to musicians and models, to pro ball players. He knew some of everybody.

The fast pace at which Swift had me moving had my head in a whirl. At the end of each day, Swift would take me to a nice restaurant or we'd hit a party with his industry friends. I loved L.A.

183

and my new life. My decision to relocate to the West Coast, at Kevin's insistence, had been simple when he generously offered for Destiny and me to live in his guest house for as long as we liked. It was just as comfy as his home, only a smaller version. He tried convincing me to stay in his house, claiming that we had separate rooms so it wasn't a big deal; but just as hard as he tried to convince me that it was okay, I was just as persistent in proving to him that shacking up was something my belief in God wouldn't let me do.

Life with Swift was like getting a college education with an internship. As he schooled me on the business side of the industry, I also got my first real taste of fame when I sang hooks on his artist's track and appeared in the video, which was a combination of R&B, Christian hip-hop, and my new urban contemporary gospel sound. After the appearance, people dubbed me America's sweetheart. My spot in the hip-hop and gospel arena was solidified.

Swift and I were becoming an unofficial item, too. I loved walking into parties with him. It was all eyes on us when we entered the room. I knew his artist Cartier was jealous by the way she peeped me out every time the three of us were in the same room. I'd read the articles about her and seen the pictures of her on Swift's arm at different events, but if it was all that, I'm sure he wouldn't have invited me to events as his guest. I guess it made her day to finally get the stress off her chest that had been causing her to turn up her lips every time she saw us together.

"You know what?" she asked, leaning against the wall next to me as if we were involved in casual conversation. "Don't think just because you've sung a couple of jingles that you're 'bout to be running things," she said, sucking her teeth. "And whatever you got going with Swift, he's gonna dis you when he gets tired of you, just like he does all these other broads."

"Oh, really?" I asked, "Is that what he did to you?"

184

"Look, you're out of your league, sweetie," she ignored my question. "If I were you…"

"You're not," I cut her off mid-sentence. "Why are you tellin' me all this anyway? Are you concerned about my welfare or does my presence threaten you?" I asked sweetly.

"I'm just looking' out," she said, walking away as Swift approached.

"What were you two talkin' about?" he asked, walking up with a frown on his face. "Is she over here trying to spit venom?"

I laughed. "I guess her insecurities got her buggin'. Maybe she's just digging to see what we got goin'. If you were *my man*, I wouldn't want any other females trying to take my place either."

"Well, you don't have to worry about that, Mami, 'cause I am ya man and nobody's gonna take your place," he said, his eyes fixed on mine.

"Oh?" I asked, smiling coyly.

"Look, Ma, we don't have to play games with each other. I'm diggin' you. I like your style and I like how you carry yourself. I've been wantin' someone like you by my side. Don't you want to be happy again?"

"Of course I do."

"And don't you think you can have that with me?" he asked.

I nodded.

"Come here," he pulled me close. "Don't be scared alright?" I'm not going anywhere and I'm not going to let anything happen to you," he promised hugging me. "Alright?"

"Alright, Swift."

"So it's official?" he asked, looking down with a questioning grin.

"Yes, it's official."

"That's my girl," he said, kissing my forehead. "That's my girl."

185

* * * * *

Falling in love with Swift came as naturally as breathing. Whenever he walked into the room, my heart skipped a beat. I tried to resist the feelings, but he treated me like a queen, catering to my every desire like I was the only woman on the planet. It wasn't even two years ago that Dre' and I had been making plans for our future, planning our marriage and finding out about Destiny. There was something undeniable between Swift and me, but I felt like I was betraying Dre's memory by wanting Swift so badly.

"Baby, stop fighting it," Swift breathed into my ear, his soft lips finding mine and taking them in a kiss.

"I don't know how," I whispered, burying my head into his chest. My heart beat uncontrollably.

"I know you've been through a lot, Kayla," he was looking into my eyes, into my soul, "I promise I'm not going to hurt you. I only want to love you. Just let me," his kisses were tender, melting my fears away. "Just let me." He held me tighter than I'd ever been held before. For the first time in months, I felt safe.

CHAPTER THIRTY

Swift surprised me, coming into the kitchen and lifting me up into his arms twirling me around.

"Kevin, what's gotten into you?" I asked, laughing at his childlike exuberance.

"Kayla, guess what?" he asked, not even giving me a chance to answer before he continued. "I was in the gym watching TBN," he started.

When I first started trying to get him to watch Dr. Dollar's program, he wasn't with it. He always had excuses of why he wasn't into watching Christian TV. He didn't even understand why I was glued to it the way I was.

"Baby, I got saved!" he said.

"Are you serious?" I asked, shocked. I never even knew he'd started watching TBN or that he was seriously thinking about God.

"Yes, I'm serious. Kayla, I never felt like this about God, but seeing everything he's brought you through and making you stronger has been motivation," he began. "Yeah, I have all this stuff," he said, spreading his arms about the kitchen, "but there was still something missing and now I know *that something was God.*"

"Swift, I'm so happy for you." I said, putting my arms around him.

"I'm happy too, Ma, can't you tell?" he asked. "I mean, I know it's going to take some time for me to get my life completely right but I'ma get there," he spoke with confidence. "And watching this cat on TBN this morning tellin' about how he used to bang and how God intervened in his life, spared him from death, Kayla, then seeing what God has done for you….I felt like it was time to give in."

187

"So how do you think this is going to affect your business?" I asked, curious as to how he was going to handle the pressures of the industry as a Christian.

"I don't know. I mean, I'm going to keep doing what I do, who knows, maybe me being in the position I'm in is part of God's plan. I mean, He's already been using us to help each other."

"You're right," I said, thinking about what he'd just said. "Maybe that's it." And I felt God's love stronger at that moment than I had in a long time.

*   *   *   *   *

"Kayla, let's do something fun today," Swift suggested as Kayla entered the room.

"Fun, like what?" She asked, her eyes beginning to show that sparkle that Kevin had fallen in love with. Dang, Kevin couldn't believe he'd actually allowed himself to think it. He'd never been in love for real before, but baby was *tight*. She was different from the countless chicks he'd kicked it with in the past. Something about her definitely stood out. She wasn't even in the same class as them. It was like God knew everything he liked and packaged it all up into her.

"Just leave it up to me," he smiled. Not giving her any clues. I just hope you're not afraid of heights." Her eyes got big as saucers.

"What, you're going to take me on top of a skyscraper?" She laughed nervously.

"Something like that."

"Dang, Swift, don't keep me in suspense," she said, playfully tugging at his arm. But he wasn't giving out any more hints.

"Just go get dressed,' he said, not giving in to her pleading.

"I'll be back in an hour," he kissed her cheek and disappeared down the hallway.

Swift was back in an hour as promised, finding Kayla patiently waiting out on the deck, sipping her Fiji water, giving him that smile when she saw him.

They sped off in his Jag, Kayla still wondering what he had planned and Swift offering no clues.

When she saw they were at the airport, she couldn't help but to really begin to wonder what he was up to. He parked the Jag and came around to her side, opening the door.

"Are we going somewhere?" she asked, accepting his hand as she rose from the car. "I didn't bring anything!"

"Baby, you don't need anything," he reassured her, amused at her curiosity. As they walked toward the small airport, Kevin pointed towards a small plane sitting there waiting on them.

"Wait, what's with the plane?" she asked.

"Just trust me, Kayla, I wouldn't put you in any danger," Swift said, trying to put her at ease. "I just want to take you for a ride." He squeezed her hand reassuringly.

"Swift, I don't know about all this."

"Come on, you just gotta trust me, Ma," he smiled. "Come on," he said pulling her hand. She couldn't believe she was letting him convince her into getting into the plane, but she was.

"Where's the pilot?" she asked, looking around curiously.

Swift climbed in beside her and settled into the pilot's seat, put on headphones and confidently began checking the various dials as she observed. He flipped a dial and an engine roared to life. He stroked her hand.

"Are you ready?" he yelled above the roar of the engine.

She put her head into her hands. "I guess I'm ready as I'll ever be."

He flipped the different dials and the propeller began to rotate, then another and she closed her eyes as he slowly began to pull a lever back that moved the plane forward.

"I can't believe you actually know how to fly," she said, her voice not really sure.

"Yeah, my uncle gave me a lesson yesterday," he joked. "He said that I was such a natural, I should be able to go up by myself today." He saw the fear creep into her eyes. "Relax, baby. I'm just messin' with you," he laughed as she breathed a sigh of relief. Thou she'd known he was joking, she played along. The plane began to pick up speed and soon they were taxiing down the runway. It was awesome as the plane began its ascent into the sky.

"Oh my goodness, we're flying," she gasped as the plane leveled off. She could see the small airport in the distance becoming a little speck as they soared into the clouds. She couldn't help but to admire him. Even though they were thousands of feet off the ground and her life was literally in his hands, she'd never felt safer.

* * * * *

To my surprise, I'd enjoyed the plane ride. It had definitely been unexpected. Swift was full of surprises and I loved it. He was like none other and I loved him for it. He'd promised me a spectacular dinner afterwards and as the door to the restaurant opened and we stepped off the elevator at the top floor, I turned to Swift in awe amazed by the sight of the table with the single rose decorating it. The single table, positioned in the center of the room, soft music and candles set the romantic ambience that caused me to turn to Swift gratefully, embracing him with thanks. The waiter brought a bottle of champagne to the table and filled our glasses.

"To the love of my life," Swift said as we touched glasses, then he came around the table and took my hand in his. He gently pulled me to my feet. "Come here," he said lovingly and I obliged. "I love you, Kayla," he said taking me into his arms and bringing me close to him.

"I love you too," I breathed against his chest. "I love you so much." I felt the smile on his face as he kissed my forehead.

190

"I knew from the first time I saw you that you were special," he said. "Right before you came out of nowhere, I'd been thinking how I felt like something was missing from my life." He paused, gently lifting my head so that our eyes were locked together. At that moment, nothing else existed. I wasn't aware of anything but the sound of his voice as he continued.

"I thought about all the females I'd ever kicked it with and none of them ever made me feel the way I feel about you, Kayla." He looked deep into my eyes and I was lost in the promise I saw in his. "Now I know what was missing because I found it in you. You're beautiful, you're sweet, you're intelligent and talented. I don't want to live another day without you. I want to be with you, even when we grow old. I want to have children with you. I want us to take trips together around the world *and* I want to give you the world."

I was speechless as he proceeded to get down on bended knee, never letting go of my hand.

"Will you marry me, Kayla?"

A dam burst behind my eyes as he said the words.

"Yes. Yes, I'll marry you," I cried, pulling him to his feet and wrapping him in a hug. I kissed him over and over and over and his eyes glistened, too. We stood there hugging and kissing and crying for what seemed like a lifetime. Kayla Swift. I thought it had a harmonious ring to it. Kevin and Kayla Swift.

CHAPTER THIRTY-ONE

I awakened to the wonderful sound of birds singing outside my window. What a beautiful song to wake up to. Swift was still asleep but I didn't let that stop me from leaning over to breathe in his familiar scent. Cuddling up against him, I planted a kiss on his cheek as I professed my love for the millionth time since I'd become his wife.

"Good morning, Mami," he greeted me back, rolling over to face me with a smile decorating his handsome face.

"Good morning, Papi, I didn't mean to wake you." I managed, sitting up, stretching my arms with a loud yawn.

"I've been awake for awhile, I was just waiting on you to wake up," he smiled, folding both hands behind his head.

"Why, what's up?" I asked, turning to face him, my curiosity setting in.

"I've got to fly out to Cali tonight to meet with Philip." He started. Philip was his attorney. "I'll be back tomorrow morning right after."

"Cali?" That changed my whole mood. After we'd gotten married and our newest addition to the family, Mikayla, had arrived last month, Mark Shepard had the gall to send a congratulatory bouquet of roses to Cedar's Sanai Center where I'd birthed our daughter. After the incident, Swift, the kids, and I had taken up residence in our Atlanta home. I knew it was silly for me to not want him to go, but I didn't. Ever since Mark Shepard had sent those flowers to the hospital, I'd been on edge. I knew I couldn't let him control my life, but not knowing where he was and that he knew how to find me was *scary*. Kevin made me feel secure and I needed him here with me. I loved knowing that he was here to protect me, but with him going back to Cali, the fear began to rise up inside of me.

"Kayla, you know I'm not going to let anything happen to you, no matter where I am," he began. "I wish I didn't have to go without you, and I wouldn't if we didn't have that little angel in the other room."

"I know," I shrugged. "I just feel so much safer when you're here. But I know I can't expect you take care of your business and watch over me 24/7, it's just that you're my protector, you know?" I didn't want him feeling guilty for leaving me when he had to travel. I mean, traveling was a part of being in the music industry, especially for a man like him to stay on point. I couldn't be mad at that. I knew if we didn't have a newborn baby, I'd be right there with him. I felt like a big baby.

"*Baby, you can expect that,* you're my wife and I'll do anything for you." He said, lifting my chin and looking directly into my eyes.

I felt stupid now, seeing the love in his eyes and knowing I did want him to feel kind of guilty for leaving me. I knew I was being selfish, but he was my baby, I whined to myself silently.

"I know, baby, I hate feeling like this," I said, exasperatedly. "I mean, I don't want that lunatic to have this kind of power over me."

"Kay, you've been through hell, I don't expect you to act like none of that stuff happened because it did," he said, scowling. He pulled me close to him, so that my head was lying on his chest. "You're strong. The average chick would be in much worse shape after living through what you went through so you don't have to try to pretend like it doesn't scare you. I was there remember?"

I nodded. Of course I remembered. Even though well over a year had passed, the memory haunted me just like it had happened yesterday.

"I know how you feel, baby, it's like we can't even get too comfortable because that fool is still out there. But don't worry,

Mami, I promise I'm gone take care of him. I promise," he vowed, kissing my forehead tenderly.

"What do you mean when you say, 'take care of him'?" I questioned.

"Don't be naive," he said, calmly. "The only way he's gonna be out of our lives is if he's dead," he answered casually, like I'd just asked him about the weather.

"Do you really think I'm going to let that cat just roam about out there knowing that he's terrorized you and if he could he would do it for the rest of your life?" he asked as he turned to sit up on the side of the bed, running his fingers through his short curly hair.

I couldn't believe he was being so blunt. I could tell he was dead serious, though. I knew exactly how he felt, if not more. Killing Mark Shepard had crossed my mind on numerous occasions. He had no right to be walking around while I felt like a prisoner in my own life, but I also knew we had to trust God. I just prayed we wouldn't be put in a situation where Kevin would have to carry out the threat. It would be a relief when he was out of the picture, although my faith in God made me believe that he would take care of it without us having to risk our salvation.

I couldn't even relax knowing that my husband would be out of town for the night. Tika had flown to Atlanta to help us with the baby, though, and that provided some consolation, just knowing that I had someone to talk to in Kevin's absence. Kevin had security on the grounds too, but nothing and no one made me feel safer than having him physically present with me. I guess I didn't have anything to worry about though. It wasn't like I would be here alone, so I tried to get Mark Shepard off of my mind. Besides, it *was* only for one night. But as Kevin's departure time grew nearer, my apprehension about the whole thing grew. On top of that, it had clouded up and began sprinkling outside. I turned to the weather channel and learned that a storm was on the horizon.

Before Mark Shepard, the rain had never bothered me but, now, as soon as the sky began darkening, so would my mood. An uneasy feeling would creep up inside of me from deep down in the pit of my stomach. The sound of the rain reminded me of that dreadful night that I'd escaped the clutches of that crazed maniac. It was crazy, on the worst night of my life, I'd met the person who would be the best thing that could've happened to my life. I guess, ever since he'd rescued me, I always felt safer with him by my side, especially when it rained. Kevin had been my knight in shining armor, even though he'd come in a Benz rather than on a horse.

Kevin was in his closet packing his overnight bag, as I sat on the bed, observing as the rain pelted down against the skylight.

"Kevin, do you *have* to go tonight, in the rain?"

He stopped packing and came over to me, taking my hands and lifting me off of the bed and into his arms. He pulled me close and looked into my eyes.

"Kayla, everything is going to be alright," he assured me.

"I just hate for you to fly in this rain, there's supposed to be a storm," I said, saying anything I could think of in my attempt to persuade him to postpone his meeting.

"Yeah, I know, but it'll be okay, baby," he began. "I'm going to call you from the plane to check on you, I don't want you to worry your pretty self." He said tilting my chin upwards and kissing me, gently, melting some of the fear away. I lay my head on his shoulder. I needed to soak in all the security I could. I felt silly. I couldn't expect him to be here every time there was a storm, though up until now, he had been.

Those stupid nightmares were to blame. Ever since I'd started having them, anything that reminded me of Mark Shepard caused me to become a bundle of nerves. I was constantly on edge, experiencing the flashbacks of the tragedy. It didn't seem fair that he'd been out there killing people, innocent people, having no more regard for their lives than the life of an insect. But he was still out there, roaming about freely.

He'd killed those people in Jersey, Nicole and Monica Banks and the *real* Karlos Day, yet *he* was still out there. I couldn't comprehend how the police could not have caught him by now. The FBI was even on his trail for kidnapping me and transporting me across state lines, but they'd been unsuccessful in hunting him down, too. It made me furious. It made me wish I'd killed him myself when I'd had the chance, but could've, should've and would've *wouldn't* make it so.

Now I had to live my life with my nerves constantly on edge, never really feeling safe, never knowing if or when he would show up. It was a terrible way to live, to have my new husband, a new life, with everything I'd ever wanted, and not be able to fully enjoy it all because of this crazed psychopath.

I just had to put my faith in God and now was a good a time as any. He'd come through for me before when he'd allowed me to escape from that raggedy shack and sent Kevin down that dark road to rescue me. If He could do that, then anything was possible.

Kevin had finished packing and let me know he was about ready to leave. I was going to take him to his office so he could retrieve his paperwork and then his driver would transport him from there.

I was silent, as Kevin maneuvered the Escalade through the rain. We pulled up in front of Kevin's private entrance to the building and he hopped out to pull his bag from the backseat. I met him around the rear of the truck.

"I love you, baby." He stated simply.

"I love you, too. Don't worry about me." I wanted him to know that I wasn't upset about him leaving so that he'd be able to relax. "Just have a safe trip."

"Alright, Mami," he smiled, wrapping me up in a bear hug. His lips met mine in a juicy kiss. I really didn't want him to go now, with his sexy self. It was still hard to believe sometimes that this sexy, fly, GQ man was my husband. He was sexy, fine and, best of all, mine. But the sooner I let him go, which I did reluctantly, the sooner we'd be reunited. We squeezed each other a little tighter and enjoyed another kiss before he grabbed his bag and headed towards the door.

The rain pelted down harder against the car windows as I entered the freeway to head back home. I was glad that my cousin, Tika, was staying with us. She was at the house right now with Kevin's right hand man, Victor, who she swore was her soul mate after the first time they'd met.

Victor and Tika's presence at the house lessened my feelings of loneliness and gave me more of a sense of security than if it were just me and the kids.

Driving back up the driveway to the garage, I tried to focus my mind on Kevin's return rather than his absence. I could go in and soak in the Jacuzzi and hopefully get some writing accomplished.

I called out to Tika as I entered the house through the garage, but she was obviously tied up with Victor. As I climbed the staircase, I saw her and Victor running around the back of the house, playing like two kids out in the rain.

I checked in on the girls, who were asleep for the night and then headed back towards my bedroom to prepare for my mini vacation. I turned on the radio, but they were playing Cartier's song, which I quickly replaced with my India Arie CD. That home wrecking tramp made me sick to my stomach. True, thanks in part to her record sales, Kevin and I were able to enjoy the comforts of this nice home, but I still didn't like her. She'd gone out of her way to make trouble for me and my husband, but nothing could break our bond.

I sang along with India, erasing the image of Cartier from my mind.

The aromatherapy candle calmed my senses, melting all my cares away. I took a deep breath as I slid into the hot water. The rain continued to pound against the skylight and the lightning made its presence known as it lit up the murky sky.

I closed my eyes and fantasized about Kevin and me alone on a secluded tropical island with no distractions, no phones, no business and definitely no plotting vixens. The threat of Mark Shepard wouldn't exist there. But it wasn't just about getting away from all of the drama, but the two of us being able to honeymoon again. The first time had been wonderful. Kevin was everything I'd ever dreamed of. I imagined his lips sucking at my neck, kissing me, his muscular arms wrapped tightly around me, caressing me. I imagined his deep brown eyes, savoring me as if I were the only woman that existed. I loved him more than words could express, so I did my best to show it with my every action. I was lost in the reverie for awhile as I let the soothing sounds and bubbles lull my body into relaxation.

I finished my bath and slipped into my pink Victoria's Secret loungewear and set the phone on the arm of my chaise lounge, just in case Kevin called home. I cued up a track that Kevin had given me to write to. Songwriting was my therapy and I needed a session to calm my mind. If Kevin were here, we could go into our studio and vibe; the soundproof walls would keep the storm at bay. But in reality, the thunder reminded me of its presence as it crackled in the background, startling me. A splash of lightening lit up my bedroom and caused the lights to flicker.

"Dang, just what I need." I mumbled to myself. A flashlight would be perfect right now, just in case. I scurried down the stairs towards the kitchen, only to be stopped in my tracks, as the lights flickered again and then went out. This whole scene triggered that same fear in me that Mark Shepard had imbedded in my mind at the time he abducted me. I tried to suppress the memories that threatened to resurface, but the thoughts sent a cold chill down my spine.

"I hate storms!" I mumbled under my breath, feeling my way around in the dark for a flashlight in the utility drawer. I should've just stayed in my bedroom under the covers, where it was safe.

Where was Tika?

It was hard to believe she would still be outside in this weather. But this house was so big; they could be in any one of the more than a dozen rooms and still have complete privacy. I'd laughed at the two of them playing around like two kids earlier but, now that I needed them, they were no where to be found.

"Tika?" I called out. "Victor?" No response. There was no telling where Tika had taken Victor. I called out again into the darkness and still they didn't respond. I finally found the flashlight. A streak of lightening zigzagged through the pitch black sky. This was freaky. I paused in the darkness; I could've sworn I saw a shadow against the wall.

"Victor?" I sighed with relief. "Where have y'all been?"

The hairs on my arms rose to attention and the smile quickly faded from my face as I turned on the flashlight and standing there, legs crossed, arms folded, with a wicked grin planted on his leathery face was my worst nightmare, Mark Shepard.

"Hi, Kayla," he grinned. "I've been waiting so long to see you," he confessed, taking a step towards me.

I felt like I was inside a nightmare. The sound of my heart pounding inside my chest was undeniably loud. Boom boom! Boom boom! Only it was going in slow motion. In my mind, time had stopped. I couldn't move. I couldn't open my mouth. I couldn't even blink. I tried backing up, but my legs felt like rubber bands. I heard horrible little gasping sounds and realized they were coming from me. I squeezed the flashlight that, amazingly, I was still gripping.

"What are you doing here?" I questioned in a small child-like voice that quivered with fear.

"*I came for you*," he answered. His voice was filled with tenderness, giving off the impression that he'd expected me to be anxiously awaiting his arrival. He was still sick and twisted if he thought that I wanted anything to do with him. He took another step forward, extending his hand towards me. I turned and bolted towards the staircase, hearing him gasp in disbelief as he lunged towards me. I turned just long enough to smash the flashlight into the side of his face.

"Uh, uh, not again!" He muttered, through gritted teeth. But I was taking two steps at a time to avoid his hands clamoring at my heels. I made it to the top of the stairs and hid behind one of the columns at the top of the staircase at the entrance to the hallway.

I felt helpless against the surges of fear that soared through me. I dared not breathe, out of fear that my hiding spot would be discovered. I could hear his footsteps creeping up the staircase. If I was really quiet, I could let him pass me and then get back downstairs and somehow get help.

I held my breath as he crept past me like a thief in the night. I released a silent sigh of relief. I'd gone undetected and was about to make my getaway when the sound of the phone ringing from my robe's pocket signaled Mark Shepard to my hiding spot. I tried to silence the ringer, but my efforts were in vain, I'd been discovered.

"Hello, hello?" I heard on the other end. It was Kevin. "Kayla?"

Mark Shepard's voice was deliberate, filled with evil, as he approached me. He planted himself firmly in my get-a-way path as he raised the phone to my ear.

"Answer him," he demanded, "and if you try anything, I'm going to snap your neck and don't forget about those pretty little girls," he whispered.

I nodded and gulped.

"Hello, hi, baby, I'm here." I stuttered, putting the phone to my ear. Mark Shepard gave me a warning look.

"Hey, Mami, what's up, is everything cool?" he asked, a hint of concern in his voice.

"Yeah, baby, everything's cool," I answered, trying my best to sound calm, cool, and collected to keep the fear out of my voice.

"You sound funny, Baby. This storm is crazy! I know you must be buggin'." He sighed. "Are you sure you're alright?"

"Yes, baby, actually, it's exactly what I needed," I responded, desperately hoping to trigger an alarm within him. "You know, I feel so silly for how I acted earlier." I said, apologetically. "I just needed something to take my mind off of you being gone and the storm just helped me to chill out and relax. I think I'm just gonna cuddle up with a good book and probably call it a night in a little while," I added.

"Baby, you're not making sense. Now you *like* storms?" he asked, confusion filling his voice.

"Yeah, baby, don't be silly."

Mark Shepard's presence almost caused me to crumble but the thought of him near our children… I couldn't even bear the thought.

"Yeah, alright," he said, not sounding quite convinced. "I was just calling to let you know my flight was cancelled and I'm on my way home."

"Alright, I'll see you Friday. I love you, Swift."

"I love you too," he said, before disconnecting.

*　　*　　*　　*　　*

201

Kevin ran through the rain to the truck waiting outside for him, demanding Reggie, his trusted friend who also provided his security needs, to trade places with him. He was barely behind the wheel before he slammed the accelerator to the floor and sped off towards their mansion. He pounded the horn, weaving in and out of traffic like a madman. He couldn't believe what was happening. As soon as Kayla had thrown those little hints, he knew that something was wrong and there was no telling what would happen if he didn't get there, and fast!

He almost wrecked the Escalade in his pursuit to get to Kayla. Meanwhile, Reggie had pulled out his .45 automatic and was checking the clip, making sure it was fully loaded. It was time for this fool to get handled. Kevin had already clued everyone in his circle in on the Mark Shepard situation and they all had his back in case he ever was out of town and anything went down with Kayla.

"Damn!" Kevin shouted, gritting his teeth and pounding his fist into the steering wheel. "I should've never left her. She begged me not to go!" Swift growled to himself, frustrated that his truck couldn't fly. He knew Kayla must be losing her mind. The kids were there. Aw, naw, the kids! He could barely see the road in front of him as rage overtook his body. He'd tried to stay faithful to his vow to God but his mind was cluttered with wicked plots of how he was going to kill Mark Shepard.

Reggie pulled out his Nextel phone and chirped his homeboys. "Man, I need y'all to get over to Swift's crib. It's goin' down, now! That fool has his wife. We just left the airport. Just wait outside until we get there and make sure that fool doesn't go anywhere. Put a beam on his head if you got to." He ordered. "I'll hit y'all back when we get there."

Kevin tried Vic's phone again. Where in the hell was he? There was no answer and Vic was supposed to make sure that nothing happened to Kayla.

"He'd better be dead somewhere, because if he's not, I'm gonna kill him!" Kevin shouted.

CHAPTER THIRTY-TWO

"You wanna know why I killed him?" Mark whispered, smoothing my rain soaked hair away from my face as I cringed with disgust.

"Killed who?" I cried, confused at his incessant rambling that he'd been doing ever since I hung up with Swift.

He dragged me down the stairs, "Kayla, I don't want to hurt our kids but I've had to hurt people I loved in the past," he said in a low voice, threatening to harm my babies if I resisted.

"Owwww!" I cried out, bumping my head on a corner of the door as he forced me into my Escalade and drove back towards the guest house, demanding that we sit on the deck, in the pouring rain.

"Your precious Dre'," he said out of the blue, cynicism dripping from his every word.

"What?" his unexpected comment confused me.

"I said do you want to know why I killed him?" he asked as calmly as if he was asking me to pass the salt. "I'm admitting it." He threw his hands up in defeat. "I killed him," he said.

"*You* killed Dre'!" I shouted, not able to digest what he was saying. My breathing turned to labored gasps at his life shattering admission. *He* was the one who'd stolen my fiancé, robbing my daughter of her father? There was no justice. "You're sick! I hate you!" I screamed, lunging towards him with swinging fists. "I wish you were dead!"

"Kayla, you really need to get over that attitude," he warned, grabbing my hands. "A beautiful girl like you has no business letting that kind of filth come out of her mouth," he scolded me like I was some child.

"You killed Dre'. I wish *you* were dead!" I screamed.

"Is that what you really want!" he prodded, pushing me to the floor.

"No," I just miss my family." I sobbed. "But I can't even enjoy my family 'cause you're bent on destroying my life. I want to know why." I cried. As hard as I tried to maintain control over my frustration, I couldn't and the salty tears burst from my eyes. "Why me? Why did you have to do it? Why are you so bent on destroying my life?" I demanded. "Why won't you just leave us alone?"

"Destroying your life?" he laughed. "That's a joke, right?" he laughed. "She thinks I'm destroying her life!" he shouted up, as if this question would yield some miraculous answer from heaven. He sank down onto the floor next to me and looked off into the distance as if all the answers lie there.

"If you really want to know, I'll tell you," he paused, "and then you'll understand why you and I are meant to be together." He smiled, "Then you'll understand everything." He promised.

The rain's pounding intensified, splashing against the deck in huge drops, my nightmare unfolding again as it had so many times as I slept, but this time it was real. And he began his story, supposedly the story that would change everything, that would somehow miraculously explain this twisted plot that he'd devised to convince me that we were soul mates.

"You want to know why I killed Dre'," he started slowly, pronouncing each word slowly. "I did it because Dre' stole everything in life that was supposed to be mine." His piercing eyes seemed to look right through me, daring me to challenge his statement.

I took the bait. "Do you even realize how crazy that sounds?" I asked. "Everything you accuse Dre' of is everything you're guilty of doing. You're the one that stole *his* life! You stole my husband. You robbed my daughter of the opportunity to know her father. He didn't even…"

205

He put his hand up to silence me. "Let me finish!" he demanded. "For once, can't you just listen?"

"I'm listening," I answered.

Then calmly, he began again. "I only took back everything that was stolen from me." He muttered in disgust, spitting the words out at me. "Your *boo* stole the life *I* was supposed to have," he stated matter-of-factly.

He was still so blinded by his insanity that he actually thought Dre' was responsible for everything, when all Dre' had ever done was warned me against him.

"Yeah, you think I'm crazy but that's because you don't know everything," he said through gritted teeth. "Your precious Dre'," he looked off into the distance, "was just like a thief in the night. You think I'm the bad guy, but Dre' was the devil."

I clenched my fists, wanting to clock him in the eye for disrespecting Dre', but I fought to keep cool, not knowing what his insane accusations were leading up to or if he would smack me in retaliation.

I focused my thoughts on getting away from him. He was on edge as much as he was the first time he'd taken me away from my family. The night he'd killed Monica. I was so close to home but I felt alone and helpless. Where was Swift? I'd warned him that I was in danger; I knew he wouldn't leave me hanging.

"I said, listen to me!" he shouted, interrupting my thoughts.

"I am, I am," I replied with the child-like voice that his presence commanded, attempting to prevent his temper from flaring up to the boiling point. "I just don't understand why you're accusing Dre' of being the cause of your unhappiness. He never stole me from you, we were already together when I met you," I tried to explain. "Don't you remember that night I sang at the nightclub?" I asked, trying to jog his memory. "Dre' and I were together that night."

206

"Kayla, Kayla," he said, sadly, shaking his head. "This isn't just about that night, this goes way back, even before you," he said. "You were just the icing on the cake," he grinned.

My confusion must've been etched in my face the way he looked at me as if my expression pleased him. He gave voice to a pitiful little laugh.

"Do you know that ever since I was a kid, all I ever wanted was a family...a mother...and a father?" He said, his voice cracking.

"No, no, I didn't know that," I stammered.

"Yeah, I wanted my mom's to be happy...and my dad...he was the only one that ever held the key to her happiness. Do you have any idea what it's like to grow up with her always blaming' me for everything bad that ever happened to her?" he asked. "Do you?" he demanded, hollering.

I felt like telling him yeah, because that's how I felt about the way he blamed Dre' for everything wrong in his life.

"No," I finally answered, "and I'm sorry that you had to grow up with that burden on you." I cried, trying my best to sound compassionate.

"That's right, you couldn't know," he began weeping, "Anthony this and Anthony that!" he went on, mimicking his mother's voice. "And Dre'...he had everything, but that wasn't good enough." He snarled.

I cried for Dre', seeing the hate that Mark had for him, I know he must've been so scared knowing that his life would end as a result of Mark's hatred. Knowing he would never see me or our unborn baby was probably worse for him than taking those bullets. I hated Mark Shepard. He ranted and raved about Dre', but he was to blame for causing me pain. He went on about Dre' stealing his life, but he was the thief. He was the one who deserved to die for everything he'd done and everything he'd stolen. His ranting continued and he seemed to become angrier with every breath.

"He ruined my life! He stole everything from me!" He screamed at the top of his lungs. His breathing became labored and he started pacing the deck frantically. I didn't know what to do or how to respond. Anything could cause him to explode on me. Remaining calm was my only option. I'd seen him like this once before, on the night I'd escaped after he'd realized that I'd tricked him to get those handcuffs around him and make my getaway.

He stooped down in my face and stared at me. "Why are you crying? I'm the one who should be crying after everything I went through." He said, getting up and putting his hands on his hips, pacing the deck. He looked at me with a look of scorn etched into his features. "Don't tell me you're still crying over Dre'," he laughed.

"But *you* killed *him*," I cried, rocking back and forth with my arms wrapped around me as if they were a security blanket. "Why did you have to do that?"

"I had to," he explained, his teeth gritted, "The life I was supposed to have…his life was supposed to be my life and it was all because of him and Anthony that I suffered. His father was supposed to be my father." He emphasized his statement by pounding his fists to his chest.

"His father chose him over me. He abandoned me and my mother and he chose Dre'," he said angrily. "I was taking back what was rightfully mine!"

I didn't believe any of his lies. He lied so much, he had made up a so-called fantasy to rationalize his satanic behavior.

"Dre's dad was a good man. He would've never done the things you're saying."

"A good man, huh, why…because he went and turned into a preacher?" he laughed. "Why do you think he did that, Kayla? It was to erase the guilt of what he did to my mother. How you gonna wait 'til it's too late to try to make things right? Do you know he even had the nerve to try to say a prayer for me before I cut him down?"

I covered my mouth to stifle the horrified gasp that threatened to escape from my throat. "You killed Dre's dad?" I asked, horrified at his confession.

"I had to, Kayla," he admitted. "And if you think I'm crazy, it's because he made me this way. How would you feel if all while you were growing up, all your mother ever talked about was Anthony and how he left us for his other family?" he asked. "I had to listen to how he made sure his other son had everything and then the son grew up and had the girl you were supposed to end up with and then to rub it in, he gets you pregnant and tries to make you his wife!" he said in disbelief. "He violated," he raised his hands up exasperatedly.

"Dre' was out here violating while we struggled everyday. And on top of that, I had to deal with a crack head for a mother, constantly blaming me for ruining her chance at a real life with Anthony. But he denied us that, so I was gonna make it happen for myself. *All I wanted was a family.* And you were so perfect. You reminded me so much of how my mama would've been if Anthony wouldn't have been so caught up with Dre' and his mama," he went on.

"Kayla, you can't deny it was fate that brought us together. You're beautiful. You sing like an angel. How come you couldn't just forget about Dre' and be a family with me. I told you I loved you. I even made it so we could be together without Dre' always blockin'." Each confession he made was sickening, but he continued. I didn't want to hear any more.

"Then you have the nerve to go and get married on me again?" He asked. "How was I supposed to take that? Then this other dude comes along trying to pick up where Dre' left off, taking you across the country and then bringing you way down here. You think I was gonna let him steal everything I worked for?" he didn't even give me a chance to respond.

"Now do you see how Dre' stole my life? Do you realize what it did to my mother when my dad chose Dre' and his mother over me and my mother? Do you know he tried to beat me out of her stomach? He's the one that turned my mother on to crack…to try to kill me!" he shouted. "And you think I'm wrong?"

"It wasn't Dre's fault, you didn't have to kill him," I cried. "He never would've hurt you, he would've loved his brother." My shoulders shook, my eyes burned from his scorching words. I hated him. He took my baby away and I hated him for it.

"I hate you!" I screamed at the top of my lungs. "You're crazy, I hate you," I sobbed, uncontrollably, swinging at his face as hard as I could.

"You think *I'm crazy*?" He asked in shock. "I tell you the truth and you still call me crazy?" His eyes became dark and his nostrils flared and he reached back growling angrily and smacked my face with the back of his hand. I heard an ear piercing scream that I realized came from me. The rain mixed with my tears and burned as they fell down my face, which pulsated like a beating heart and stung as it began to swell. I tasted blood in the corner of my stinging lip.

The glare of the truck's bright lights blinded me and before I knew what was going on, Mark had his hand wrapped around my arm, pulling me up roughly. The lights were fast approaching the guest house slinging mud as the tires raced through the grass.

"Get up, get up!" he demanded, pulling harder. He forced me to my truck and into the passenger side, climbing across me and burning rubber as he raced to dodge the headlights.

"Shut the door, shut the door!" he demanded, grabbing my hair to prevent me from hopping out.

I was still stunned from the blow he'd dealt me, unsure of whether or not he'd cracked my jaw, unable to comprehend as we raced around the guesthouse, trying to avoid the lights that were swiftly approaching. I could see the red truck through the foggy haze and rain. It was Swift!

Mark tried to avoid a head on collision with the truck, swerving all over the grass to avoid impact causing my truck to almost tip over on its side as we slid back onto the driveway. Mark laughed; getting a thrill from the chase, as he raced down the drive until he saw two cars full of Kevin's muscle bound homeboys waiting for him. He growled angrily, stomping on the gas pedal, heading straight for them. Seeing that he was going to run them down, I reached out and grabbed the steering wheel in an attempt to avoid them. I heard two loud blasts and then the sound of glass shattering as the truck jumped forward, went airborne, and rolled once, then again, as metal crashed into earth and glass shattered. We skidded around on the trucks roof until we hit something that caused us to spin furiously before it came to a halt in a dark pond filled with muddy water and smoke. I tried opening my eyes but I felt like I was still spinning out of control until everything became still and darkness engulfed me.

* * * * *

"Felony, Kane! Find Kayla," Swift ordered the two canines. They took off obeying their master's command.

Seconds later, the animals masculine barks alerted Kevin that they were on the trail. He hopped back in the SUV and took off towards the pool house, following the animals. He arrived just in time to see Mark Shepard forcing Kayla into his truck. From a distance it looked like she was handcuffed! Swift raced towards the house, his tires slinging mud as he sped off.

* * * * *

Mark checked himself. He was still alive. Looking over, he rubbed his hand over his face as he saw Kayla unconscious with a stream of blood flowing from a gash in her head. He ripped a piece of his shirt and pushed it against the gash, trying to stop the bleeding.

He could hear voices and barking in the distance. "I'll catch you later, baby," he told Kayla. His door was jammed. Swift's boys called themselves trying to stop him and look what they'd done.

He kicked his Timberlands furiously at the windows, forcing the glass from the truck's windshield leaving a big enough hole for him to crawl out of. Mark ran up the street of the upscale subdivision before Swift and his homies could catch him. He heard the animals in hot pursuit and ran towards the sub-division's north entrance. Just his luck, a chick was pulling up in her drive as he watched from her perfectly manicured bushes. She was unaware of his presence as she parked and gathered her purse. Her curly red hair was so fiery it was visible even in the darkness. She strutted towards the massive front doors as if the walk leading to it was a runway. Mark admired her beauty as he descended on the damsel from out of the bushes.

"Don't scream," he demanded, placing a gloved hand around her mouth. She shook her head in agreement as he slowly removed his hand.

"Turn around," he demanded again, observing her fear filled eyes. "Give me the keys!"

She was captivating and Mark wanted to take her as his own, but his loyalty lie with Kayla at the moment, even though he was standing here, thrust into the middle of another crime because of her.

He allowed his eyes to quickly travel over her body, observing the voluptuous curves. Her body was up there with Beyonce's. If it didn't work out with Kayla, he'd definitely be back to scoop this beauty.

CHAPTER THIRTY-THREE

She stepped into the dimly lit town home that greeted her with the sweet, spicy aroma of baked apples drifting from a scented candle on the sofa table. Walking through, she observed the warmly decorated living room, done in rich shades of brown and burnt orange with its cozy oversized sofa sitting across from the fireplace, made for cuddling couples to enjoy romantic evenings on the sheepskin rug.

A photograph of Kayla hung above the brick fireplace enclosed in a chocolate colored frame embellished with flicks of gold throughout. The picture reminded her of a royal painting; Kayla's beauty had that kind of effect on people. She was sure that Kayla's flawless beauty contributed to her being the object of his affections and America's sweetheart.

Children's furniture in the pink bedroom along with a toy chest filled with dolls, catered to the fantasies of giggling little girls. The twin beds were decorated with pink bedspreads and fluffy pillows. Pictures of Minnie Mouse hung on the walls and stuffed animals were strewn here and there, giving the room a lived in feel. The empty home longed for a happy family to fill its interior with love, laughter, and happiness.

She looked around a bit more, letting her fingers travel along the walls, picking up his energy as she traveled into the bedroom. The master bedroom held a massive king sized bed, with its canopy flowing around the exterior, enclosing the bed like a private sanctuary. A woman's silk bathrobe lay across the bed along with a matching pair of slippers that had been set at the side of the bed. Kayla's, she presumed.

A framed photograph of the Urban Elite Magazine cover he'd done with Kayla at the beginning of her career decorated the black lacquered dresser. To the average spectator, the photograph may have revealed two people, reveling in their impending success. But she saw the distance Kayla intentionally exerted between them with her slight lean to the side, away from him. Nevertheless, she managed to captivate those who would soon embrace and adore her, tagging her hip-hop gospel's sweetheart.

Mark's gaze was fixated on her, devouring Kayla with his eyes. It was unmistakable, whatever she'd done; he was sprung. She laughed faintly at his love sickness.

She caught a glimpse of herself in the mirror as she observed the subjects in the photograph.

"What are you doing here?" she asked the reflection. She knew the answer. She was on a mission and there wasn't much time. He'd be back soon, possibly with Kayla. He'd been so occupied with hunting Kayla down, intent on alerting her to his presence that he was unaware that he was being followed. But justice had to be served. She knew the FBI was hot on his trail, too. But their brand of justice was too good for the pitiful crimes he'd committed. He'd done too much and stolen so many people's lives, dealing fatal blows to their dreams. Now it was his turn.

He was so confident that he wouldn't be caught and couldn't be stopped. He'd convinced himself that he was invincible; but the time had come. She couldn't stand by silently while he ruined another family. It hurt to think what she was about to do. A deep ache arose in her chest as she realized that once done, her actions would be irreversible. As much as she despised him for being a killer, she was about to be one too. The thought brought along with it a migraine. Knowing unbearable guilt could engulf her after the act was committed threatened to stop her from carrying out the plan but it was now or never.

She emptied the syringe into the vial and tucked it neatly back into the refrigerator. The hole was so tiny, she was sure he would never notice that it'd been tampered with. It was done. She fought the urge to dispose of the Pavulon filled vial, the urge to spare his life quickly squashed by the thoughts of the lives he'd disposed of so easily. She wondered if he'd ever had second thoughts, but she knew he hadn't. He'd become accustomed to dealing death. It was in his blood.

She left just as quietly as she'd come, pulling the black hood back over her stocking-capped head to disguise her identity just in case any onlookers got the urge to drop a dime. She took a look around once more before turning the knob with her black leather gloved hand.

"Sweet dreams, Mark," she whispered, adding a dose of "pimp" to her walk for the benefit of any would be witnesses.

CHAPTER THIRTY-FOUR

I couldn't remember going to sleep but I must've, because when I awakened, everything was different. The right side of my body ached terribly and pain pulsated through my throbbing temples. My eyelids felt heavy and I couldn't see clearly for the haze that obscured my vision. My surroundings were unfamiliar. The air swooshing around the room was cool, despite the fever that warmed my blood and my lips felt dry and crusty. An eerie silence filled the room. The only sound was an irritating hum that, even in its minuteness, permeated the thick cloud of silence.

"Kevin?" I called out, but the sound became an unrecognizable moan. Oddly enough, he recognized the pitiful utterance as his name.

"I'm right here, Mami," he answered, his hand squeezing mine in assurance. Despite the darkness and the haze covering my eyes, masking his face from me, I gained comfort from the sound of his voice.

"What's going on, I don't feel right?" I asked, trying to turn towards him, but my temples throbbed as I attempted to reposition myself. "Ow!"

"Baby, just take it easy," he said, concern filling his voice. "Just relax."

"What's going on?" I asked again, the words becoming muffled once again.

"I'm just happy your back," he buried his face against my cheek. "I thought you had left me."

What was he talking' about? Back from where? I wondered. I tried to comfort him. I'd never heard him cry before. I wanted to embrace him, but my arm movement was restricted and ached when I tried to move it. Kevin tightened his grip around me and buried his head deeper into my bosom. Even though my ribs screamed in pain, Kevin's head lying against me was all the comfort I needed. My eyes burned as tears filled up in the corners, spilling down my face. I didn't know what to say or how to react to Kevin's grief. I didn't know what was happening, only that it was bad enough to land me in a hospital bed in agonizing pain with a grieving husband crying because I was hurt. In all the confusion, I hadn't even asked about our babies.

"Mami, I love you, I love you," Swift kept repeating with his head still buried in my chest.

"Kevin, you're scaring me, tell me what's happening! Is it the girls?"

Kevin seemed dazed as he wiped his eyes and looked at me. "No, no, it's not the girls." He assured me. "They're fine, they're at home."

"Then what is going on? Tell me!" I tried to shout, but it came out as if I'd mumbled the words.

"Baby, I'm sorry, I don't mean to scare you. The girls are fine but you..." he paused, "you've been in an accident."

I tried to remain silent but the minutes ticked by slow in the painstaking silence that hovered over his words as I waited for him to continue. He was choking up, fighting to maintain his composure.

"You're in the hospital," he continued. "Do you remember *anything*?" he inquired.

"No," I shook my head as much as my injuries would allow. "I don't remember being in any kind of accident. Am I going to be okay?" I asked, groggily.

"Yeah, baby. For awhile, you had us all scared, but you're gonna be okay." He assured me. He pushed the bedside button and a nurse's voice answered.

"Yes, Mr. Swift?"

"Kayla's awake," he said, hoarsely. "She just woke up."

"I'll be right down," the nurse announced.

217

Kevin laid down the receiver, not taking his eyes off of me the entire time. I closed my eyes trying to recall something. I remembered being in my own bed just this morning because the birds had been singing, the sun was already shining, and it was the first morning that I'd awakened from a peaceful night's sleep in over a week. I remember Kevin telling me that he was going on a business trip and...that was it.

I tried telling Kevin but my throat was dry. He held the straw while I sipped on my water. I tried relaxing, hoping it would help to fill the blanks in my memory.

"I dropped you off this morning," I started, "for you're trip." I remembered soaking in the tub and listening to India Arie's CD and feeling relaxed, but my body tensed as I recalled the thunder that crashed loudly from the sky, shaking the house like little earthquakes. I gripped Kevin's hand as tightly as I could.

"Do you remember?" Kevin asked softly.

I looked up at him, unable to answer, as my body succumbed to the frightening memories. Uncontrollable quivering overcame me in my attempt to escape the frightening memories, until I gave in to the darkness swallowing me up as the walls contracted around me and the room gave way to darkness.

"I've given her a sedative," I heard an unrecognizable female voice mumble before I drifted back to sleep.

* * * * *

"Whew," he breathed a sigh of relief, adrenaline still pumping as he stood on the inside of the door to his home. He laughed, feeling that he had reached safety. He'd barely dodged death this time, he thought. The only thing was he still didn't have what he'd risked his life and freedom for.

Kayla's husband and his goons had shown up, throwing a monkey wrench in his plan. He thought that Cartier chick would've provided him with more accurate information about Swift's trip to California, especially after she'd revealed the

218

location of Swift's hide-away-home in Stone Mountain. He'd deal with her later though. Show her the price of disloyalty. Later for that. He had to get out of here now that they knew he was in the city. They probably had a manhunt going trying to locate his whereabouts. He congratulated himself at his own cleverness thinking about how flawlessly his plan had begun. He'd outsmarted everyone. When he was surprised by Tika and her boyfriend, he'd even handled that by dealing him a blow to the head with the barrel of his nine millimeter and smacking her into a corner as she tried to fight back. He shook his head, laughing at their mishap, wondering if they'd escaped yet or if they'd been discovered in the guesthouse where he'd left them bound and gagged.

He grabbed his bag from the front closet where he'd packed it away for a quick getaway. He just had to take his insulin and he was outta here. He hated having to stick himself, but it was the only way to stay healthy and he had to be healthy to make a baby with Kayla. It would be soon, too. Even with this setback, he'd find a way.

That reminded him he had to find out what hospital she was in and if she was alright. But first things first, he filled the syringe with the clear liquid and injected it into his groin. Now he could focus on another plan to get his woman back.

*   *   *   *   *

When I awakened again, it was dark in the room, except for the television and a florescent light illuminating the hallway. Kevin sat on the edge of the bed, a blank stare on his face.

"Kayla, you're awake," he said, kissing my cheek, a look of disbelief forming on his face.

"Yeah, I remember what happened too." I said.

"I'm so sorry, baby. I'm sorry I wasn't there to protect you," he apologized. "I promised to protect you and I didn't," he said, nodding his head.

"Kevin, *you were there*." I began. "If it hadn't been for you, there's no telling what might've happened to me. I'd probably be dead."

He shook his head. "Nah, don't say that. Don't even think it," he ordered.

"I have something to tell you, baby," he started. "They found Mark Shepard," he said, pointing to the TV.

"They did?" I exclaimed. "How? Where?" I asked. My prayers had been answered. Oh my God. This was like a dream come true after all this time.

"In Decatur," he started. "He was renting a house there," Swift explained, "Look!" he said, pointing to the TV. A reporter stood in front of the townhouse reporting the story of wanted murder and kidnap suspect, Mark Baker, who'd gone by the aliases Mark Shepard, Karlos Day, and Chaos. FBI agents had found him dead in the home earlier that afternoon after receiving tips from neighbors.

"He was always so nice," a middle aged woman commented as the reporter asked how neighbors felt about this wanted felon who'd been hiding out in their quiet neighborhood. "It's a shame folks act like this. It makes you wonder who you can trust," she said, nodding at the idea of having someone like that living that close to her.

"Oh my God, it's over. It's over," I cried, and Swift and I held each other tight as my body released a long awaited sigh of relief. My body still ached from the ordeal Mark Shepard had taken me through, but my soul rejoiced. I finally had my life back. "Thank you, Jesus!" It was finally over.

CHAPTER THIRTY-FIVE

I'd arrived from the hospital to find an unaddressed letter waiting for me on my desk. *Kayla,*
You don't know me but, nevertheless, I want to offer you my apologies. I cannot express how sorry I am for what Mark put you and your family through. Despite what you may think, Mark was not always the monster that he was perceived to be and had transformed into over the years. Can't lie, though, it did begin to peek when he was just a lil' boy, longing for the presence of his daddy and forsaken by my love. You see, his daddy was partly responsible for my drug addiction. Indirectly. But in my attempts to redeem myself, I embellished the story, leading Mark to believe that his father had forced me into the lifestyle that I'd chosen after he left me. Mark always vowed to make him pay. Always said he was going to reclaim what was rightfully his. Found out that meant he was going to have the family that he felt he was robbed of by his daddy's absence. His fixation on restructuring the family began with trying to kill me first. Yeah, I'd shamed him so much that he actually tried to strangle me to death in my sleep. Chile, I got out of there. Never looked back either. But not before clubbing my own son over the head with a bookend. That didn't stop him though. When I heard the news of his daddy's death, I knew he was responsible. I really believe he would've gotten ahold of his father's son, Andre' had he not been away at school. Andre' had everything he wanted: a beautiful mother and his father. He was set on marrying the perfect woman, too, once he'd gotten rid of those past ghosts. That's when he met that poor girl, Nicole Banks. She was everything he wanted me to be. She was pretty, smart, and sang like an angel. I knew he'd picked her thinking they would make a perfect family. His plans didn't take into account that she

may not be a willing participant. He became so frustrated. And her boyfriend…" Kayla paused taking it all in. She took a deep breath and continued reading. *"he didn't make matters easier. Just made everything fall right into place. It was 'bout that time that you and Andre' began making headlines. I truly believe that's when my son re-emerged as his victim, Karlos Day, and maneuvered his way into your life, just as he had with Nicole. Just like I knew he was responsible for his daddy's death, I knew he was the one that got rid of Andre', too, clearing his path to make you his. It took me a long time, but I finally caught up with my son and I followed him until I knew his routine frontwards and backwards like clockwork. I knew if he ever recaptured you, even if he didn't mean to, he'd eventually snap and maybe even kill you. Yes, even though you were the perfect woman and fit right into his dreams, he'd have eventually hurt you, too. Just his nature. Kayla, my own son, who murdered our first loves and tried to snuff out our lives, was unaware that while he was executing his attempt to carry out this obsession he had with you being his wife, I was in his apartment, lacing his insulin with a lethal drug. Making certain that he'd never ever hurt anyone again. It's finally over, chile. Go 'head, breathe a sigh of relief. I read 'bout how you were a servant of the most high. Knew that even though you wanted my son outta the picture, the God in you wouldn't allow you to take it into ya own hands. Wished with all my heart there would've been another way. I created him and much as I loved him, I just couldn't let him keep hurting' people. He wasn't gonna stop. He promised that he was gone get me too, even if it was the last thing he did and he would've too. He always had revenge in his heart. I realize you may even choose to turn me in, but nothing could be worse than the nightmare that I've survived and knowing' that I have to live with what I've done. Do as you will with this information, but know that you are finally free!*

The letter was signed, Brenda Baker.

222

"So, whatever happened to Mark Shepard?" Sonji asked. "Did you do it Kayla, did you kill him?"

I looked her in her eyes and answered truthfully, "No."

"Well," she sighed, "I must admit, you're a strong sister, 'cause if it had been me, I wudda sent that brother straight to hell!"

"Sonji, believe me, I wanted to, many, many times, but if it hadn't been for my experience with him, I probably wouldn't know God the way I do now. So even with all the pain he caused, God used what the devil meant to kill me to make me stronger." I testified.

"Yes, he really did," she extended her hand. "Thank you so much for sharing your story with me, Kayla."

"Thank you for giving me the opportunity to share my story with the world," I said, knowing that neither of us deserved the glory, only God, because had it not been for His goodness and mercy, I wouldn't have made it.

Sonji left and Swift and I snuggled in front of the fireplace, finally able to enjoy the marriage that God had pre-destined for us.

"So, what are you going to do with this?" he asked, handing me the mysterious letter that bare Brenda Baker's confession.

I took the envelope and threw the letter in the fireplace, watching as the last connection I had to Mark Shepard disintegrated into the flames.

THE END

ACKNOWLEDGEMENTS

To my children, I always prayed to God to allow me to be a successful writer and entrepreneur to enable us to live a prosperous life—Thank you for having patience as I pursue my dreams.

To Gram—Thank you for ALWAYS believing in me.

To all my Family & Friends who believed in me enough to donate to making this novel a reality. I love you ALL. Thank You for helping my dream become a reality.

To all the models who took part in bringing my vision for this book cover to life: Tim Ferguson, Briana Broadnax, and Gabriel White; my hairstylist: Kassandra Buyck; and models makeup artist: Alex Zhander—God Bless You All.

To Chad and Michael at Promotions Ink, thank you for hooking me up with a tight cover.

To Valorie Burton—without her inspiration I may have never picked up a pen to write, but through her God-given gift, not only did I write, I took steps that landed me directly in my purpose...writing, motivating, and inspiring—Thank You.

To everyone who buys and/or reads this book, my prayer is that you be enlightened, entertained, and inspired—Thank You for your support.

To God, my Lord and savior, who supplies all my needs, Thank you for fulfilling your promises in my life.

—I Love You for ETERNITY!

Platinum Dreams Publishing

ORDER FORM

 # COPIES   **TOTAL**

Platinum Dreams—A Novel by Jacki Kash   ___ x $14.95 $ _____

Shipping: (3.95 first book, $1.00 each add'l.) $_____
Sales Tax: Add 6% sales tax to books shipped to Michigan addresses $_____

Total Enclosed $ _____

SHIP TO:

Name

_____

Title

_____

Company Name

_____

Address

_____

City_____State_____ Zip_____

Phone (   ) _____ e-mail_____
Send this order form and a check or money order payable to:

Platinum Dreams Publishing, Mail Order Department
P.O. Box 320693
Flint, MI 48532

Allow 1-2 weeks for delivery

visit our website at
www.platinumdreamspublishing.com

About the Author

Jacki Kash, a Flint, Michigan native, is the founder and Publisher of Platinum Dreams Publishing and CEO of Ka$h Rules Entertainment. She is working on her next novel and the discovery of talented authors and entertainers. She resides in Flint, Michigan with her children.